Georgia Bottoms

ALSO BY MARK CHILDRESS

One Mississippi
Gone for Good
Crazy in Alabama
Tender
V for Victor
A World Made of Fire

Georgia Bottoms

A NOVEL

Mark Childress

LITTLE, BROWN AND COMPANY
NEW YORK   BOSTON   LONDON

Little, Brown and Company
Hachette Book Group
237 Park Avenue, New York, NY 10017
www.hachettebookgroup.com

First Edition: February 2011

Little, Brown and Company is a division of Hachette Book Group, Inc. The Little, Brown name and logo are trademarks of Hachette Book Group, Inc.

Library of Congress Cataloging-in-Publication Data
Childress, Mark.
    Georgia Bottoms : a novel / Mark Childress.—1st ed.
        p. cm.
    ISBN 978-0-316-03304-6
    1. Women—Southern States—Fiction.   2. Single women—Fiction.
3. Man-woman relationships—Fiction.   4. Baptists—Fiction.   5. City
and town life—Alabama—Fiction.   6. Alabama—Fiction.   I. Title.
    PS3553.H486G46 2011
    813'.54—dc22   2010026157

10   9   8   7   6   5   4   3   2   1

RRD-IN

Printed in the United States of America

To the memory of my father, Roy Childress,
and my friends Oakley Hall and James D. Houston

Georgia Bottoms

1

If only Eugene didn't run on so long in his sermons, Georgia thought, a person might not have time to think about how hot it was in this church. Beads of sweat were trickling a very personal path around each vertebra, into the waistband of her panty hose. It was September, but still summer held Alabama in a death grip. Georgia did not give a damn about global warming, because she knew Alabama couldn't possibly get much hotter than this. Although everyone said it was not so much the heat as it was the humidity, the heat alone was enough to drive you out of your mind. And then the mosquitoes would swarm in to finish you off.

The only way to survive summer in Alabama was to sit yourself down sometime in April and hold still until October. Or get out of Alabama entirely. Or follow the rest of the South into the embrace of the one true religion—A/C—with which the First Baptist and most of Six Points were still, at this late date, unblessed.

It's hard for outsiders to believe that even in the year 2001, there was a town so far from the interstate, so far behind the times that it had no cable TV, no Walmart, McDonald's, or Starbucks, and hardly any A/C. Most people in Six Points were happy to lag a few steps behind the rest of the world. They liked sitting out on their porches, cooling themselves with a glass of iced tea. They liked having something as dependable as the heat to complain about.

Georgia's house was the only one on Magnolia Street with central A/C. Neither neighbor on either side had it. The Pinsons two doors down had a window unit for their bedroom, but the Simpsons didn't have any A/C at all, nor the Wallers, nor even Billy Russum on the corner of Cedar with his flashy Lowndes County girlfriend Dawn, who you'd think would be the first one to want it. No, in Six Points there was a general opinion that A/C only makes a hot summer hotter, because every time you go out in the heat, you're just counting the moments until you get to go back in where it's cool. Judge Barnett always said A/C is for people who don't have the patience to be hot.

Georgia thought that was ridiculous and they were all idiots. A/C was the greatest invention in the history of mankind. In July and August she kept her thermostat on 68, kept that big Carrier plant in the backyard humming like a dynamo. She wished she could bolt out of this sweltering church right this moment, go home and crank the thermostat down so low she'd feel a chill and need a blanket for her feet. She would turn on her propane firelog and have a nice cup of tea while the rest of town was perspiring into its Fruit of the Looms.

Could she crank the thermostat low enough to give herself frostbite? If they had to amputate her fingers and toes, could she get a job operating a computer with one of those headset things you blow into?

"If we take an interpretational view, we begin to realize," came the wandering monotone of Eugene Hendrix, "why Paul's attitude in his answer to the Ephesians is one of puzzlement, almost as if he is thrown into doubt by their lack of faith. As if their agnosticism is a contagious disease, and he has come down with a bad case of it himself."

If only Eugene didn't throw around those ten-dollar seminary words, "agnosticism" and "interpretational" and such. He was not bad to look at, even handsome in his nervous, bookish way, but as a preacher he could use a good dose of Shut Up and Sit Down. His little cowlick was cute, standing straight up. The John Lennon spectacles reinforced the boyish aspect. The problem was that his sermons tended to drone on and on until Georgia felt this terrible urge to rush out the door. If only Eugene would thumb through the *Reader's Digest* once in a while, find something halfway witty or clever to keep a person awake, not intimately focused on the rivulet trickling down the valleys of her silky underthings.

Georgia's mother had a saying on the subject of sweating in church. *Sweating like a...* Georgia flipped to that card in her mental Rolodex, but it came up blank. She was turning up more of these blank cards lately. Was that a normal sign of aging?... Or beginning to age?... She was hardly old enough to start worrying about that. There was not a trace of gray in her naturally blond and beautiful hair. Thirty-four is not even old!

But then—it's not as young as thirty-three. And a good bit older than twenty-nine, the last age she remembered not thinking constantly about her age.

She had noticed the trend in that department and it was not good. The numbers all seemed headed in one depressing direction: up. She saw how a person could become obsessed.

Georgia had not quite admitted to herself that getting older

5

was something that would actually happen to her. Just because everybody else did it didn't mean she had to. Perhaps it was one of those things you could prevent if you ignored it hard enough.

That was one secret to Georgia's cheerfulness: she thought about the things she wanted to think about, and blotted out everything else. Another secret: she was the exception to most rules. A woman without a husband isn't supposed to be happy, but Georgia was. A woman alone is not supposed to have fun... but Georgia had it all, and then some. Women are supposed to hate the idea of getting older, but Georgia knew she would be fine if it ever did happen to her. She would give up makeup and dieting, sit all day in front of the TV, happily eating peanut M&M's. Hell, bring it on!

Just not yet. She wasn't ready quite yet. There was still a bit of juice in the lemon.

She had plenty of time to chase the question out of her mind, while Eugene Hendrix took a detour around the subject of what kind of stamps Paul might have used on his letter to the Ephesians.

There were plenty of things everybody believed in, but not Georgia.

She never missed a Sunday in church. There had to be other doubters in the crowd, but Georgia was fairly certain she was the only one who attended every Sunday without believing a single word of it: not God, not Jesus, not the Bible, not one word of the whole fantastic giant marshmallow everyone else had swallowed whole. What a whopper! God talks from the sky in the voice of John Huston! Nails his son to a cross to save *you!*

Yeah and I've got a bridge here I think you might like.

Every Sunday morning at five minutes to ten, Georgia sailed

through the First Baptist vestibule looking for all the world like a true believer. If that made her a hypocrite, so be it. She was in good company. Everybody else gave the appearance of believing, but in their day-to-day lives, she knew, they were no godlier than she was.

She hugged and howdied her way to the fourth pew, seated herself among the believers. She bowed her head in a practiced imitation of prayer. She mouthed the words to the hymns in case anyone was watching.

In Six Points, a woman had no choice but to go to church, especially a woman of a certain age who was as yet untouched by marriage. Otherwise who knows what they would say about you? (A small town looks sweet from the outside but not when you grew up there, not when everybody's got the dirt on you.) Members of Georgia's family had sat in this pew for generations, since before her grandmother Big Sue changed the family name from Butts to Bottoms because she thought it sounded more genteel.

(Big Sue died before Georgia was born, but Georgia always felt grateful to her for the change. She was happy not to go through life as Georgia Ethel Butts.)

Week after week, month after year, Georgia sat in that pew, upholding the good Bottoms name, tuning out Eugene Hendrix's sermon to the best of her ability. She used those fifty-five minutes every week to think about her hair, her manicure, the dress in the window at Belk's, the heat versus the humidity, the phone calls she planned to return and the ones she never would, the ever-lengthening list of things she wanted from life.

Georgia was not a bad person, really. But if it turns out there really is a vengeful God like in the Old Testament, he probably has a special hell for women like Georgia who use their time in church to make lists of their worldly desires.

1. *New dress, navy striped twill (Belk's)*
2. *New teakettle w/ whistle so I can stop almost burning down the house*
3. *New shoes, Gucci, Aug. Vanity Fair*
4. *New Orleans*

She noticed a stray beam of sunlight bedazzling the white collar of Eugene Hendrix's shirt. On his neck just above the collar she saw a mark. You would see it only if you knew where to look—a little bruise in the shape of a flying saucer, or a kiss.

Everyone else came to church to improve their souls and reflect on Jesus. Georgia felt certain she was the only one studying the hickey she had made on Eugene's neck while he stabbed helplessly at the air with his big fat—

A good Christian woman would not sit here thinking about sexual intercourse with the preacher. But how could she help it? It was just a few hours ago!

It must be even harder for Catholic girls to keep their minds pure in church, with naked sexy-looking Jesus hanging right there in front of them.

Georgia pictured Eugene's face scrunching up in that earnest grimace as he reached the end of his efforts: a comical mix of pain and surprise, like a little boy whose toe has just been pinched by a crab. Georgia had to close her eyes to keep from laughing. One time she'd laughed, and Eugene pouted for a week.

She was always so careful not to leave any marks.

"Are we not every one of us filled with the same doubt as Paul, as Mary, as Jesus himself in the garden at Gethsemane when he let out his great peal of doubt—'O Father, why hast thou forsaken me?' Listen to that cry! Doesn't it sound familiar? Don't we all feel a little bit forsaken, every morning when we wake up?"

No we don't, Eugene. The congregation sat unmoving, and unmoved. Forsaken, my foot! Too depressing! Snappy sayings, little stories, easy lessons they can take home and turn over in their minds—that's what the people want. Marshmallows, fluffy and light. Not this sticky theological molasses. The only one interested in feeling forsaken is you, Eugene Hendrix, and you really need to cheer up.

Eugene in bed was much like Eugene in the pulpit: earnest, sincerely grateful for your attendance, but always wandering off down these unproductive side alleys. It took him forever to get to the point. You might think he'd have learned something from all those Saturday nights with Georgia, but the lovemaking abilities of most men were fixed in stone before Georgia got her hands on them. A man learns to tie his shoes one way, and that'll keep him for life. He's perfectly happy to shave his face with the same exact pattern of strokes, every day.

Georgia could never be satisfied with just one way. She liked to keep her list fresh and updated. She liked to add new items from time to time.

Normally in church Eugene avoided her with his eyes, but now he glanced directly at her. "Where can we find these moments of beauty," he said, "these hopeful shoots of green poking up from the dry rocky desert of our daily lives?"

Georgia answered him with her brightest smile.

His gaze ran away from her, quick as a fish running away with a hook. It skimmed over the heads of the congregation to the plump shoulders of his wife, Brenda, in the second pew. Lined up beside Brenda were the four little Hendrix girls, stairsteps from ten years down to two, perfect posture like their mother, frilly dresses from the American Girl catalog. Brenda Hendrix's shellacked Clairol-blond pouf was so flawless and stiff that Georgia wanted to throw a coin at it, to hear the *tink!* as it bounced off.

Eugene was making cow eyes at his wife, so the congregation might think he meant Brenda was the hopeful shoot of green in his life. Only Georgia knew who he really meant.

"The loving embrace of a family is a fine place to find those green shoots," he said. "But family love, the love of our children, even marital love cannot be our only comfort. We must turn to the Lord. He wants us to give up our lives of sin, and search for a holier way to live. But do we do that? No. We keep right on sinning, don't we? Every day we have to ask God to forgive us all over again."

Oh for God's sake, Eugene, tell the whole world, why don't you? Georgia's thought echoed so forcefully that for a moment she thought she'd spoken out loud.

The navy dress in Belk's window had a slimmer waist and a deeper neckline than Georgia's usual style. At least she had the figure to pull it off. Unlike Brenda Hendrix, who was built like a can of Campbell's soup.

When Eugene came over on Saturday night he definitely did not want to talk about Brenda. Once you got him out of his preacher suit, Saturday-night Eugene was a flirt and a big old tease. A sweet-talker, a smoothy. He looked sexy flung out on the four-poster bed in the black silk boxer shorts Georgia had given him for Christmas. He only wore them at Georgia's, of course.

She kept them for him in the seven-drawer highboy during the week.

Last night he was there but not there. Staring at the wall, off into the distance. Georgia offered him a penny for his thoughts. He was worried about his sermon for today, he said. Trying to fit the pieces together.

It was sad how hard Eugene worked on his sermons. Would the people pay more attention if they knew how he slaved over each sentence? Would they at least make an attempt to keep from falling asleep?

You couldn't listen to Eugene's voice without drifting into that pleasant trance that can lead to...if you don't...make yourself sit up and...

Georgia pinched her thigh, hard. She blinked and sat straighter in the pew.

"Take me, for example," Eugene was saying. "If you want to see someone who's been walking down the wrong road, brothers and sisters, take a good look at me."

Georgia clicked full awake.

While she was dozing, Eugene had somehow wandered out of his sermon and up to the brink of catastrophe.

A warning bell shrilled in her ear. Any confession from him would pretty much have to involve Georgia, would it not?

Last night—he clung to her long past time for him to go. He pulled her in close, snuggling under the comforter, out of the arctic blast of the window unit.

Then he answered a question she hadn't even asked. "No," he said, hooking his feet around her ankles. "This is perfect, right here."

Now he was staring down, his fingers gripping the sides of

the pulpit, a fierce battle under way behind his John Lennon specs.

Georgia had seen this look in the eyes of other men. Occasionally one of them lost his mind, fell ridiculously in love with her, and decided to throw over his whole life for her. (He always seemed to come to this decision without consulting Georgia.)

She saw how this was going to go. Eugene meant to confess his infidelity right here in front of God and everybody. In front of Brenda and his lovely daughters and the congregation, he intended to declare that he loved Georgia too much to keep on living a lie.

It was the same old story: middle-age fever. A man's desperate attempt to feel young one last time before beginning his slow topple into the grave. But Eugene was only thirty-two years old—and a coward. He had to make his declaration in front of witnesses. Otherwise he wouldn't go through with it.

What he didn't realize was that he was risking much more than Georgia's reputation. One word could ruin a lot more than that.

She had to stop him.

A glance at Ava Jean McCall drowsing at the organ brought to mind a *spitball,* a word Georgia hadn't even thought in twenty years. She opened her purse—yes she did have a straw from the Dairy Dog, a cash-register slip she could chew the corner off… aim for Ava Jean's ear, startle her into producing a noise that would stop Eugene from making the biggest mistake of his life.

But what if Ava Jean brushed the thing off her neck? What if she yelped, but Eugene kept talking?

Georgia had to stop him. Before he had a chance to say her name.

"There's a heavy burden on my spirit, and I need you folks to help lift it off me," he said. "This has not been an easy decision."

Georgia rose from the pew. The quick way out was to the left, but she had to make Eugene notice her. She grabbed her large jingly purse and plowed the other way, toward the center aisle, forcing everyone in her pew to turn their knees to let her by. Geraldine Talby glared at her, annoyed.

Georgia batted her eyes and concentrated on appearing woozy. She was a splendid actress. Anyone could see her face growing paler by the moment.

"I've lied to you all, and I've lied to myself," she heard Eugene say. "The more I have prayed over this, the more I've come to realize...I just can't go on living this lie."

Georgia made sure she was well into the aisle, clear of the pews on both sides. She didn't want to get hurt. Her eyelids fluttered. Her gaze turned upward. All the muscles in her body went limp. She collapsed in a heap on the carpet runner—a most convincing and ladylike faint.

She heard screams, a male shout of alarm: "She fainted!"

In every crowd there's one genius, Georgia thought.

She fell into a pose of prostration, one arm stretched artfully over her face. She felt thunder through the floor as people sprang to help her.

The rules of fainting required her to keep her eyes closed, her jaw a little slack—not unattractively, of course, and just long enough to be convincing.

Actually it felt rather nice, stretched out here on the carpet. A bit cooler than sitting in the pew. She hoped no one would try to splash water on her face.

The real purpose of her maneuver would be obvious to anyone who'd been paying attention to Eugene's sermon. Georgia hoped no one had been.

One thing was certain. He wouldn't be finishing that sermon today.

"She looks all right to me."

Georgia recognized the serrated edge of Brenda Hendrix's voice. She could feel the weight of Brenda's shadow pressing down on her. She was glad she had chosen her most form-fitting sage green Ann Taylor suit. Even sprawled on the floor she must look fantastic, and that would be making Brenda sick with envy.

"Mommy, is she dead?"

"She just fainted, honey," said Brenda. "Ladies do that sometimes."

"Stand aside, folks, give her some air!" The courtly baritone of Judge Jackson Barnett came with the smell of peeled garlic, which he carried in his pockets and nibbled all day as a snack. No vampire would ever get hold of Judge Barnett. Georgia heard his knees pop as he crouched to take her hand.

She let her eyes swim open. "Well hey, Judge. Where am I?"

"Right here, Miss Georgia. In church." The judge hid his concern behind a smile. "I believe you have swooned. Did you eat a good breakfast this morning?"

"Why, I'm sure I did, I always do." She tried to sit up but the men all said no! not yet! She let them talk her into lying back down. "How embarrassing! It's the heat, I guess. I felt light-headed, I was going to get a drink of water, and next thing you know..." She made a keeling-over motion with her hand.

"It's not so much the heat," said the judge, "as it is the humidity."

"You have a point," Georgia said.

"The important thing is, you're fine," said Brenda Hendrix. "If it were me, I would want to get up off the floor, get the blood circulating."

It must be killing Brenda to see Georgia at the center of all this attention. Look at the array of concerned gentlemen who had rushed to her side—the judge, Sheriff Allred, Lon Chapman of the First National Bank, Jimmy Lee Newton who owned the *Light-Pilot,* and here came Dr. Ted Horn to take her pulse. The most powerful men in town, shouldering one another aside to make a fuss over Georgia.

Their wives were clucking over her too, offering their own stories of fainting. Everybody in Six Points loved Georgia. They had loved Little Mama when she ran the town switchboard, before private phone lines came in. When her daughter Georgia grew up to be beautiful and cheerful, they loved her too. She was all over town her whole life, mixed up in everything Six Points had to offer. How could anyone fail to love her? She hadn't set out to become a star, but in a place like Six Points it was inevitable that someone with her qualities would either rise to the top, or get the hell out of town.

"You think she'll be all right, Doc?" Jimmy Lee Newton's high-pitched giggle only came out when he was nervous.

"Pulse is good," said the doctor. "Georgia, you stay right here while I get my bag from the car."

"Oh Ted, come on, is that necessary?"

"I think it is. Be a good girl, now."

Georgia had started this. She had to let it play out. She noticed Eugene Hendrix standing—no, *hiding* behind his wife, hands tucked into the folds of his black robe. When Georgia looked at him, he turned away. "Take her to the choir room," he said to no one in particular. "There's a sofa in there."

"Now Reverend, nobody needs to take anybody anywhere," Georgia said in a tinkly voice. "Y'all, I'm *fine*. Would you let me sit up?" This time no one stopped her. "See? Much better. I just had a little spell, that's all."

"The vapors," said Martha Barnett, Mrs. Judge. "Lord knows we've all had 'em." The other ladies agreed.

The judge and Jimmy Lee helped Georgia to her feet. Half the congregation had crowded around to make sure she was all right. The other half were fleeing to their cars in case Eugene got a notion to resume his sermon.

Georgia let them help her up two steps to the choir room. There was a sagging couch covered in green corduroy, beneath a decoupaged plaque of Jesus overturning the money changers' table. The room reeked of Wednesday-night fellowship hall lasagna. Georgia hated the thought of her Ann Taylor suit steeping in that smell, but that's why God created dry cleaners. She sank down on the sofa to wait for Ted Horn.

Louise Gingles brought a cup of water and a damp paper towel. Martha Barnett told how her mother-in-law fainted at her own wedding, cracked her tailbone and spent her honeymoon in the Mobile Infirmary. "And sure enough, she was a sore-ass the rest of her life," Martha said, her whiskey cackle punctuated by a cigarette cough, *HA!*

"The Lord works in mysterious ways," Georgia said. "I'm just lucky I didn't break anything." She couldn't wait to call Krystal and describe the scene: Six Points' most prominent Baptists milling about the choir room, Brenda Hendrix patrolling the door to keep her precious Eugene away from the hussy on the sofa.

Krystal didn't know all the complications of Georgia's life, but she knew more than anybody.

"Have to ask you folks to step out, please." Brandishing his doctor bag, Ted Horn cleared the room. He shut the door, and turned to Georgia. "Now, then. Are you pregnant?"

"Oh *hell* no. No, Ted. Not possible."

"Anything is possible in a young, healthy, sexually active female, which pretty well describes you, if I'm not mistaken."

"I'm glad you managed to work 'young' in there," Georgia said. "I am not pregnant." Not a chance. She took precautions, overlapping layers of precautions.

Ted unlimbered his stethoscope. "When you passed out—it looked like somebody just switched off the lights. Probably just an everyday vasovagal syncope, but I'm going to examine you to be sure."

"This is so silly. Don't you have any real patients who need you?" Secretly Georgia was thrilled that her performance had fooled a medical professional.

Ted slid the steel disk of the stethoscope inside her blouse, his palm warm behind the cold circle. "When was your last period?"

"Ted. Listen to me. I—am—*not*—pregnant. You hear me? You know how careful I am."

He grinned that rabbity grin. "Just answer the question."

"Two weeks ago? Two and a half. God. So personal."

"I'm your doctor." He thumped her chest and listened.

"I know what you are," she said. "You are bad."

"Yes I am." His voice softened. "I am very bad. I've been naughty."

"You have. A very naughty doctor. You need to be punished."

"Shhh..." He moved the stethoscope to her back. "Okay,

Mark Childress

deep breath—let it out slow. And again." He sat back. "Listen, why don't we go to my office and run an EKG. Just to be safe."

"Ted. I'm fine. Don't ask me how I know, but I know. I fainted. It's over. Case closed."

"I don't tell you how to be Gorgeous Georgia. Don't tell me how to be a physician." He massaged her jawline, feeling her nodes and glands. "Come on. Quick little EKG."

"I can't! You know somebody has already called Little Mama, she'll be hysterical any minute, I have to drive Brother to his meeting and my September luncheon is Tuesday—"

"Okay, okay." He poked a nozzle into her ear. "Were you listening to that sermon?"

"Not really," she lied.

"Sounds like Preacher Eugene's feeling a little guilty about something."

"I wouldn't be surprised," said Georgia. "Probably cheats on his wife."

"You call Debra first thing in the morning, she'll work you in. I want to run blood, check a few things."

Georgia crossed her fingers where he could see them. "I promise."

"You better," said Ted. "And, uhm—Wednesday?"

"Of course Wednesday," said Georgia.

He snapped shut his bag. "Go home and put your feet up. Read a book. Don't do anything else today. That's doctor's orders. And tomorrow I'm getting that EKG. If I have to come over there and drag you to my office."

She shook her head. "You just want me out of my clothes."

He fixed her with a look: *I won't dignify that.* He opened the door to reveal Brenda Hendrix's ear more or less pressed against it.

18

"Oh hey, Dr. Horn," she sang, bustling in. "How's our little patient?" No one could have missed the note of fake concern in her voice.

"Much better, Brenda," said Georgia. "Thank you for asking."

Ted waved, and ducked out the door. Georgia's mob of well-wishers had dispersed. Eugene was nowhere to be seen.

Brenda planted her fists on her hips. "You get up from that couch."

Georgia felt a twinge of panic. She never intended to be left alone with Brenda Hendrix. "I beg your pardon?"

"We both know there's nothing wrong with you. Physically, anyway."

Georgia batted her sapphire eyes with the long, long Maybelline lashes. That would drive Brenda crazy with her squinty pink pig eyes and that pig nose on her face. Georgia wondered what could ever have attracted Eugene to this woman. Even fifteen years and four children ago, that would not have been a pretty face. "Brenda, is something the matter?"

"Don't you play innocent with me. I know what you've been up to with my husband."

"All this heat must have gone to your head," said Georgia. "Bless your heart, you're delusional."

So Eugene spilled it all to his wife without a word of warning to Georgia? How typical!—to take for granted that Georgia would be standing by, ready to upend her own life to help him through his midlife crisis.

Every man thinks any woman would be lucky to have him. When it's *always* the other way around.

"You didn't fool anybody with that display out there," said

Brenda. "You knew what Gene was going to say, and you wanted to stop him."

"I did stop him." Georgia maintained her smile. "You should be glad I did. Or did you want him to blab it to the world?"

"Oh, he has to tell," Brenda said. "It's the only way he can come clean with his Lord. Gene knows he got his own self into this mess. And he's going to need the help of not just the Lord but his whole church family to get out of it."

"That is really so interesting," Georgia said.

"You didn't stop anything," said Brenda. "You just postponed it."

Poor Eugene. To let himself be run over by this bulldozer— and for nothing! Georgia didn't want to marry him anyway! He was a nice diversion on a Saturday night, but one night a week was enough.

He must have had to do some big-time confessing when he got home last night. Which is how he wound up in the pulpit with this gun to his head.

Georgia was tired of acting ladylike. She was ready to move on to the slapping and hair pulling. She was strong, she could take this tub of lard with no difficulty. "I don't think there's any need for a scene, do you, Brenda? You want your girls to hear?"

"How dare you. You leave my girls out of this!"

Georgia spoke softly. "That's what I'm trying to do."

"Damn it, Brenda!" Out of his holy robes, in khaki Dockers and a white shirt, Eugene Hendrix looked unmistakably mortal. "I told you I'd talk to her!"

Brenda whirled on him. "Where are the babies?"

"Outside. There's plenty of folks out there to keep an eye on them."

"You left them by *themselves?* Are you out of your mind? Have you forgot about JonBenét? You go back out there this instant! I'm handling this."

Eugene looked relieved to have an order to obey. He turned to go.

"Eugene, don't you move," Georgia said. "You told her about us?"

He stopped. His face flushed red. "She found out."

"He was calling you from our *home,*" Brenda wailed, "like I'm too stupid to listen in on the extension?"

Georgia turned to Eugene. "Dummy, if you wanted to leave your wife for me, don't you think you could have discussed it with me first?"

She couldn't quite decipher the look on his face—confusion and something oddly out of place. Sympathy? She plunged ahead.

"I did the only thing I could think of, Eugene. I couldn't sit there and let you ruin my life—and your life, too! What were you thinking?"

"I have to come clean," he said. "This sin is weighing so heavy on me. It's pressing down on my soul. I've been living a lie, Georgia. I can't go on like this."

He didn't sound at all like himself. He sounded like the guy who'd had to explain it to Brenda last night.

"Eugene, listen to me. I don't *want* you to leave her. I don't *want* to marry you. Do you understand?"

"Marry? That's a hoot," Brenda said. "What makes you think he would ever leave me? And our babies? For a tramp like you?"

"Now come on, Brenda," Eugene huffed, "there's no need for that kind of thing."

Georgia said, "One of us is crazy, Eugene. Who is it? Her or me?"

"Tell her, Gene," cried Brenda, "tell her what you were going to say when she put on her little fainting act."

Eugene's eyes didn't make it all the way up to meet Georgia's. He pressed his lips together, looked at the floor, and sighed as men do: *None of this is my fault.*

That's when Georgia understood the truth. Brenda was not the fool in the room. Georgia was.

Eugene was not leaving his wife. He was staying with her.

No doubt this was mostly Brenda's doing, but Eugene had to be in on it too. They'd worked it out between them. In a desperate attempt to save their marriage, Eugene intended to denounce Georgia in front of the congregation as a home wrecker, a wicked woman. Never mind that he was the one skulking down the alley to Georgia's garage apartment every Saturday night, it was always Eugene who came to see Georgia. *Never* the other way around.

Georgia didn't know why she was attracted to men like this— the good-looking, nice-seeming, treacherous type. She vowed to start working on that as soon as she got the hell out of this church.

"What we did was just plain wrong, Georgia, you can't argue with that." That was Eugene, trying to convince himself.

"If that's the way you want it," said Georgia. "But you better not go making any public statements. There might be a few things you might not want told."

Brenda made a face. "Like what?"

"Like that cowboy hat you wear when you're riding the horsey, Brenda." Georgia winked. "What is it you always yell? Giddyup? Go horsey?"

"Gene!" she shrieked. "You told her that?"

"You can't make this stuff up," Georgia said. "And if you think I'm too shy to go tell it on the mountain, you might want to think again."

"Oh, now you're threatening me?" Brenda cried.

Georgia said, "I've been coming to this church all my life. Y'all have been here what, five years? I'll be sitting in that pew when the two of you are just a vague memory."

"I don't think so," said Brenda.

"Brenda. You want your husband?" said Georgia. "Take him home. Good luck keeping him there, by the way." A nagging voice said, *Get out of here, Georgia. Fix this later. Just go.*

Brenda wasn't quite finished. "You put on all these airs like some pillow of the community. Prancing around like you own this town. People ought to know exactly what kind of woman you are."

Eugene winced at his wife's misapprehension of the word "pillar." He looked embarrassed that Georgia had this close-up glimpse of the woman he'd been married to for fifteen years.

Until this moment Georgia had felt mostly sorry for him, but that wince made her hate him thoroughly, all at once. How dare he look down his nose at his fat unattractive wife, who put up with his cheating and his endless wandering sermons, and gave him four lovely daughters! He must have known what a cow she was when he married her. How dare he wince at her now!

Georgia whirled on him. "You spent three hours at my house last night and couldn't find a moment to mention this to me? What the hell is the matter with you?"

"Last night?" Brenda began squawking, flapping her wings. "But he—Gene, you were at Fellowship Circle last night!"

"Oh no, it wasn't a circle," said Georgia. "Although we definitely did have some fellowship. How many times, Eugene? Was it three? Look at that hickey on his neck, Brenda, did you even notice? Of course not. You really should pay more attention." Georgia pushed up from the couch. "He spent half the evening lying to me, then he went home to lie to you. That's the one thing he's really good at. Believe me, honey, you do have a problem. But I ain't it."

Eugene looked horrified. His hand went to the spot on his neck. He must not have noticed in the mirror this morning, but his hand knew just where to go. "Now wait a minute," he said.

Georgia sailed out the door. "Y'all have a nice day."

2

Four little Hendrix girls sat on the curb beside their father's rust-colored Dodge minivan. They looked perplexed by the absence of anyone telling them what to do. Georgia started to call out, *Don't worry, your parents will be out soon, get up off the dirt in those nice dresses*—but why should she trouble herself with those brats? Let them sit there all day. Who cares?

The nerve of some people! A good cloud of anger had built up in the back of Georgia's head, a cumulonimbus with a broad purple base. She stormed over the heat-shimmering asphalt, thinking how little she needed a lecture on morals from the fat wife of Preacher Eugene, who stood by watching the confrontation with all the authority of the shriveling organ he had turned out to be.

Georgia climbed into her four-wheeled Honda oven, cranked the engine, turned the A/C to MAX. Anger would get her nowhere. She must not let it overpower her.

The hot air blasting from the dash began to pale into coolness. Georgia buried her face in the airflow, massaging her temples with the pads of her thumbs.

What was the name? A name from long ago. Friend of Little

Mama's, a big man, used to come to town all the time to visit a cousin. Another Rolodex card coming up blank.

Jolly Santa Claus cheeks and a boisterous laugh.

She was still trying to visualize the letters of his name an hour later, as she lugged the sacks from Hull's Market through the deep-freezer porch. Whizzy the white-spotted mutt whined, swatted his tail, and twisted around to put himself as much in the way as possible. "Get out of here, Whizzy, go on! Mama, who was that man from the Baptist convention?"

Little Mama looked up from the pan of purple hull peas she was shelling. "What man?"

"That friend of yours, Mr. Big Shot Baptist with the big gold knuckle rings. You said never trust a Baptist that wears that much gold."

"Aw, you talking about old Teebo Riley," said Little Mama.

"Teebo! That's it!"

"His real name was Clarence, or Horace or something."

Georgia kept her voice casual. "Wasn't he some big to-do at the Southern Baptist Convention, in Montgomery?"

Little Mama nodded. "He's the right-hand man of the one that runs the whole shebang."

"I wonder whatever happened to old Teebo," Georgia said.

"He's still around, called me last year on my birthday. Least I think it was him. Might have been somebody else." Little Mama's memory was getting spottier, but she filled in the gaps with her imagination. She'd been working the same jigsaw puzzle for years, but if it didn't bother her, so what?

"You still got his phone number, Mama?"

"I think so."

Within minutes Little Mama was cackling on the phone with

ol' Teebo. Georgia listened for a while at the edge of the conversation, to make sure Mama got the details right. Then she poured herself a fat glass of red wine and carried it into the chill of the sunporch to celebrate.

She looked forward to the smoothing effect of the wine. Her body felt achy and tingling, leftover trauma from the shock she had received at church—as if she'd touched a live wire, or had fainted for real. Eugene's attempted betrayal was not only shocking, but humiliating. Georgia was not accustomed to having her private life dangled in a threatening way in front of the congregation. The first sting of rejection had been quickly replaced by a sense of resolve.

Either party in an affair should have the right to break it off at any time, Georgia believed. That's one reason she never married— she liked keeping her options open. People are so naturally fickle that she understood why some might want a binding legal contract to enforce a promise of the heart. But Georgia's life, at least, was too complicated to put in writing.

If Eugene wanted to break it off, okay—but to shout it from the pulpit for the whole town to hear? She simply couldn't allow it. She conducted her affairs discreetly; no one had any idea what she was up to. Rarely did she have to bring the hammer down on anybody. It was nice to know she still could if she had to.

She sipped her wine and waited. Presently up the hall came the walker with split tennis balls mounted on the front legs for traction. "All done, baby."

"Mama, you are a miracle worker. Remind me to buy you a mink coat for Christmas."

Mama snorted. "I could use one, cold as you keep it in here. Ain't your feet freezing? My toes are like niblets of ice."

Little Mama never asked why her daughter might want her to make such a call. Simply did as she was told. Eugene and Brenda would never know what hit them.

Little Mama halted her walker at the sofa.

"Put on socks if you're cold," Georgia said. "Go around barefoot, no wonder." Thumbing through the Montgomery yellow pages, she settled on "Charlie Ross Regal Moving" because she liked the cartoon of Charlie Ross wearing a jeweled crown as he rode and whipped his moving van like a bucking bronco. She appreciated a moving company with a sense of the ridiculous. She dialed the number and explained the situation to a pleasant woman called Shirley.

"And your name is?" said Shirley.

"Brenda Hendrix," said Georgia. "I know this is awful short notice. Can you really get a truck here first thing in the morning?"

"It's your lucky day, we had a cancellation," said Shirley. "I'm sending you down my best crew."

Georgia thanked her and hung up. She consulted the yellow legal pad with the list for her September luncheon, three handwritten pages of closely spaced items still to do. It was only forty-eight hours until the first guests would begin parking their cars along Magnolia Street. "What you think, Mama? Chicken salad or pimento cheese?"

"For what?"

"Finger sandwiches for the table in the front hall."

"Chicken salad," Little Mama said. "Nowadays some people can't tolerate cheese. I don't get it—nobody used to be against things like cheese. If we still had a colored woman, you could just tell her to make both of 'em and then people could have whichever they want. It's all because of that damn Rosa Parks."

"Now don't start..." Little Mama was a lethal bore on the subject of Rosa Parks, whom she blamed for every form of misery that had come into the world since 1955. If uppity Rosa Parks hadn't sat down on that bus in Montgomery, things might have stayed as they were when Little Mama was young: gasoline was nineteen cents a gallon, a white woman had privileges, you could have a colored girl do your housework for nothing. Little Mama didn't invent that way of living, but she sure as hell preferred it to the way things were now. There were plenty who agreed with her, but mostly they were senile or dead, or keeping their thoughts to themselves.

Outside the house, Little Mama had to stay quiet about her opinions, but inside she let fly, mainly to irritate Georgia, who was like her father, a yellow-dog Democrat on the subject.

They used to have the most terrific dinner-table wars, Little Mama roaring that Paw was a worse nigger lover than Eleanor Roosevelt, Paw roaring back that she ought to put on a hood and a sheet and go night riding, if you're going to be a Klucker do your duty, woman! They raged like that for decades. Paw lost the argument—or got out of it, anyway, by dying. Georgia tried not to argue with Little Mama if she could help it. There were at least three African-American women in town she would be perfectly willing to invite to her luncheon—Dr. Madeline Roudy, for instance, the pediatrician at the county free clinic, a good-natured person, attractive, intelligent—but Georgia didn't dare. Little Mama would find a way to bring up Rosa Parks.

"She wasn't even a seamstress, that was all just *publicity*," Mama announced. "What she was was a Communist agitator. I've seen the pictures of her in the Communist training camp in Tennessee."

Mark Childress

"Yeah, Ma, I know, just leave it alone. You're right, I'd better make both pimento cheese and chicken salad, or somebody is bound to be disappointed."

To Georgia, the silliest argument of all was this endless wrestling match over race. As far back as she could remember, everyone in Alabama had been re-fighting the Civil War, a hundred forty years later. Someone was always trying to send the black man back into slavery, or raise him up higher than he was ready to go. To Georgia, the solution seemed simple: Everybody just forget about it. White people, get used to it. Black people, stop dwelling on it. Let's all just *pretend* we're equal, and get on with our lives.

People, thought Georgia, should aspire to be more like ants. Ants make no distinctions based on color.

Georgia had this thing about ants. She'd spent much of her childhood on her knees with her nose near an anthill. She liked to pick out one ant with her eye and follow its travels as long as she could, imagining its life from beginning to end. As a grown-up she watched every ant documentary that came on public television.

She was fascinated by the way ants passed complex chemical messages down the column. A bad message could get them dashing around in a panic, tiny mobs going berserk. Whenever Georgia got to feeling alone, maybe a little bit useless, she reflected on the "Ant Connection." Ants work their whole lives for the good of the species. They don't need words to speak to each other. They don't mind being one speck among millions—or do they? Maybe they don't realize how tiny they are. Maybe they seem as large to themselves as we seem to us.

There were lessons to be learned: One ant doesn't matter

much. We are tiny, but we are connected. We all have to work for the good of the Ant Connection.

"I'm too busy to drive Brother. Why can't he just walk over there?"

"You know he'll just call that Bailey boy to come get him. And they'll wind up in jail again."

"I have a to-do list twenty feet long, if that matters to anybody," Georgia said. "Are you done shelling those peas? You want me to put 'em on for your supper?"

Little Mama said, "There's a piece of fatback in some foil in the back of the icebox."

Georgia went to put on the peas. She cranked up the soft rock on WBGR, *woo woo no baby please don't go . . .* She fanned out her *Southern Living* cookbooks and launched into the first major round of cooking for her Tuesday luncheon.

She roasted and peeled a large pan of red peppers, then dragged out the food processor, a hunk of cheddar, and a huge tub of mayonnaise to whip up her famous pimento cheese. She plopped two chickens into a pot to be boiled, cooled, and deboned for Curried Chicken Salad with Grapes and Candied Pecans. She sliced, mixed, and stirred, opening can after can of ingredients for the fancy casseroles and layered salads that would anchor the main buffet table in the dining room. She peeled and grated a pile of Granny Smiths for the Fresh Mountain Apple Jell-O Compote that Krystal swore was the best thing she had ever put in her mouth (since Billy Satterfield, ha ha).

Georgia didn't own the fifty shot glasses needed to give each guest her own serving of the Lobster Scallion Shooters. In a burst of inspiration she'd had Fred at Hull's Market order two cases of votive-candle holders, which she now had to wash, dry, and scrape the price tags off until her thumbnail was a ragged rim of gray sticky cheese.

Once she repaired the nail with a clipper and emery board, she set into making a double batch of Taco Cheesecakes, which were so labor-intensive that she only bothered because they were such a major hit last year.

When the cheesecakes were in the fridge setting up, Georgia constructed Miss Angie's Five-Layer English Pea Salad, and a vat of Cranberry Ambrosia Cream Cheese Spread for stuffing into Endive Boats.

She began dicing cantaloupe for the Pizzetta Bruschetta and was swept by a sudden wave of hunger. She ate a big hunk of melon just like that, ripe juice dripping down her chin. Generally she tried to avoid eating—that was the only way to stay slim—but sometimes hunger took over her hands, made her do things. Awful things. She ate half the cantaloupe in four bites, *mluph mluph*.

The last count on her invite list showed forty-four yeses. Plus the inevitable last-minute RSVPs, and those who would show up without bothering to reply. That meant at least fifty women roaming the house, hungry as bears, eating everything down to the lace tablecloths. Georgia could lay out chips and store-bought onion dip, and they would consume it all without saying a word—to her face—but oh Lord later how the phone lines would sing!

Over the years, Georgia had set a certain standard with her September luncheon. Husbands were said to be jealous that only their wives were invited. Georgia put out the fanciest food, the most dazzling flower arrangements, the cleverest centerpieces. She inscribed each guest's name on a place card in her impeccable hand. Each would depart with an elaborate homemade goody bag. Year after year Georgia kept raising the bar, although she claimed her only goal was to give the kind of party to which she would like to be invited. The pressure was tremendous.

The preparation was the part she enjoyed. The party itself was always a combination letdown and blur.

Now that she had the dishes washed and stacked, the kitchen under a semblance of control, she slipped out the back door, over the broken bricks of the garden path. The sun was setting but the air was still heavy and hot, bugs zipping around. A blue jay raised a piercing alarm.

If Georgia kept at it without a break, she thought, she had just enough time to clean the apartment before driving Brother. Who you'd think could get himself across a town as small as Six Points without help from his sister.

The big houses on Magnolia Street all had these back buildings, which some called "dependencies," or "slave quarters" if they were being historically accurate. The Bottomses had always called the first level of their back building "the garage," though it was built as a stable and had never been a garage, and the upstairs was "the apartment," though no one had lived there since slavery times.

The garage's double-arched doorways were large enough to admit a horse and carriage. Now it served as the laundry, and a repository for croquet sets and broken lamps.

Georgia grabbed a mop and bucket and headed upstairs. An iron gate prevented anyone from seeing past the landing. Only inside the gate could you peer into the long, high-ceilinged apartment with the four-poster bed, green velvet chair, the skinny seven-drawer highboy dresser. A bathroom had been added in the 1920s, but otherwise the room looked as it had for a hundred years. The chimney was gradually disintegrating, sprinkling clay-orange brick dust on the floor every morning. The floor sloped toward the chimney from all sides. Over time, the heavy chimney was sinking into the soft earth, dragging the rest of the house into the hole with it.

Along the front of the building ran a balcony with an elegant wrought-iron rail. Anything that happened in the apartment was hidden by a pair of honey locust trees with foliage dense and thorny enough to prevent anyone from climbing up or seeing in.

The apartment smelled musty—God help us, the leftover funk of Eugene Hendrix. Georgia threw open the French doors, stripped the sheets, carried them downstairs, and stuffed them in the washer. She went back up and put fresh sheets on the bed, and set into a radical cleaning, from one end of the room to the other. She vacuumed the rugs, hung them over the railing, and beat them with the broom. She swept the sloping plank floor and mopped it twice.

In a Hull's Market sack, she collected the remnants of Eugene—silk shorts, pack of Camels and a lighter, the shiny blue polyester bathrobe he smuggled in early in their affair when he was thinking of himself as some kind of Hugh Hefner type. A pair of black candles. A paperback called *The Imaginary Christian* that she had tried to read, at his suggestion. An empty Gallo Blanc de Blancs bottle (the religious ones always need alcohol to get the motor running) and a crumpled bag of Funyuns, his favorite. That reminded her to retrieve his toothbrush and mouthwash from the bathroom sink. And the box of Magnum XL.

One thing about Eugene she would miss.

She fished the little key from its hidey-hole at the back of the highboy dresser, turned the ingenious rod-and-pin mechanism that unlocked all seven drawers at once. One drawer for each day of the week—Eugene was the bottom one, the Saturday drawer. There was nothing left in it but one white crew sock, a can of athlete's-foot powder, and a Christian tract: a hand-sized comic book called "This Was Your Life!"

Georgia flipped through, recalling how the Campus Crusade girls used to hand out these things at football games before heading up under the bleachers to make out with boys.

She slid the photo of grinning Eugene out of the silver frame. She set the frame back on the bedside table, and dropped the photo in the Hull's sack. She carried the sack down to the alley and stuffed it in the garbage can.

Night was falling through the trees. She went back upstairs to turn on the lights.

Eugene Hendrix had arrived in Six Points with two strikes against him: (A) he was from north Alabama, practically a Yankee, and (B) he had come to replace the Rev. Onus L. Satterfield, beloved pastor of the First Baptist of Six Points for the past forty-three years.

Eugene managed to ingratiate himself that very first Sunday by preaching on the subject of whether God would root for Auburn or Alabama. In the end, he satisfied the whole congregation by concluding that God was probably an Auburn man—like most of the men in the church, coincidentally—while the rebellious Jesus no doubt would have sided with the Crimson Tide just to irritate his father.

Georgia put down the paper towels and Windex. She retraced her steps downstairs, to the garbage can. It was full dark now, crickets fiddling in the trees. She retrieved the crumpled-up Hull's sack and carried it to the backyard, the barbecue pit.

Grandpa Speeler and Uncle T.C. built this pit from stones they lugged in croaker sacks from the river bottom. Georgia fished Eugene's cigarette lighter from the sack, placed the sack on the grate, and fetched a can of lighter fluid from the garage.

She squeezed the can with both hands, enjoying the *goonk* of the liquid glugging out. She used a good bit more fluid than was necessary. She flicked the lighter and tossed it, *WOOF!* It blew bigger than she'd thought, a Wizard of Oz belch of flame that lit up the whole yard and the trees in the neighbors' yards. Georgia jumped—a faint smell of burning, the light hairs crisped on her arm.

She picked up a stick and poked at the sack until she was satisfied it would burn completely, then headed back toward the garage.

"Cookin' weenies?" Brother jumped from the shadows.

She tried to act as if he hadn't startled her. "Don't touch that. I'm just burning some trash."

"I'm hungry, Georgie. Cook me a weenie!"

"Hush. The whole neighborhood can hear you."

"You gonna drive me?"

"Give me five minutes, okay? I'm almost finished upstairs."

"I'll wait in the car," he said. "Give me the keys so I can listen to the radio."

If she gave him the keys he would drive off in her car. "Can you just wait in the house until I'm done?"

Brother huddled in the flickering firelight. "Aw come on, I won't wreck your car," he whined.

Maybe not, she thought, but when you get pulled over with

your license revoked, whose car are they gonna impound? Not yours, because funny thing, you haven't got one, because you would have to have a job or at least some money of your own, which is something that will never happen.

All she said was, "Forget it."

"Why you so mean to me, Dimmy?" Brother made a face like a demon.

She shook her head. "Go wait for me in the house, Linda Blair."

He pulled his sweatshirt hood over his head and vanished in the darkness of the side yard.

It was not a good sign, Brother going back to his old sneaky ways. When he was twelve, his favorite game was to sneak up on Georgia to scare her. He hadn't done it since the night she was carrying scissors and nearly stabbed him in the eye.

Brother spent most of high school in detention. Every time the authorities got hold of him, they handed him back in worse shape. He wasn't in school that long, or jail that long, or the army that long, but each of them did a real number on him. He went into the army a beautiful kid, slightly dumb, all mixed up. That was eight years ago—look at him now. Twenty-six years old. In the mornings he looked forty. He existed on cigarettes, Fritos, and beer, which is what he drank when he "wasn't drinking."

At first the meetings seemed to be doing him good, but he was backsliding all the time. He missed appointments with his parole officer. He wasn't supposed to leave the house after nine p.m., but he breezed in and out all night long without bothering to hide it. Brother thought of his screwups as amusing anecdotes he could use to entertain his low-life friends.

You can't help who you're born as, Georgia often said to herself. *But at least you can try to rise above it.*

She got the sheets humming in the dryer, and headed upstairs. Warm floral exhaust floated up through the cracks in the floor. She shook out the white comforter. Eugene had said its whiteness made him nervous, always afraid he would spill wine on it, or worse.

She went to the highboy. The top drawer, Sunday. She slid the judge's photo out of its waxed-paper sleeve and put it in the silver frame where Eugene's picture had been. She brought out three framed prints—angled views of Gen. Robert E. Lee on his horse, Traveller—and placed them on the mantel. She draped an antique lace panel across the back of the velvet chair.

She wound the mantel clock, then unfolded a linen towel on the dresser for his mother's silver hairbrush and hand mirror. Georgia didn't use these objects, but she laid them out for him to see. His eyes always went to the dresser to make sure they were there.

Georgia filled the lamp with oil and lit it, closed the French doors, cranked up the window unit. She turned off the electric lamps, and slid the soundtrack of Ken Burns's *The Civil War* into the CD player. Two logs on the grate, a twist of newspaper underneath. A fresh box of matches ready to strike.

One turn of the key locked all seven drawers. She put the key in its hidey-hole in back.

The judge thought the room always looked like this. Each man thought the same thing. None of them imagined that Georgia changed the decor every day, along with the sheets on the bed and the picture in the frame.

Each man thought he was the only one. That was essential to

Georgia's arrangement. She never let herself get cavalier about the details. Only by observing strict rules of separation was she able to keep all these plates spinning on sticks.

It wasn't just for herself she was doing this. It was for Little Mama, who'd had three husbands but never one who left her a nickel...and for useless Brother...but mainly for someone who waited for a sum of money every fourth Saturday at the Western Union, Poydras Street, New Orleans.

An old debt Georgia was still paying down.

In the highboy were seven drawers, one for each day of the week. There was a man for each drawer except Monday. Monday was her night off.

Now, though, the cleaning out of Rev. Saturday left two drawers empty.

These men were not Georgia's lovers, exactly, although she let them think they were. Each one thought he was helping to support his mistress.

To Georgia, they were more like clients. Or patients. She thought of herself as a kind of scientist, or therapist. A counselor employing nontraditional methods. She had rescued more than one marriage in Six Points, she knew that. Didn't the men say she was the only reason they were able to stay with their wives? Every one of them told her that, sooner or later.

Pay attention was her big lesson from today. She was appalled to think of herself daydreaming in that pew, admiring herself in the mirror in her head, oblivious to the unfolding threat. She should have seen Brenda Hendrix coming from ten miles away.

Good God, she had teetered on the very edge of disaster! What if Eugene had blurted her name?

There they sat in the pews, listening to that sermon—every one of them. Sunday the judge. Tuesday the president of the First National Bank. Wednesday the doctor. Thursday the newspaper publisher. Friday the sheriff. And of course the one who was preaching, the man of the Lord: Mr. Saturday Night!

3

Preachers have been hypocrites since before the time of Christ, Georgia thought. She pictured the decoupaged plaque in the choir room. Who do you think invited those money changers into the temple? The man in charge. A preacher. So why did it come as such a shock when Eugene turned out to be the worst kind of hypocrite—

Oh let it go! It's over and done.

But if you don't learn from the past, it can come back to bite you. Georgia had made a major mistake. She had let herself get a little thing going for that man.

So? Mistakes were made. Lessons learned. Time to move on.

"What are you muttering about?" Brother said.

Georgia started. "I'm not muttering."

"Ah Georgie, somethin' is definitely up with you. First I find you out back, settin' fire to mysterious objects. Now you talking to yourself like some ol' crazy woman."

Georgia touched the brakes. "You want to walk?"

"It's okay for Mama to lose it," Brother said, "but can't both of you lose it at the same time. I can't take care of you both."

She snorted. "Like you ever took care of anybody. You can't even take care of yourself!"

Zing! Got him! He flinched.

Georgia hated how she sounded, like some naggy old hag of a sister. She took a deep breath and tried again. "If you would just make some attempt, Brother. There's Help Wanted signs all over town. You don't have to really get a job—just look like you're trying to get one. That would be enough to satisfy Mama."

"No it wouldn't," he said. "She won't be satisfied till I'm dead, or she is. And even then, you wait—we'll be trying to put her in the ground and she'll be telling us we're doing it wrong."

"Bite your tongue." Georgia flipped on the turn signal. "What on earth would we do without Mama?"

Brother said, "Well, for one thing, we could breathe."

"I am breathing just fine, thank you. If you're not, maybe you should give up smoking."

"Here is good," he said. "I can walk from here. Thanks for the lift."

Georgia stopped the Civic one block short of the T. C. Looney Community Health Center. Apparently they were back in high school and he didn't want to be seen accepting a ride from his sister.

Ahead, Georgia made out the lighted doorway of the low-slung brick building, the silhouettes of people catching a smoke before the meeting. The most prominent shape was Sims Bailey in his big-bellied overalls, flannel shirt, Red Man cap. The "anonymous" part of AA didn't count for much in a town as small as Six Points. Everyone knew who the regulars were: Candy Lemmon and her husband Ralph, Davis Sanders who owned the antique shop, Carl Wilmot, Raylene Coombs, the Boxley kid (Ernest? Ernie?), J. T. Cobb of the savings and loan, and of course

Ted Horn, Georgia's own Dr. Wednesday, who was good to let her know when Brother was skipping meetings.

"I'll see you here in one hour," said Georgia.

"Don't bother," said Brother. "Me and Sims are gonna go shoot some pool afterwards, or something."

"Come on, Brother. You can't be going out drinking after your AA meeting."

"What, are you my parole officer now?"

She leaned across the seat to shut the door. "If you're not here in an hour, that's who you can talk to about it."

He tucked his thumbs in his armpits, and waggled his wings at her. "What happened to good ol' Sister Georgie? She was a lot more fun. I really miss her."

Would it ever be possible for Brother to address her without that snide mocking tone? Remember when he was the cutest little boy, when he loved his Sister Georgie more than anything in the world?

"One hour," she said, and drove on. She glimpsed him in the rearview, strutting up to Sims Bailey. Still such a beautiful kid— that angel face, those sunny blond curls had gotten him into more trouble through the years. Nobody could ever say no to that face. Nobody ever imagined that a boy with a face like that could be up to no good. That's how Brother wound up the front man, the lookout, driver of the getaway car.

Am I my brother's keeper? Not on your life.

Georgia had to focus on what was important: it was the Sunday evening before the Tuesday luncheon, and she was out of waxed paper. You cannot make Chow Mein Noodle Cookies without it.

She hated to drive all the way out to Hull's for one item, so she drove across the tracks behind the water tower to the Kwik-M Mart knowing she'd pay double, then they didn't have waxed paper, so she had to go to Hull's anyway. It would have been a total waste of an hour if she hadn't come back downtown via Camellia Street and spotted Krystal's forest-green Subaru in its spot behind city hall. Georgia slid her Civic in beside it. Twenty minutes of Krystal was as good as two hours of anybody else.

"Girl, don't you come in here wasting my time," Krystal crowed when she saw her. "You know some of us peons have to work for a living."

"This is what you call work?" said Georgia. "How many times have you beaten Sol today?"

Rhonda Peavey smiled up from the desk at Krystal's door. "Well hey Georgia! Don't you look good!"

"Thanks, Rhonda. I can't believe she drags you down here on a Sunday night just to watch her play Sol."

"I ain't playing no Sol!" Krystal rose up from the huge cherry mayoral desk, her arms spread for a big friendly hug. "I've been down here since church, doing the people's vital business. And here comes you, waltzing in to mess me up." Krystal went to the Methodist, as her family always had. "Mmm, you smell as good as you look. What is that, Calvin Klein?"

Georgia settled into a wooden armchair. "Don't tell me you don't recognize Chanel Number 5."

"That ain't Chanel," Krystal said. "Too fruity."

"You're just smelling my Juicy Fruit," Georgia said. "And don't say 'ain't.' It makes you sound country."

"I am country, and I truly do not give a shit who knows it." Krystal was barrel-shaped: wide, round, low to the ground. Twice a year she came back from Montgomery with another load of cropped mayoral jackets and industrial-strength wool suits from Dillard's. Being a short, portly lady mayor in lower Alabama was definitely a fashion challenge. Occasionally Georgia tried to offer suggestions, to lighten her look with a scarf or a colorful blouse— but it was like putting a feather on a battleship. Anyway Krystal had gotten herself reelected three times with this look. It was pointless to change.

Through the door Georgia saw Rhonda pretending to file a piece of paper while hanging on every word of their conversation. Georgia asked Krystal with her eyes: *Can we shut the door?*

Krystal pantomimed, one hand cupped to her ear, *If we do, she'll just listen through the crack.* They were such old friends they didn't need words to communicate.

Krystal cleared her throat. "Rhonda, could you run over to the judge's office and see if Shelley's got that ruling yet?"

"She didn't, when I talked to her ten minutes ago," Rhonda replied.

"Well, maybe she does now. Run over there and wait for it, would you please, ma'am?" Lady mayors had to be five times more polite than anyone, Georgia thought. Even to subordinates.

Georgia said, "Don't you know only sinners work on Sunday?"

Krystal explained that it was all Judge Barnett's fault, goddamn garlic-reeking old dinosaur. He had been working nights and weekends to thwart Krystal's annexation plan. She was awaiting a copy of his latest ruling so the city attorney could file an appeal. The whole thing was so complicated it made Georgia's head swim, millage rate differentials and periodic fee adjustments...Krystal's goal was to bring city services to the black, unincorporated side of town, East Six Points, commonly known as "East Over," as in "east, over there." Her annexation plan had run into a wall of white male dinosaurs who didn't want their tax money going for fire hydrants for shiftless blacks who used their food stamps to buy Doritos at Hull's Market. Georgia didn't think it was anybody's business what people bought with their food stamps. She was glad there were people like Krystal to fight these things on her behalf.

Rhonda went off on her errand. Krystal and Georgia caught up on each other's news. Georgia told about her confrontation with Brenda Hendrix, and Eugene's startling decision to stay with her.

"You didn't honestly think he would leave her?" said Krystal. "Damn, George. A preacher, married, four little girls—how much more unavailable can a man be?"

"That's not the point. I don't even want him! The point is, he chose her. Over me. Now, why did he do that? Am I losing my charms? Tell me the truth."

Krystal rolled her eyes. "Please. You've got entirely too many charms for your own good. Listen to me—Eugene is a man. Automatically that makes him an idiot. And you know that wife of his pushes him around like a baby stroller. Anyway, you're gonna be seeing his face in the pulpit every Sunday from now on, so you'd better just get over it."

Georgia couldn't help a little smile. "Maybe not."

"What does that mean?" Krystal tilted her head. "Georgia. What did you do?"

Even when she confessed, Krystal didn't quite believe her. She couldn't believe Little Mama could make one phone call and have Eugene assigned to a rural circuit in southeast Arkansas, or that Georgia would be so bold as to dial up the movers and pretend to be Brenda. "I swear to God, Georgia, is there anything you wouldn't do?"

Georgia smirked. "Don't cross me, hear?"

After much clucking and shaking her head, Krystal began to describe her adventures at the Mayors' League meeting in Atlanta. "There was this girl mayor from Kentucky, Louise Massengill—"

"Like the douche?" Georgia snickered.

"*You're* the douche! God, are you juvenile!" Krystal leaned across the desk to deliver a fake smack on the arm. "Anyway she was a nice gal, so pretty and smart...We wound up in that revolving bar, you know, the top of the Peachtree Plaza? Lord, we must have had about fifty of them revolving margaritas. Turns out girl mayors have more in common than you might think. Next thing I know, Louise goes, 'Come on, hon, let's go out and get some fresh air,' so I said hell why not, and we—"

"I can't believe you can drive by yourself in that Atlanta traffic," said Georgia. Sometimes you had to stop Krystal from telling more than she meant to.

Krystal registered the interruption with a little downward smile. "Nothing to it, as long as you stay in your lane." She shook her head and changed the subject. "Hey, shouldn't you be getting into a panic about now? Two days till D-day, you're supposed to be freaking out."

"Oh no," Georgia said. "Everything's under control." She ticked off all the food she'd already made. "If I wasn't sitting here waiting on my alkie brother to finish his meeting, I'd be home making Chow Mein Noodle Cookies instead of falling behinder every minute."

"They're called 'haystacks.' I guess you're too ignorant to know that," said Krystal.

Georgia laughed. "Haystacks! Well, that does sound appetizing. Here, have a bite of some hay!"

Krystal said, "I'm bringing those blue-cheese tea biscuits whether you want me to or not. They are absolutely the best thing I ever put in my mouth—"

"Since Billy Satterfield?" Georgia finished. That joke went back to high school. It still made them laugh.

"Oh Georgia, you are a big ol' mess," Krystal said. "Let me back to my stupid spreadsheet. You want me to come by tonight and help you cook?"

Georgia pondered. "I could really use you more tomorrow—to set the tables, do your arrangements? You're so good with the flowers and linens and all."

Krystal smiled. "Why, thank you. That's nice of you to say."

"Don't get the bighead," said Georgia. "I'm just stating a fact."

She knew Brother wouldn't come to meet her. She went to the rendezvous point anyway, so she could hold it over his head. She waited precisely five minutes, then drove around the front of the T. C. Looney Community Health Center. Ralph Lemmon leaned against his car, smoking, talking to J. T. Cobb of the savings and loan. Georgia started to roll down her window to ask, but no, they were "anonymous." Besides, it was no mystery where Brother had gone—to shoot pool with Sims, like he said. If he wanted to violate his parole, let him. Let him go back to jail if he had no more self-control than that. Georgia always got a better night's sleep when he was behind bars, anyway.

She pointed her Honda toward home. This was the first evening that actually had a feeling of September: angled shadows, a touch of gold in the light, a river of blackbirds streaming overhead. Just when you thought you couldn't take another minute of summer, here came the first hint of cooler, longer nights ahead.

All this golden light raised a lump in her throat. The old town seemed suddenly lovely: long green lawns stretched out under live oaks, sprinklers chattering, flinging arcs of bright glitter. Some of the clapboard cottages were as old as the live oaks. Kids made skateboard racket on the broken sidewalks.

At home, Georgia stirred up a pan of cornbread to go with the peas. She propped Little Mama in her chair with her blanket and supper and the Channel 12 news from Montgomery. Little Mama loved to rail against the black weather girl, Gwen somebody, who was actually very pretty, Georgia thought. Well-spoken.

"Look at her," said Little Mama. "They all dress like prostitutes these days. Look how low cut that blouse is!"

"I'm gonna go get my bath," said Georgia.

Little Mama said, "Did you bring the Mentholatum?"

"It's right there by your hand. If it'd been a snake woulda bit you."

"I thought you forgot it again." Little Mama opened the jar, put a dot of ointment on her upper lip. She used vats of Mentholatum but never had a cold. Georgia suspected the smell reminded her of all the Kools she used to smoke.

Mama waved a claw at the TV. "Would you look? Everything she's got is hanging out!"

"I know, Ma. You hate poor ol' Gwen. You've hated her for years."

"They used to have that nice gal from Evergreen, whatever happened to her? Oh, that's right—she was white, so they took her off. Everything for the Nigroes these days."

"Yes, Mama. You're right." You had to agree with her, or she would never shut up.

"They never let one of 'em have their own show until that

Diahann Carroll. Now they done taken over the whole damn TV! I mean, come on! Give 'em a channel of their own, I don't care. But do they have to be on every last one of our channels too?"

"Yes, Mama, they do. It's the law now. They have to be on every channel."

"It's that goddamn Rosa Parks."

"That's exactly who did it," said Georgia. "They should never have put her in charge of television."

"Did you bring my Mentholatum?"

Georgia peered at her. "Mama. It's next to your hand."

"I thought you forgot it again," Mama said.

Georgia didn't say if it had been a snake it would have bit her. She loved her mother, although when she tried to think of reasons why, all she got was a headache. She hoped Little Mama would have a happy old age, but secretly she also hoped it didn't drag on and on, like some mothers. Even if you love them, you don't want them hanging around forever, do you?

Also, Little Mama was a terrible patient. You could not do a thing to suit her. She used to say, "When I get old, I hope you just take me out in the woods and shoot me."

She hadn't said it lately. Probably thinks I'll take her up on it, Georgia thought grimly.

Ah, well, it's part of the Ant Connection, everybody working for the good of the anthill, the strong ant helping the weaker ant, daughter ant helping mother ant—and Brother ant—daughter ant giving and giving, day in day out, working working working until she gets so exhausted she drops the crumb. Some other ant snatches it up and carries it down the hole. And that's how the world goes around!

Georgia turned the shower as hot as she could stand it, to make her skin glowy and warm. She slathered her body with rose milk, sudsed and conditioned and rinsed her hair three times. She dried her hair and brushed it out, tied it back with a silk ribbon. She applied oils and potions, elbow cream, knee smoother. She poured a little puddle of eau de toilette in her palm. Drawing two fingers through it, she painted twin stripes of lavender fragrance up her heel, her calf, the back of her knees. She painted the curve of her rib cage, between her breasts, to the nape of her neck.

When she smelled even better than God made her, she slipped into the peach linen chemise with clusters of tiny chiffon roses at the bodice. At the waist she fastened a short, scalloped petticoat of cream-colored flannel, followed by a longer petticoat of white-starched cotton, a third petticoat, a fourth. Over these layers she drew a satin dressing gown—the same shade of peach as the chemise—the embroidered silk-velvet belt, and matching slippers.

These clothes were a gift from the man who would be removing them shortly. He had ordered the complete ensemble for her in three colors—peach, ivory, and a soft rosy pink—from the Civil War reenactors' superstore in Myrtle Beach. Perhaps tonight he wouldn't undress her all the way. Some nights he just liked to play part of the game. Some nights the whiskey made him sleepy and he dozed off in his chair while she rubbed his shoulders. Or he might start to undress her carefully, layer by layer, but fall asleep before he got down to bare skin.

Georgia swished this way and that in front of the mirror, swaying her skirts like a bell. She loved the rustle of stiff cotton against her legs. When the judge wasn't sleepy, he could be downright frisky.

A glance at the clock sent her downstairs in a hurry. Whizzy ticked up the hall to greet her.

"Mama, you need anything? I'm going up to work on my quilt." Georgia used to take such pains to confine her costumes to the apartment, but these days Mama barely noticed whether it was night or day.

"How's the new one coming, baby?"

"Beautiful." Georgia kept walking down the hall. "You're going to love the colors in this one."

"Did you bring my Mentholatum?"

"It's beside your right hand." Georgia held the scrabbling dog inside with one foot while the door hissed shut on its piston. She knew it was risky, blowing off her mother that way. One day she would come back to find Mama dead in that chair—God, wouldn't she feel guilty then!

But it would be just one or two days of guilt. In exchange for years and years of blowing her off. A decent trade, overall.

Every year or so, Georgia drove halfway across Alabama, to a bend in the Catfish River where a little settlement of old black women made quilts. Some of the women were so old they were the granddaughters of actual slaves. The quilts were beautiful: brilliant colors, stark geometric designs. Somebody had wised up the women to the folk-art angle, and now they were charging up to two hundred bucks per quilt—but they charged Georgia half that because she'd been buying their quilts in bulk for years.

She started by giving a few as gifts to well-placed friends. Everybody wanted one after Susan Chastain showed off hers on the Holiday Parade of Homes. Now Georgia sold the quilts with a hefty markup in Alma Pickett's gift shop, Treasures n' Stuff, on

Court Street downtown. Georgia's quilts were famous in Six Points. Everyone assumed she made them herself, though she had never claimed that in actual words. Every couple of weeks she would bring a new example of her handiwork downstairs to show Mama and Brother before driving it over to Alma's shop.

Everyone in Six Points was eager to believe in Georgia's quilting ability. People knew to leave her alone in the evenings. That was quilt-making time, Georgia time. The rule was, you didn't disturb Georgia when she was at work in the apartment unless blood was flowing and the ambulance was already on the way.

What if those old colored women ever stopped making quilts? She barely knew how to thread a needle.

She struck a match to light the lamp, and touched it to the paper beneath the firelogs. She turned the A/C to LO. One last glance around the room told her everything was perfect. A perfect night from a hundred fifty years ago. Georgia was good at this game.

She flipped the switch that turned on the light in the alley. One if by land . . . That was the signal.

Immediately she heard a car door slam. She smiled. He was sitting in his Town Car, waiting for the light. Waiting for her.

Nothing felt quite so stirring as being the object of desire. Georgia had tried most of the known thrills, and this was the one she liked best.

She met him at the iron gate. His fingers curled around hers. She shushed him, hurried him in, stayed behind to lock the gate. She tucked the key in the pocket of her dressing gown.

She found the judge gazing down at his mother's hand mirror, eyes aglow. From the other side of the room he looked forty years old—okay, fifty. You had to get close to see the ruin of years in his face. He had kindly gray eyes and a livid complexion, flushed pink as a ham, blue veins spreading across the crumbly skin of his nose. "My God, woman," he said, "you are a positive vision of heaven."

"Why, Cap'n Barnett, how you do flatter me!" Slipping his seersucker jacket off his shoulders, she steered him to his chair. "I just threw on this old dressing gown till I make up my mind what to wear to Twelve Oaks tonight."

He beamed. "Are you going to the barbecue?"

"Why, you know I am!" she cried. "Don't be a horrid old fool, Jackson Barnett, you know perfectly well you're taking me to eat barbecue, and I don't want to hear another word about it!" She grabbed her Japanese fan and swatted him.

The judge hunched over to untie his shoes. "I'm happy to see you feeling better, Georgia. It looks as if you've recovered completely."

"A girl who faints in the morning is always more lively by evening." She poured whiskey from the crystal decanter on the desk. "Just put that silliness out of your mind."

"I was afraid you might—thank you, darlin'." He wrapped a meaty hand around the glass. "After the way you were stricken, I thought you might not feel up to our rendezvous tonight. It made me realize all over again how precious you are to me. There I sat in the dark—in my carriage, you know—waiting like some lovesick swain. Anxiously awaiting the light in your window."

"You're a sweetheart to wait for me, Captain. I'm a very lucky girl."

His gaze settled upon solemn old Robert E. Lee astride his horse. "No, I'm the one who's lucky. Sunday is the best day of my week, by a long shot."

She agreed that it was for her, too.

She was waiting for him to take a swallow of bourbon, to cut the garlic so she could move in closer. Garlic was the major drawback of Judge Barnett. It was not by accident that she saw him on Sunday and kept Monday free... an extra day for airing out the apartment. "Do you think the Yankees can possibly win the war, Captain?"

His brow darkened. "Not a chance. Our brave boys... Why, it takes three of those Yankee bastards to whip one of ours." He took a sip from the glass. "I did see a dispatch today with glorious news from the front."

"Oh, tell me about it."

"Well, it seems General Lee has whipped the Yankees at Chancellorsville. Sent them reeling back into the woods. The obnoxious Joe Hooker was caught with his trousers down. The word around Washington is he's to be sacked!"

"Wonderful," Georgia said. "I can't keep all the details straight in my little ol' head, but it sounds like great news for our side."

"Oh, it is." The judge patted his knee. "Come sit, my little flower."

"Most gladly," she said, "but—shouldn't we be a tiny bit discreet?" She tugged the sash of the curtain, unfurling a velvet curtain across the French door.

The judge's eyes brightened. Georgia walked the length of the front wall, letting down each panel in turn, until they were inside a candlelit green-velvet tent. She reached into the armoire to press the button on the CD player. A wistful violin sang the melody of Ken Burns from hidden speakers.

It's all about happiness, Georgia thought. Look at the light in his eyes. See the years melt away. It's the little things—the flickering fire, the glow of the oil lamp, the way velvet muffles the tick of the clock.

She perched on his knees, slid her arm around his neck. She pressed her lips to his temple. "Hey darlin'," she said.

His hand stroked her waist, sneaked up her back. "You're delicious."

"You too." Like a slice of garlic bread, she didn't say.

He patted her shoulder. "But you're wearing too many petticoats. Please remove them at once."

She hopped up from his knee, mock-offended. "Captain! Remember yourself!"

He laughed. "You're so good at this. You missed your calling. You should go to New York and be an actress."

"New York? Why should I go to New York?" She considered it her duty to stay in character, even when the judge slipped out. "I have no use for Yankees or snow, either one. But Lord, it is so hot down here. I feel a little feverish, do you mind?" She toyed with the topmost button of the outermost petticoat.

He encouraged her with a grin.

She undid the buttons and danced over to his hand. With two fingers he snagged the waistband. He held on as she twirled, unwinding herself.

The judge gathered the lacy cotton to his face and breathed. "Oh, when this cruel war is over," he said.

"Try not to think about the war." She started on the next row of buttons. "Just think about us, here, tonight."

The fire crackled and spat sparks, a tiny fireworks display. The violin line turned and meandered, mournful as a gray rainy day, but somehow the room felt cheerful. Georgia really did love the old man in a way. She danced close so he could grab the waistband and twirl her, peeling her—she loved the eagerness in his eyes when they were into the game. He was never this young with anyone else, she knew it. Even a ruined old judge has a right to feel young again, once in a while.

Thoughts like these—the rightness of her cause, the good she was doing—helped Georgia transform herself most nights. It took a special kind of woman to slip out of her own skin into a man's fantasy, then back into herself, night after night without losing track of who she was. Sometimes she had to be the most sensitive, sharp-seeing person on earth. Other times it was better to be blind. It took Georgia years to learn this. Right now she had the judge's motor running, and she knew how to put him in DRIVE. She danced to the bathroom and came back with an oval blue pill and a Dixie cup half full of water. "Here, Captain, a tonic for that big ol' headache of yours."

"Thank you, darlin', gettin' bigger every second." He placed the pill on his tongue, tipped his head back, and tossed it down. "Aw yeah. Where were we?"

She made a pouty face. "Well, I was going to get myself all beautified, and let you drive me over to Twelve Oaks to eat barbecue. But I believe you have wickedness on your mind."

He patted his knee. "Damn right I do."

"I don't think it's right, you taking advantage of an innocent girl this way." She batted her eyes. "It's just not gentlemanly. I may have to tell Daddy!"

"Long as you don't tell my wife," he said with a snort. His large sausagey fingers struggled with the buttons of her second-to-last petticoat.

Georgia was afraid he would pop them. She closed her small hands around his. "Let me help you."

"Ah, you're not as innocent as you like to pretend!" His eyes gleamed. "You can't wait to get your skirts off so you can disport yourself like some wild hussy from Savannah!"

She slapped him on the cheek—hard enough to sting. "How dare you! I am a lady and you will treat me as a lady. Do you understand?"

He grinned. "You come here," he growled, yanking her down to his lap, smooching her neck, nibbling up to her ear.

He enjoyed playing strongman, pinning her in place with one hand. She let herself be pinned. They both knew it was playacting. The judge made the decisions in his courtroom, but in this room Georgia was the boss.

He lapped at her earlobe, her throat. She floated up out of herself and thought about the male urge to overpower. She saw it all the time, cropping up in different guises through the week. Men love to prove themselves stronger. To overcome female resistance. Nothing turns a man on like a struggle, even in make-believe. Maybe that's a Darwin thing, an animal thing, an urge all male creatures have in common…part of the great Ant Connection? Are all males rapists in the secret part of their souls? Why else do they like it so much when they get to overcome a woman resisting?

Darwin might point out that the stronger, more dominant male reproduces more often—the satisfaction that comes with conquering the resisting female is selected into the species—but how would Darwin explain a man pretending to be strong as a pretext for a woman to humiliate him? How would you work that out in an anthill? Men are slightly more complicated than ants—but every anthill is ruled by a queen. Not a king. A queen rules the workers, soldiers, and drones. In the world there are billions of anthills, each one ruled by a tiny female dictator.

At least that's how it looked from the perspective of the judge's lap. Why else would the human race be 52 percent female? Women are winning, that's why. We're better at surviving.

In a surge of lust the judge tried to lift Georgia and carry her to the bed, but lost his strength and toppled back to the chair. Georgia spilled to the floor. "Unruly monster!" She scrambled up. "Control yourself, sir!"

"My God, you are one hot number." He staggered to his feet and chased her around the chair, giggling like a boy. "Stop that! Come here and accept your punishment."

"You're not going to spank me again, Captain! I've been so good!"

"You little fornicatress," he growled. "Following the army— pretending you're a lady—it's downright immoral!"

She wished she hadn't noticed the glassy strand of drool dangling from the corner of his mouth. Something like that could let all the air out of an evening. You had to avert your eyes, fight off the image, and keep going.

Georgia was thankful for the blue pill. Really, it was the miracle of the age! It put hours back into her evening. What used to take two or three hours could now be wrapped up inside of forty-five minutes. But you had to be careful—it could also be a little blue hand grenade. Once you pulled the pin and set it ticking, you'd better be ready to move—

And move they did, more or less together, to the big squeaky four-poster, where the last of her petticoats came off with no help from anybody. Georgia was down to her pale peach chemise. Judge Barnett's suspenders were hopelessly snarled at his waist.

She caught a gust of garlic as she clambered over his legs, laughing, pushing his hands away. If she undressed him all the way, it would add at least half an hour to his visit. She couldn't help thinking of the twelve dozen figs she had to stuff with Gorgonzola and wrap in prosciutto before bedtime. She reached for his zipper and tugged.

"Wench!" he cried. "Can't keep your hands off me? What is it you're wanting?" His face was even pinker—the first flush of the medication. "You can't even wait to get your—wait, no, let me— let me help you."

A discreet glance at the clock told her she had given him exactly thirty-five minutes of top-quality foreplay. It had been a few Sundays since they went all the way, what with his sleepiness and the shoulder rubs and all, so he was really ready. Three or four minutes, tops. She yanked down his trousers and his baggy boxers, hauled out his stubby pink thing, rolled a rubber on it, and climbed aboard.

His tough little willy was not as significant a drawback as the garlic. Neither was it any sort of added attraction. Women who say size doesn't matter are lying through their clenched, frustrated teeth. Even under the engorging influence of the blue pill, Georgia felt little more than a stirring down there, a kind of rhythmic poke-poke. She hipped and hollered and made the bedsprings squeak as if she'd never endured anything quite so splittingly huge.

Another! Satisfied! Client!

The judge bucked and wallowed around with a sloppy grin on his face. Georgia dragged the coverlet back and made sure his flabby butt was on the sheet where it belonged, then she tightened down on him, speeded up and brought him home, hey hey *BANG!* And then yep! There it was.

"Hooeee! Damn, woman! Yeah!" He threw his hands up as if he'd just crossed the goal line. "Oh yeah!"

She leaned down to kiss him. Garlic. "Mmmm, my goodness, Jackson," she hummed into his mouth. "You are simply over-powering tonight."

"Careful, careful—don't—wait, my—" He groaned and shifted. She detached herself.

She slipped into the bathroom to perform a quick hygienic procedure, came back with towels and a steaming washcloth. She got him washed up, tucked away, purring like a happy old cat. This was his usual pattern—as soon as it was over, he turned into a sleepy kitty craving a nap and the comforting stroke of his mistress's hand. Sometimes Georgia had to perform fancy tricks to get him dressed and out the door before he dozed off for good.

No man was ever allowed to spend the night. A steady rotation under cover of darkness was essential to the successful application of the system. Sometimes Georgia felt the passing urge to snuggle up and spend the whole night in the arms of one or the other. It had been a long time since she had allowed herself that. Her life was too complex. She had responsibilities. She had plates spinning on sticks.

"Time to go, Captain," she said in a quiet voice. "Daddy's on his way home, and if he finds us in this situation—there's no telling."

"Oh Georgia," he said, buttoning his shirt. "What would I do without you?"

"Or I, you?" She kissed his pink cheek. "Will you excuse me? I'll be back."

Her second trip to the bathroom was a signal, as specific as the light in the alley, although Georgia had never discussed it with the judge. She closed the door, turned on the water in the sink, flushed the commode, hummed a little tune. She sat on the toilet lid, giving him time to remember that he needed to reach into his coat for the envelope and place it atop the highboy.

This was the only part of the game that made Georgia uncomfortable. There was no completely unembarrassing way to go about it. It helped to remember a few important facts:

1. She never asked anyone for money. Whatever happened to be left atop the highboy was a gift, freely given. Not a payment for anything.
2. She never asked for any money.
3. The money was a gift.

As long as everyone remembered these facts there could be no misunderstanding. What you had was a simple exchange of gifts. Georgia gave the gift of her time, her complete attention, her kisses, sometimes more. She gave these things freely, willingly. They were hers to give.

In return—no, not in return for anything, but of their own free will, with no connection to any action of Georgia's—the men offered gifts of their own. They knew she was not wealthy; everyone knew the Bottoms fortune had dried up shortly after Big Sue changed the family name. Everyone knows it's expensive to keep up a big old antebellum falling-down house with a sick old mother and a worthless brother in tow. So they gave her gifts.

In the movies, men gave their sweethearts diamonds, or roses, or fancy kitchen appliances. Georgia liked cash. No fuss, no raised eyebrows at the bank. If there was one thing we all learned from Richard Nixon, she thought, it was the importance of avoiding a paper trail.

Sometimes it took a bit of extremely subtle hint dropping to get a man to come up with the idea on his own, to realize after the third or fourth date how lucky he was to be spending one night a week enjoying the lady's company, and it might be the gentlemanly thing to offer up a little—a little gift, just to help with the upkeep of the place—not that she was his mistress, which would make her beholden to him, but—after all she had been so kind, and there she was in that big old rambling house with the mother and the useless brother. What harm could there be in a gift?

He was clumsy the first time, trying to press a wad of bills into her hand or some such, so that she had to pull back in a huff and refuse, horrified by the very idea, whatever he meant to imply she was definitely not that kind of girl! Of course he would rush to reassure her he hadn't meant anything at all. A gift! That's all. Just a gift. Eventually he would come to insist that she take it, practically force it on her, to prove it was only a gift. With no strings attached.

And although she resisted, acted hurt by the very idea and turned her face away, eventually she came around to telling him how awfully kind he was, how sensitive to notice that her family was not exactly made out of money. She discreetly let him know that any such gift would not go for dresses or frivolous things, but directly to the stack of household bills.

She was so honestly, quietly grateful that the man would be moved to offer the same gift every week.

Each man thought he was the only man. Each thought the whole idea was his idea, his gift the only gift. That was the secret to making a living, the Georgia way.

4

Emma Day Pettigrew's Florida room had a great view of the relevant side of the parsonage, the front door, driveway, and garage.

Georgia considered each of the four houses that backed up to the church property before deciding that Floyd and Emma Day's Florida room had the best view. With its fifties-style screened windows, frosted glass slats that cranked open to let in the heat of the morning, sitting in that room felt like being in a garden with no bugs.

Once Georgia made the calculation, it was only a matter of how to get herself invited to Emma Day's house at ten minutes till eight on a Monday morning.

Thank God Emma Day said, "Of course, come on over, I've been working in my garden for hours." When she answered the door, Georgia led her through her own house, singing the praises of the Florida room all the way there. She sank down on an elegant wicker settee.

Emma Day was a morning person, in a morning-gardening outfit straight out of *Southern Living:* cute turquoise flip-flops, white pedal pushers, white cotton sweater with pink stripes, and a little more makeup than is advisable in broad daylight. Her hair was a blond ball of cotton candy. Her skinny white pedal pushers bore not the first grass stain, not a mark of any kind. How could you garden in white pants and stay that clean? Perhaps she had run inside to change when Georgia called.

Here she came dragging a folded-up card table as if it was too heavy for a woman of her petite build. "Is one table going to be enough?" Emma Day said. "We have a couple more in the garage."

"One is plenty," said Georgia. "I hope you know you're saving my life! I didn't even know my card table had a bad leg till I went to set it up this morning. Talk about the eleventh hour! Hey, and this is a nice one, too. Much nicer than mine, I think Mama ordered it from Sears a hundred years ago. You better remember to ask for this one back, or I'm liable to keep it. Where'd you get it?"

"Let me think." Emma Day looked pleased to be asked. "I think the Tar-jay."

"The what?" Georgia said.

"The Tar-jay? You know, Target. In Mobile. Everybody calls it Tar-jay like in French. Cause it's like a fancy Walmart."

"I never even heard of it," Georgia confessed. She prided herself on keeping up with the latest trends in retail, even if she did live in a hick town that didn't have any better store than a half-sized Belk's.

"Oh my God, Georgia, in that case we've got to go! They have the greatest stuff. It feels more expensive than Walmart, but really it isn't." Emma Day seemed excited by the notion of the two of them going off on a shopping trip. She'd sounded thrilled on the phone when Georgia asked for the loan of a card table for her famous September luncheon.

Georgia and Emma Day were friendly enough, but they didn't socialize. Emma Day had more money; Georgia was more popular; on looks, Georgia probably would win. Georgia had to invite

Emma Day to the luncheon because she was best friends with Trisha, Krystal's first cousin, who couldn't *not* be invited.

"This coffee is delicious," Georgia said. It was some kind of milky cappuccino, a sprinkling of cinnamon on the foam.

"Isn't it good? Oh my God, Georgia, I never thought an expresso machine could change my life, but it absolutely has. Do you have one? You have to get one. It keeps me so wired I get twice as much done! Some nights I used to find myself pining for a double expresso after dinner... Now I just go in and make one! I can get the whole house clean before bedtime!"

Emma Day would make a great spokesmodel, Georgia thought.

On a pedestal in the corner of the Florida room stood a sculpture of a fawn, a rough-hewn bronze Bambi grazing in the bronze grass at its feet. To Georgia it looked tacky. But she didn't know the first thing about art. Anything that came with its own pedestal and spotlights must have cost a fortune.

She wondered where Floyd Pettigrew got the money. His job with the highway department didn't pay enough to buy bronzes of fawns, or fancy white wicker furniture, or his-and-hers Infinitis. If there was family money it must have come from Floyd's side. Emma Day was a Windham from right here in Six Points. Nothing wrong with the Windhams but they never had any more money than anybody.

"If I drank coffee I'd never get to sleep," Georgia said.

"I drink it all day and never have a problem," said Emma Day. "I guess if you're an addict like I am... I give myself a workout in the yard, with my roses and all. I really am kind of obsessed."

"I work out sometimes too," Georgia said, picturing herself snuggling onto Eugene's lap. "But it doesn't help me sleep. Sometimes it gets me all worked up, you know? The opposite effect."

Emma Day laughed. Once you got past the cotton-candy hair, Emma Day was all right. Georgia had wondered if her hairstyle was ironic, the way some modern girls favor old-fashioned cat-eye glasses, or corny decoupaged purses shaped like steamer trunks. One look at the bronze Bambi and Georgia knew Emma Day did not have an ironic bone in her body. She should have guessed, from the two perfect children who sat between Emma Day and Floyd every Sunday, the only kids in church who actually seemed to listen to the sermon.

"You really do have the most beautiful flowers, Emma Day. How do you keep 'em looking so good?" To Georgia there was no more boring subject on earth. Who cares what grows in the dirt? The lowliest worker ant has a thousand times more brainpower than the smartest flower on earth.

Georgia smiled and cocked her head as Emma Day chattered on about coreopsis and clematis and the importance of natural rainwater and nitrogen in the soil.

From the bottom of all sound came a rumble so low it trembled the floor beneath Georgia's chair. Outside, something large was moving—okay yes, here it comes, first the grille then the tractor of a huge moving van sliding out of the shade of the pecan tree, a long trailer with a cartoon cowboy on the side, wearing a crown, riding a truck that snorted and bucked like a bronco. Charlie Ross Regal Moving.

Georgia checked her watch: eight on the dot. The truck slid to a stop in a pool of sunshine at the end of the church driveway. The engine continued rumbling. Two men climbed down and went to drag open the sliding door. A third man tucked a clipboard under his arm and walked up the driveway to the parsonage.

Emma Day was chattering on and didn't notice. Georgia had

the weird sensation that the truck was some kind of mirage, a piece of theatrical scenery that had been rolled into view. It was so big it didn't look quite real.

She knew she couldn't go on staring out the window. She locked her gaze on the tip of Emma Day's nose.

Now came a small commotion, raised voices in the vicinity of the parsonage door.

Emma Day placed her cup in its saucer, and swiveled neatly on her wrought-iron chair. "What in the world?"

"I heard a rumor they were moving," Georgia said. "I didn't know it would be this soon."

Emma Day was shocked. "Eugene and Brenda? They're not moving."

Georgia said, "Isn't that a moving van?"

Now Brenda Hendrix was out in the driveway, hollering at the man with the clipboard. You couldn't make out individual words, but it was easy to get the gist.

Brenda still wore her hot-pink chenille robe and slippers. Georgia detected the shadow of Eugene inside the screen door. Wasn't it like him to stay inside letting his wife do all the yelling?

"My stars, Georgia! Did they make some announcement at church? Floyd tied one on Saturday night, as usual, so we had to miss."

"I heard something," said Georgia. "But not from Eugene. I forget who told me."

"Well I was over there yesterday and Brenda didn't say a word! You'd think she would...I mean, my gosh, we've been neighbors for years."

"I heard he got transferred," said Georgia. "To—I don't know, Oklahoma? Arkansas? Somewhere like that."

Now Eugene pushed open the screen door and stepped out-side. He was moving so slowly it was obvious he didn't want to come out at all. Teebo Riley had promised Little Mama he would call Eugene immediately with word of his new assignment. That meant the Hendrixes had had all night for the truth to sink in. Still, the moving truck at their door the next morning must have come as a shock. And Eugene was not a morning person.

For a time, Brenda seemed to be yelling at both Eugene and the clipboard guy, who had subtly backed up a few steps. The other men hung back at the truck.

Suddenly Brenda ratcheted up the pitch of that cutting voice so that everyone on the block could hear. "I don't give a god-damn what he said, Gene, this is *not* the way people get a new assignment!"

Eugene said something—undoubtedly telling her to keep her voice down, don't take the Lord's name in vain.

"Oh God, I *hate* you!" Brenda slapped him across the face and charged into the house. *Bang!* went the door.

One of the men at the truck let out a whistle.

The bang of the screen door broke the spell. Emma Day turned to Georgia. "My stars. Did you see that?"

"I sure did."

"Okay—I just—I guess I'm not believing my eyes."

"Does she hit him like that a lot, you think?" Georgia said.

"Not that I'm aware," said Emma Day. "Not that I've ever seen, anyway. But you never know what goes on behind closed doors."

"I just don't understand married people," Georgia said. "Per-sonally I wouldn't put up with too much of that before I'd be out that door."

"Well, you do what you have to, I guess," said Emma Day.

The clipboard man motioned to his associates. They came warily up the drive, as if Brenda might fly through the door and set upon them next.

Emma Day gazed at Eugene, quietly conferring with the clipboard guy. "But Reverend Hendrix is such a sweet man," she said softly.

Georgia shrugged. "Looks can be deceiving...although he has been a good preacher, he sure has. A little depressing sometimes, but good in his heart."

She knew Emma Day couldn't wait for her to leave so she could run across that yard and find out what was what.

Georgia had felt a swell of pleasure when Brenda slapped him, but after that she felt a little bereft. Something was ending, one chapter of her life closing for good. She would have no trouble finding someone to occupy her Saturday nights, but it would not be Eugene.

Here came a moving man out the door with an end table in each hand, and another bearing a stack of dinette chairs. The clipboard man wedged something in the hinge to hold the door open.

"It does feel like eavesdropping," said Georgia. "As much as I'd like to stay and visit."

"Oh, don't go," said Emma Day, without much enthusiasm. As pleased as she had been to improve her friendship with Georgia, the tableau across the lawn was much more interesting.

Georgia kissed the air by Emma Day's cheek, picked up the card table in one hand, and crossed another item off her to-do list.

5

Midnight Monday was the moment of transition from the well-thumbed pages of the to-do list to the crisply annotated timing chart. Once Georgia posted the chart on the fridge, she knew what she had to do every minute until the first guests arrived at 11:30 a.m. Tuesday to ensure that each dish reached the proper warmer or ice tray at the ideal serving temperature.

Georgia approached the luncheon with scientific attention to planning, execution, detail. Any ring of the doorbell before 11:30 was strictly ignored, a hard-line policy Krystal thought hilarious. "You really leave 'em standing on the porch until eleven thirty on the dot?"

"I only invite people who know how to read," Georgia said. "The invitation doesn't say eleven fifteen. If I didn't draw the line, they'd show up the night before with sleeping bags. Besides, there are very nice rockers on the porch where they can sit while they wait."

The chart allowed precisely five hours for Georgia to sleep. But putting her head on the pillow as scheduled at 1:50 a.m. didn't stop her mind from whirling in circles, recurring images of Eugene stepping out from behind his screen door to face the consequences of his actions, dinette chairs going past in the moving men's hands, rank after rank of prosciutto-wrapped figs marching toward the horizon...

Georgia desperately needed a good night's sleep, so everyone would remark on how wonderful she looked. She needed a pink, well-rested complexion to set off the gorgeous emerald-green Lauren by Ralph Lauren dress she had special-ordered from the big Belk's in Mobile.

She smiled at the memory of how good she looked in that dress, and snuggled down in the soft warmth of her pillow.

Sometime after three a.m., Brother came stumbling in drunk, third night in a row. He thundered upstairs like a horse busting out of his stall, colliding with every wall and banister on the way to his room.

Georgia got up and went down to find the door standing open, inviting the whole world to come right on in.

Whizzy was standing guard. The sight of Georgia started his tail wagging. She bent down to scratch behind his ears, and shut the door.

It took a while to drift back to sleep. The next time she started awake, the digital clock was cheeping and it was dawn. She felt a pulse of excitement, like Christmas morning when she was a kid. She sprang out of bed without pausing for her usual sigh— God, how she looked forward to this day! She loved being the Perle Mesta of Six Points, her house overflowing with ladies oohing and ahhing at the excellence of the food and decor. She loved overhearing their compliments when they didn't realize she was eavesdropping. Georgia was a long way from wealthy, but once a year she got to feel like the richest lady in town.

The phone was ringing when she stepped out of the shower.

She threw a towel around herself and dripped into the hall. It was Lon Chapman at the bank. He always called before his tellers got in if he needed to make some adjustment to their Tuesday night appointment.

Georgia was careful to maintain legitimate friendships with the men in her life. It was easier than sneaking around trying to hide their calls from Little Mama. Georgia kept her money at Lon's bank, for instance, so he had a good reason to call.

"Hey there," she said. "How's the money business?"

"Come jump in, the money is fine," Lon said with a laugh. "How's the beautiful business?"

"Oh, you flatter me, Lon! And don't let me stop you."

Lon laughed. He was a fun guy—bushy steel-wool hair, wide homely face, a big booming laugh that went off at intervals like a cannon. He talked tough, like a TV detective. He wore swanky clothes (dark shirts, white satin ties) and fancied himself a kind of Six Points playboy, divorced twice when he was younger and single ever since. Several times a year he drove his flashy gold Cadillac to New Orleans for God knows what kind of lost weekend. A few times he'd invited Georgia along, but she'd told him she had no interest at all in New Orleans.

That was one of her biggest whoppers ever. She hadn't been to New Orleans, but she knew it better than some people who lived there. She'd read all the books, studied the maps. New Orleans was Georgia's favorite place in the world. She knew it was her destiny to go there. Every fantasy she ever had about her life ended up in New Orleans. Someday, somehow, when Little Mama was gone, and Georgia's Six Points days were over, she would get down there. And then she'd never leave. She would cling to that place like moss to a tree. She would grow old there, and die there. They would place her body in one of those elegant marble tombs that hold you up out of the damp.

It would be nice to make her first trip to New Orleans on the arm of a big spendy guy like Lon Chapman, who would spring for the best cocktails and suppers, the nicest hotel—an elegant French Quarter inn with a courtyard, a fountain, and a banana tree, like the one in the souvenir brochure from Mama and Daddy's honeymoon.

"What can I do for you, Lonnie?"

"Listen, babe, I know you're busy today but I was hoping I could stop by tonight anyways. Okay? Late is fine with me."

"Oh Lon, honey, not possible, sorry. Did you forget? Today is my September luncheon."

"Yeah, but that's lunchtime, right? I'm talking about tonight. As late as you want to make it. I picked us up a nice bottle of vino in Meridian."

Georgia felt a little wave of irritation—but slow down, now, why should Lon care a thing about your luncheon? That's for ladies. Be flattered he even remembered you were having it.

"Lonnie, I would love to oblige you, sugar, but you don't know how much work it is cleaning up after all these ladies. They go through this house like a pack of wild dogs. By eight o'clock tonight, I'll be too pooped to pop." She lowered her voice. "I'll make it up to you next week."

"Aw come on, Georgia. I need to see you! How 'bout . . . right now? I could say I got a bank association meeting—"

Honestly. It wasn't a month ago Lon called at the last minute to cancel their Tuesday night, some flimsy made-up excuse, and now he wants Georgia to turn cartwheels to work him in on the busiest day of her year? Men have way too much regard for themselves. They start thinking you belong to them, you are their property, you should be ready to entertain them whenever they get a whim to be entertained.

Some girls might conduct their affairs that way. Not this girl.

"No chance, Lonnie, sorry!" She kept her voice light. "I've got a to-do list as long as your arm. Just talking to you now is making me late."

Here came Little Mama down the hall. Lately her forgetting seemed to be worse in the morning. This morning what she had forgotten was her bathrobe. Here she came out of her room in a saggy old bra and big white underpants riding up around her waist. Georgia started to scold her...averted her eyes instead. Little Mama scuttled to the bathroom and slammed the door.

Lonnie kept talking: "Come on, now, babe, you don't know how bad I been—uhm...Yes, okay." His voice straightened out. "Well, of course, with those debentures coming due, I'll have to notify the bank's attorney and then we can authorize the release of those funds. Let me call him, and I'll call you back."

Thank God for whichever teller had come in early. "Okay, Lonnie," said Georgia, "you just do that, you little sweetie. Call me tomorrow, I'll tell you all about the luncheon."

The bathroom door swung open, giving Georgia a panoramic view of her mother on the toilet, baggy panties at her ankles.

That door was out of plumb, like every damn door in this house. You had to pull up on the knob to make it catch.

Squinting to blur the view, Georgia chucked the phone onto its cradle and sprinted down the hall. "Shuttin' the door for you, Mama," she called, easing it closed. Didn't want to slam it and give the poor thing a heart attack when she was obviously not all there this a.m.

In all her careful preparations, Georgia had never considered that Little Mama might not be well enough to stand around pretending to co-hostess the luncheon, as usual. In Georgia's mind, Mama's forgetting was not that bad—not so much worse, anyway, that anybody needed to do anything. Now she found herself wishing for somewhere to park Little Mama for the afternoon, get her out of the house without hurting her feelings. She couldn't follow her around all day making sure she didn't take off her dress in front of people.

Georgia threw on shorts and a gingham work blouse. She made her bed extra neat, for the nosy ones who would "accidentally" wander into her room. She laid out the Lauren dress (so gorgeous, that emerald shade) and hung the Do Not Disturb sign on Brother's doorknob. After that early-morning arrival, she could count on him to sleep through the entire luncheon.

She hurried downstairs to look at the timing chart.

Not even started, and already ten minutes behind!

She could skip breakfast—that was five minutes. Also she had blocked out five minutes to call Krystal to remind her to bring the cut-glass plates for the Red Velvet, Jell-O, and Coca-Cola cakes. She decided to trust Krystal to remember, and bang! Right back on schedule.

At this hour, all the ladies would be laying out their nice dresses, fixing their hair. The phone wouldn't ring for the next couple of hours, which was good because the schedule kept Georgia hopping. She hurried around trimming candlewicks, smoothing creases out of tablecloths, up and down the stairs dozens of times.

Krystal's table settings had taken an extra-dramatic turn this year. She chose a nature theme, lots of twigs, pinecones, bare branches and mossy rocks, autumn leaves, darling little ponds of water in bowls. Napkins folded into decorative swans. Georgia's gold-foil goody bags sparkled at each setting, amid clouds of decorative ribbon in tones of green and brown. The big house had never looked more festive. On every mantel and sideboard were greenery runners, chains of sweet-smelling balsam, heavenly splashes of freesia. (Tommy's Dixie Florist was the big winner in all this.) Georgia filled her grandmother's Depression-glass vases with great trumpet flourishes of scarlet gladiolus.

She liked massing one kind and color of flower for impact. She had placed the glads in tepid water early to ensure they would open to the maximum red at noon.

Something nagged at her about Lon Chapman's call. Some reason she should give in and let him come by tonight. She struggled to remember. Something he could do for her?—

Another blank Rolodex card.

Damn it! Too many of those lately. Her head was overloaded with useless information—sometimes she woke up reciting the list of ingredients from a recipe.

Something Krystal had said . . .

Last night, when they were making napkin swans. Krystal looked over her specs and said, "All I need is one old bastard to cave. That would give all the others an excuse."

That was it: Krystal's annexation plan. Half the old bastards on the town council were telling her privately they wished they could go along with it. They just didn't want to be the one to go first.

Lon Chapman was one of those bastards.

Georgia went to the phone in the kitchen. No dial tone. That was surprising. The phone was the most dependable appliance in the house. She tapped the hook with her finger. Nothing.

She must have left it off the hook upstairs, when Lonnie called.

She hurried up to the phone table. Sure enough, one end of the phone sat off the cradle, at an angle. No wonder the house had been so quiet all morning.

Georgia tapped the switch hook. The dial tone returned. She took out her address book and dialed the bank's number.

Busy? She'd never known the bank's line to be busy. This was one of those mornings when nothing was going smoothly. She made a note to call him later.

Georgia didn't often meddle in the lives of her men. When she did, she was careful not to leave fingerprints. She would never go directly to Judge Barnett, for instance, and insist he give in to Krystal on annexation. In matters of money or politics, a man will listen to practically any other man before he will listen to a woman. Protest the sexism of it all you want, but Georgia knew it was true. Her method was to convince Man A to do a favor for Man B, who would pass it on through Men C, D, and E, back to A. That's how Georgia got things done without anyone in Six Points realizing she was the one doing it.

According to the chart, she was now eight minutes ahead of schedule. Her next job was to preheat the ovens and begin moving food out of the fridges and chest freezer.

Georgia went up the hall to the pine-paneled den where Little Mama spent the afternoons watching her stories. She steeled herself to look around the door—surprise, Mama was all dressed in her nice pale-blue Sunday go-to-meeting dress, thinning hair brushed into place.

Georgia said, "Don't you look pretty!"

Little Mama had even put on her best necklace, a gold locket trimmed in tiny seed pearls. She looked perfectly presentable except for the fuzzy pink bunny slippers with rolly eyes. She gazed at the TV, murmuring at low volume. "I wanted to have coffee but I heard you banging around and I didn't want to get in your way."

"Don't be silly," said Georgia. "Come on, I'll make you a cup. You ready for your cereal?"

"Naw I'll just stay in here out of the way."

"Aw come on, Mama. You must be starving."

"I'm all right…" Little Mama's voice trailed off. This pitiful act wasn't like her at all. Georgia stepped into the room to see better, and discovered what looked like blood caked at the corner of her mouth. Upon closer inspection it was lipstick that had run off the tracks.

Little Mama leaned to see the television. "I don't know why they show the same movie on every station."

"What movie?"

"*The Towering Inferno*."

"Oh, I like that one." Georgia backed out of the room. "That Steve McQueen is one good-looking man." Little Mama didn't answer. "I'll bring your coffee, Mama. You sit back and enjoy the movie."

Little Mama stared at the TV.

Definitely something off with her today. Not just the lipstick and the bunny feet, but a new frailty, a sense that she had lost ground, just since yesterday.

Ted Horn had explained that in early-stage dementia you have good days and bad days in no particular order. This wasn't shaping up to be one of the good days.

Georgia was pouring water into Mr. Coffee when the phone

rang. She reached it just in time to hear the caller hang up. The clock said 10:58. Probably a last-minute RSVP.

She slid the first sheet of stuffed figs into the top oven, set the timer, and began carrying serving dishes from the back-porch fridge to the mahogany table in the dining room.

Krystal's foresty stylings of moss and fern made the room look like a National Geographic special. She had spent all last evening dragging in bags of dead plant material, festooning every available surface with Spanish moss, garlands, dried leaves, cranberries, sprays of seedpods. Although Georgia was a little worried about ticks and spiders coming out of all that moss, she had to admit the result was lovely.

She reached into the sideboard for her camera. The flash whistled warming up. She liked to take scrapbook pictures of the table in all its perfection, before the herd came stampeding through.

The coffeemaker was gurgling, spitting. Georgia made up a tray with coffee, orange juice, and Cap'n Crunch, and carried it to Little Mama, still wrapped up in her movie. (Lately it was a struggle to confine Cap'n Crunch to breakfast; Little Mama would happily eat it three meals a day.) "Here, we need to fix your lipstick, and I brought you some shoes."

"I've already got on my shoes," said Mama.

"No, those are bunny rabbits. These are your shoes." She held them out.

Little Mama smiled on the bad-lipstick side of her mouth. "But these keep my feet warm."

"The ladies will be here in an hour. You look so pretty otherwise, you don't want to be wearing bunny rabbits at our fancy party, do you? Come on, be a good girl and put your shoes on."

Mama snapped, "Don't you take that tone with me, young lady! You are not too big for me to turn you over my knee."

"Okay." Georgia dabbed at the side of her mouth with the washcloth. "Hold still."

Mama jerked away. "I swear to God, you are gettin' too big for them britches, Missy Jean."

"Okay, Mama. I'm sorry."

"The same thing over and over," Little Mama said. "I am just so tired of it."

"Tired of what?"

"This damn movie. They keep showing the same part. I don't know what they're hoping to prove."

Georgia glanced at the screen. There was a shot of the sky-scraper engulfed in a huge cloud of fire, with helicopters darting around like dragonflies. "Hang on, Steve McQueen will be back in a minute." She got up. "I've got to get dressed."

She went to the kitchen and dialed Krystal. The phone rang and rang. This struck Georgia as odd, like the busy signal at the bank. If Rhonda was away from her desk it should click over to the answering machine. What the hell was wrong with the phones today? Ma Bell had better not be screwing around with the system on the day of Georgia's luncheon.

Georgia made multiple trips from the deep freeze to fill the galvanized washtub with crushed ice. She brought out trays of Lobster Scallion Shooters in votives and began wedging them into the ice in decorative rows, like the picture in *Bon Appétit*. It was only a hundred thirty dollars' worth of lobster *(only!)* but doled out among all those little glasses, it looked like a million bucks. One whole bright-scarlet lobster was splayed out in the middle, just for show. Spotlit at the center of the table were rows of votives containing a crimson dab of sauce and a sprig of green onion, backed by a wall of red glads. The display was awe inspiring.

Georgia stood back to admire the effect. *Girl, you have outdone yourself.* Sometimes she heard Daddy's voice congratulating her, saying the nice things he never actually said when he was alive. Daddy was one of those people who was more enjoyable to think back on than he was at the time. Even Little Mama didn't have much to say about him, and she was married to him for fifty years. Georgia never forgot how unhappy they were, all that fighting. She used to vow that she would be rich when she grew up, so she'd never have to marry a man she didn't like.

Anyone looking at this lobster display would think she was wealthy, all right. She liked that—she had restored a bit of cachet to the Bottoms family. She knew it was shallow, but to Georgia, appearances really were everything.

Speaking of which—if she didn't get dressed, the first guests would arrive to find her looking like an old ragbag. She hurried to her room, tossed off her party-prep clothes, squeezed into control tops and Wonderbra, the silky emerald Lauren dress. She ran a brush through her hair, touched up her makeup, spritzed a cloud of Chanel in the air. She had just put on her daytime diamond earrings when the doorbell rang—here we go! Eleven thirty on the dot.

Whizzy barked. Georgia called him upstairs and shut him up in Daddy's room, where he would be much happier until the guests were gone.

She paused before the gold-filigreed mirror in the center hall. She did look smashing. She blew a pouty kiss at her image, and carried a dazzling hostess smile to the door.

Wouldn't you know the first guest was Geraldine Talby, last seen looking irritated when Georgia pushed past her getting out of the pew to faint? Now Geraldine stood beaming on the porch. Her pantsuit was an awkward shade of pumpkin orange, with brown piping on the lapels. Autumnal, but not in a good way.

"Why Geraldine, how wonderful to see you! How marvelous, you're the first to arrive. Hey, that color really suits you. Come in!"

Who wants to be first at a party? Personally, Georgia would have skulked around the block ten times to avoid such a fate, but it didn't bother Geraldine. She chattered all the way down the hall. She burst out in a whoop at the sight of the Lobster Scallion Shooters. "Oh! My Lord! Would you look! At! That!"

"Why thank you, Geraldine."

"That is so *darling!* Georgia, you did this all by yourself? When you fainted on Sunday, I said, how will she ever get it together for Tuesday? But you did! How on earth?"

"I had help," Georgia said, conjuring an invisible cadre of staff, when in fact she and Krystal had been up till two a.m. hot-gluing Spanish moss to the candlesticks.

Thank God for the doorbell. That's the great thing about being the hostess—you are always needed elsewhere. "Help yourself to anything you'd like, Geraldine. I'll be back."

This was Lily Jane Mobley and her sister-in-law Jean Lardell, widow ladies, never seen in public without each other. They exclaimed over the greenery in the front room, and came down the hall echoing Geraldine's cries at the splendor of the lobster.

Georgia wished Krystal could have heard it. Come to think of it, wasn't Krystal supposed to come early to bring the cake plates and help with the hot hors d'oeuvres? No doubt she got caught up in some silly mayor thing. Luckily there were guests now to keep one another company while Georgia did everything by herself.

This party was off to a slow start, no denying it. Nearly noon, and only three guests so far. Usually the crowd arrived in a big early wave surging through the house for the first hour.

Guests were guests. What did it matter if it was three or three hundred?

Georgia brought out the first tray of toasty prosciutto-wrapped figs and stood around watching them get cold. Each lady made a show of tasting one, as if that required great courage. Jean Lardell said they were "better than I expected," a compliment so backhanded Georgia had to bite her tongue to keep from snapping at her.

The phone rang. She excused herself and went to the hall.

"Oh Georgia, it's Nadine Watson—oh honey, it's just so awful I can't believe it! After all the trouble you went to."

"Nadine, what's wrong? Aren't you coming?"

"Well honey, no, of course not. Don't you know what's happened?" She sounded hysterical, like Aunt Pittypat with Uncle Billy Sherman's artillery shells raining down upon Atlanta.

Georgia said, "What are you talking about?"

"Bless your heart, you've been getting ready all morning, you don't even know! It's too much to explain. Go turn on your TV. Oh, it's so awful!" She hung up *Bam!*

Mama came down the hall on her walker, still wearing the bunnies. "Did I hear people talking?"

"Our guests are here, Mama. Don't you want to put on your shoes? I put them in there by the TV."

"No, I don't," Mama said.

"Well, I'm not going to argue with you." Georgia turned to the dining room. "Look, everybody, here's Little Mama!"

The ladies let out high-pitched cries, the forced extra helping of enthusiasm people reserve for the elderly and small children. Little Mama accepted their hugs and friendly inquiries without comment. Georgia said something about needing to answer the door, though the bell had not rung.

She went up the hall to the front door. She peered out at the street.

No one was parking a car. No groups of ladies in party dresses were coming up the walk.

Georgia set her jaw. She went down the hall to Little Mama's pine-paneled den. The TV was still showing that same part of the movie.

She stood there and watched the scene again and again, until she understood. It was not a movie. It was news—"breaking" news, they kept saying. A blur came from one side of the screen. A cloud of orange fire exploded from a tower. A tower collapsed in a shower of dust. Panic-stricken people ran pell-mell toward the camera, chased by a boiling cloud.

Georgia thought of ants. The great Ant Connection. The anthill kicked over, ants running every which way.

She sat on the edge of Mama's chair, reading the words streaming across the screen. She turned up the volume a little.

When she looked up from the screen, Lily Jane and Jean Lardell and Geraldine and Little Mama were gathered behind her in the den, watching with mouths open.

"It's like Pearl Harbor," said Lily Jane.

"Georgia said it was a movie," Little Mama said.

Georgia held her tongue.

"I guess everybody knows about this by now," said Geraldine. "That's why they didn't come."

Georgia drifted out into the hall. The other ladies helped Little Mama into her recliner.

The urgent voices of the announcers echoed up the hallway. Georgia stood at the front door, looking out.

Things like this do not happen in Six Points. That's why we live here—to be far away from such things.

Georgia tried to grasp what had happened. It was a tragedy. A national emergency. The president was flying, they wouldn't say where. Planes crashing all over the place.

Naturally a thing like this would take precedence over anybody's September luncheon. It was much, much more important than any social occasion.

It occurred to Georgia that she might not be the only person in this position. All over the nation there must be hostesses standing at their buffet tables, waiting for guests who would never arrive.

She walked through the parlor, past pyramids of chicken salad sandwiches and pimento cheese. She remembered her twinge of dread at the prospect of the guests pawing through the beautiful food. Well, you got your wish, she thought bitterly. The dining room display sat perfect, untouched.

She picked up a dish of mixed nuts and carried it to the TV den. "Do they have any idea who did it?"

"Ben somebody," said Lily Jane. "He's the one that blew up that ship."

"The *Titanic*?" said Little Mama.

"No, a navy ship. Blew a hole in the side of it and almost sunk it. About a year ago. Remember?"

"Where was that?" said Jean Lardell. "I think I missed that."

"Somewhere over there in the Mideast, I forget," said Lily Jane. "Name a country that's in the Mideast."

"Japan?" said Jean.

"No, that's the Far East. The *Mid* East."

"Would anybody like some mixed nuts?" Georgia said. "There's so much food, oh my God. Why don't I fix y'all a plate and you can eat in here while you watch."

"Oh, poor Georgia." Geraldine Talby turned to her. "Y'all, look. Bless her heart. Her party is ruined."

The ladies clustered around to pat her arm and say how sorry they were. Georgia said a national emergency was much more important than any social occasion.

Already she was tired of being brave, tired of the TV commentators, sick to death of the terrible scenes playing over and over on a loop. Those were real people jumping off those buildings as they burned. It was just not something they should show on television, that's all.

Georgia hoped her face didn't look as crushed and disappointed as she felt—or if it did, she hoped the others read her expression as concern for the awful events, not the massively self-centered disappointment it really was.

She wished everyone would just go home so she could cry.

The phone rang.

"Hey George," said Krystal. "Are you okay?"

"I guess so. Where are you?"

"At the office. We're waiting on a conference call. The state director of public safety is reviewing our civil defense procedures."

"With all this going on?"

"Yeah, that's the point, they don't know if there's going to be other attacks," said Krystal. "There's some thought the big cities might be just the first wave. They might try to hit the small towns next. We have to be prepared."

"Oh come on. You don't really think these people would come to Six Points?"

"I can't be sure of that, can you?" Krystal sighed. "Look, the TV is saying it's a war, and everything's changed. I'm the mayor, you know, I have to take that seriously."

"I don't want everything to change," Georgia said. "I want it to stay like it is."

"Listen, the phones are going crazy down here," Krystal said. "If I need you later, could you come down and give us a hand?"

"Well of course. Just let me know." Georgia was slightly amused by the idea of Krystal defending Six Points from the terrorists, but today was not a day to make jokes.

That's how awful this was: she couldn't even joke with her best friend, with whom she could find the humor in even the darkest things. Georgia hated whoever it was that had reached around the world to get between her and Krystal. *Why can't they leave us alone? This has nothing to do with us!*

Suddenly she realized all three ladies had their purses on and were headed for the door. "Oh y'all, now, please don't go," she pleaded. "Nobody else is even coming, and y'all haven't eaten a bite." That was not the most gracious way to put it, and it was even more ungracious for Georgia to be thinking how much money she'd spent...but how do you keep your brain from thinking whatever it wants?

"Oh, I couldn't eat a thing, it's all too upsetting," said Jean Lardell.

"I'm not sure we should even go out on the street," said Geraldine Talby. "What if they start dropping bombs?"

"Nobody's gonna drop any bombs," Georgia said. "This is Six Points."

Jean said, "My sister Frances has a girl in school up there in New York. I want to call and make sure she's all right. She's just the type to grab her camera and go down there to make pictures."

"You can call from here, Jean," Georgia said.

"That's okay," Jean said. "I have that unlimited long-distance plan."

"I feel so guilty not staying to help you clean up," said Lily Jane Mobley.

Georgia forced a gracious hostess smile onto her face. "I sure do thank you for coming," she said. "We'll do it again real soon." *As soon as hell freezes over!* She knew it was irrational to be mad at the only people in Six Points, besides Nadine and Krystal, to even acknowledge they'd been invited to a luncheon. Everybody else seemed to have used the disaster as an excuse to abandon common courtesy.

She hugged the ladies' necks and watched them hurry to their cars. Geraldine craned her neck to look at the sky, then drove off, tires screeching in haste. Lily Jane and Jean waved goodbye as they pulled away.

Georgia's face was flushed, her hands trembling. She took a deep breath, let it out. She forced herself to repeat several times, *Calm down, now. This didn't just happen to you.*

The TV said thousands were dead. Maybe twenty, maybe fifty thousand. That number was too big to think about, really. Georgia couldn't think about that many people at once.

Anyway they were strangers, they were Yankees, they should be none of her concern. How were they different than anybody else on the news who died? A hundred thousand in a typhoon in Bangladesh. A million in a famine in Africa. You couldn't wrap your head around a number like that.

Georgia could not stop thinking about the stacks of sandwiches, hand-trimmed, the molded salads going soft at the edges, lime sherbet melting into the punch, a small fortune in lobster getting warm under the display lights.

The world was spinning out of control and what could Georgia do? Nothing. Wars and sneak attacks were things that happened in the movies, in the past, to Little Mama's generation—not now with all our modern inventions, the United Nations, cordless phones, windshield wipers that know when it's raining. Who allowed this to happen? Georgia suspected this latest president was a bit of a fool. Going by his scared-rabbit look just now on TV, he hadn't the first clue what to do next.

"Can we turn it off please, Mama? That man gets on my nerves."

"Fine with me. He won't say the ones that really done it. You know who it was."

"Rosa Parks?" Georgia said.

Little Mama made a face. "I didn't say that. But you know it wasn't anybody white."

Mama was fortunate not to ever have to think about anything that happened. Automatically she knew who to blame.

Georgia pressed POWER. Silence and darkness filled the house, instant gloom.

The chatter of the newsmen was better. Georgia switched the TV back on, and cut the volume in half. If the end of the world was coming, she would like a little advance notice.

6

Georgia packed up the food in boxes, coolers, and Tupperware, and loaded it into her car. In a Rubbermaid ice chest she made a fresh bed of ice for the Lobster Scallion Shooters. The votives clinked softly, like the grape-juice glasses as the communion tray was passed at church.

Just as she started to the car with the last load, Brother stumbled into the kitchen shirtless, hungover. She told him something bad had happened in New York and D.C., it was his duty to stay home and look after Mama. Go look at the TV if he had any questions.

He saw the look on her face. For once he didn't argue.

Georgia drove a loop around the courthouse square. Hardly a car in sight, no one afoot—Six Points was quieter than the quietest Sunday morning. It looked like a scene from a movie about the end of the world.

She drove out Maple Street past the hospital to the Sycamore Pointe Senior Life Village, which was the Six Points Nursing Home with a new sign.

Georgia had taken pains to be friendly with Sharon Overby, who ran the place, in case she ever needed to get Little Mama admitted out there in a hurry. Sharon was one of those who usually came to the luncheon but rarely bothered to RSVP first. The minute she saw Georgia she set about apologizing. "Oh my gosh, Georgia! I meant to call but we've been so busy. All the residents got so upset this morning, you can imagine. We had to turn off the TVs and take away their remotes."

"That's not why I'm here." Georgia set down the ice chest. "I've got my car stuffed full of food for the luncheon. If you can get somebody to help me unload it, we can feed all your people a really nice lunch."

"Oh. Oh…oh my goodness, Georgia, that is *so sweet* of you. Really. So thoughtful." Sharon looked embarrassed. "And I would love to take you up on it, but…actually we're not allowed to serve food that hasn't been inspected—well, you know, we have all this legal red tape."

"Don't be silly," said Georgia. "The food is perfectly fine. I made it myself."

"Oh I'm sure it's absolutely wonderful, it always is," Sharon said. "I've been looking forward to it so, so much."

So much you didn't bother to RSVP? Georgia shook it off. "Can't you just bend the rules for today? I mean, if ever there was a day to bend the rules."

"Oh, Georgia, I can't believe you are so kind as to think of our residents at a time like this. But we have state regulations, the county health department's breathing down my neck…I'm not allowed to serve food unless we prepare it ourselves. We could lose our operating license."

"You wouldn't be serving it," Georgia said. "I can go up and down the halls and give it away. Like a gift. People bring gifts of food out here all the time, don't they? Would that be okay?"

Sharon beamed, exactly as if she were about to say yes, and said, "No, I'm sorry."

Georgia knew full well that Sharon ran the place, she could break any rule she chose. So much for trying to do a good deed. Georgia said, "You think somebody would tell on you? Is that it?"

"You'd be surprised. A resident says something to a family member, next thing you know I've been reported to the state. It has happened before."

"I just thought, it being a national emergency and all," Georgia said.

Sharon assumed an odd, goofy smile, the kind of smile you put on for a baby to make it grin. She made a move to lift one end of the ice chest. "Let me help you carry this back to your car."

"No—*no*," Georgia said, pulling the chest away by its handle to deny her any share of it. "I've got it! You're busy. You've got a million things to do. Don't think about it another minute."

"Thank you for understanding," Sharon said. "I wish I could accept. I'll call you tomorrow, okay?"

Georgia smiled and said, "Absolutely!" and got out the door fast. She was irked by the Sharon Overbys, mindless rule followers of the world. She felt silly for trying to give her food away. She let herself stew in that feeling all the way to the courthouse.

This time, before lugging that heavy ice chest up three flights of stairs, she went up to the jail desk to ask. The deputy said no ma'am, Sheriff Allred is out on patrol, no ma'am we can't accept food for the prisoners, blah blah blah state regulations.

Georgia didn't argue. She thanked him and went back to her car.

Nobody wanted her charity. She was driving around with five hundred dollars' worth of food getting ready to spoil in her car. And no one would even let her give it away.

She switched on the radio, hoping for music to soothe her. In came the urgent voices of newscasters, panicky eyewitnesses, sirens whooping, unconfirmed reports, this just in! She lunged to turn it off. She couldn't bear the flood of anxiety pouring out of the speakers.

Georgia didn't know any poor people, but she knew Six Points had its share. Mostly they were black and lived across the bridge in East Over. She tried to think where they might congregate. They didn't have a community center or anything. That was part of why Krystal was fighting to annex them.

When Georgia pictured herself driving into that run-down neighborhood, she pictured a gang of large black youths approaching her car in a threatening manner. There might be a scuffle or stampede when they realized the white lady was giving away free lobster and other fancy food.

Anyway, wouldn't it be a little condescending to drive into somebody's neighborhood and start handing out canapés, like some honky-woman Santa Claus? Sharon Overby had made Georgia feel like an idiot. She had no desire to feel that way again.

She drove three times around the square trying to decide. Finally it occurred to her that poor people have to eat just like everyone else. In Six Points there was only one place to buy groceries: Hull's Market. The logical place to find whoever might be hungry.

It felt so essential, so urgent to give this food to somebody. Maybe it was the idea of being so scared of burning that you would rather jump to your death from high in the air. On a day when that is happening, Georgia thought, I have this irrational need to be kind to somebody I don't know. To help somebody.

She parked in front of the ice machine at Hull's Market. Yesterday's *Light-Pilot* showed on the newspaper rack:

HAWKS DEFEAT ELBA, 27–3

Everything's changed. Krystal said it. Seeing that innocent headline from yesterday, when the biggest news in town was the Six Points High football score—Georgia felt a pang of longing. That world was gone, vanished. Maybe forever. It hadn't seemed all that sweet and innocent a place until the devil stuck out his tongue and laughed at us.

Georgia got out of her car. How incredibly blue the sky was today, one of those unearthly Polaroid blues you get on the clearest autumn days. A beautiful day for a terrible thing. This would spoil all beautiful days for a while: guilt by association. Georgia wondered if the people who flew the planes into the buildings were thinking about that, if the glorious weather made their victory even sweeter as they smashed themselves to smithereens.

Here came Madeline Roudy, pediatrician at the free county clinic, the most pleasant-faced of women, even today. In her crisp white blouse and tennis skirt, she had the unstudied glamour of a young Diahann Carroll or Leslie Uggams. Beautiful brown skin with a touch of cream.

Georgia brightened. "Oh, Madeline," she said, "just the person I'm looking for."

"Hello," Madeline said.

For a moment Georgia thought Madeline didn't recognize her.

Technically that was impossible; everybody in Six Points knew Georgia. "It's Georgia," she said, to be sure. "Georgia Bottoms?"

"Oh yes, Georgia, of course, forgive me," said Madeline Roudy. "I'm kind of distracted today."

There was no particular reason Madeline should recognize Georgia, though they had gone to high school together and had been friendly ever since, hadn't they? Maybe the friendliness was only in Georgia's head. She forged on.

"Anyway, Madeline—nobody showed at my party, I've got all this food in my car and I wish you would take some of it. I can't seem to give it away." She made a comical face, an *I Love Lucy* bewilderment face to show what a ridiculous dilemma she had landed in, and to enlist Madeline's help.

Tugging down her oversized Jackie O sunglasses, Madeline stared at Georgia as if she was a crazy lady with too many cats. "I'm sorry?" she said in a voice so loud it actually rang the wire of the grocery buggies.

"Imagine if you gave a luncheon and nobody came," Georgia said. "I've got all this really nice food in my car, lobster, fancy salads and finger sandwiches, ready to go. If you wouldn't mind taking some of it home. It would make me feel good, just to know it's not all going to waste."

"Just keep it, and eat it yourself," said Madeline Roudy.

"Lord, I could never eat that much food in a year," Georgia said.

Dr. Roudy gave an impatient sigh. "Thank you, I can buy my own food," she said. Her eyes flicked ahead to the door as if she was eager to go through it.

Suddenly Georgia understood where she had gone wrong. "Oh Madeline, I get it. Of course I should have invited you to the luncheon, and I would have, too, but you don't know my mother, the way she is about…politics." Georgia was determined to straighten this out. She had always liked Madeline Roudy. She had always thought of Madeline as a friend, at least a possible friend.

Madeline drew her body up in a straight line. "You think I wanted to come to your white-lady luncheon? Is that what you think?"

"Oh my goodness. No! Madeline, you're reading it all wrong, that's not what I meant." Good God, was she really that touchy? Georgia couldn't offer a simple gift of food without her reading something racial into it? No wonder some people just give up trying to deal with these people—look where it gets you!

"So I'm not good enough to be invited to your party," Dr. Roudy was saying, "but you want to give me the food out the trunk of your car because nobody showed up? How pathetic do you think I am? God."

Georgia said, "Now wait a minute, you don't have to get all huffy. The food is good, I made it myself. If you don't want it, you could just say so."

"It's a hell of a day for you to sit out here playing the great lady," said Madeline Roudy. "Why don't you take your damn lobster and go home?"

Georgia was not used to being attacked in broad daylight. She groped for a proper response. "It's a free country," she said at last. "I don't need your advice."

"And I sure as hell don't need your *lobster,*" said Roudy in that bullhorn voice.

"Okay, then, tell the whole world about it, then," Georgia said, haughty as a fourth grader.

Roudy put up her nose and marched on. The electric eye swept the door open. A gust of cool air flowed out as she went in.

Georgia's face stung as if she'd been slapped.

Here came two more colored people the other way—two more *black* people, she corrected herself, two more *African-American persons* who might be poor or might just be wearing slovenly clothes because it's their style, God forbid I should try to do something neighborly for anyone!

Something charitable!

Georgia let these black people walk right by her and her car full of wonderful food. There was enough to feed them and all their friends for a week. She let them walk on by.

She climbed back in her car, cranked the A/C to MAX, and drove away from Hull's Market.

What she needed was a friend. What she needed right now, more than anything, was the comforting voice of a friend who would tell her she was right, or at least not that wrong.

She drove once around the square. Krystal's parking space at city hall was empty. Georgia parked and went in anyway.

The radio hummed with news. Rhonda barely glanced up from the phone, "mm-hmm, mm-hmm," making notes on a legal pad. At last she hung up. "Can I help you?"

"Where's Krystal?"

"She was trying to call you before, but your mother said you'd gone off somewhere."

The whole world has turned against me, Georgia thought. Without Krystal in the room, Rhonda didn't even bother to conceal her hostility.

Georgia tried a smile. "She said y'all might need help answering the phone. Here I am. Just put me to work."

"I didn't want your help, it was her," Rhonda said. "She's over at the water tower now, standing guard."

"Standing guard?"

"The sheriff and his men are up at the dam. They didn't have anybody to guard the water tower. So Krystal took a gun and went over there."

"Krystal has a gun?"

Rhonda rolled her eyes. "Georgia, we're really busy today."

Georgia stiffened. "Sorry to bother you. I'll find her."

She marched out vowing to tell Krystal how Rhonda acted when she wasn't around. Georgia had protected Rhonda long enough. One word from her and Krystal would fire her in an instant.

God what a day! That sky so blue it made your eyes hurt!

Rhonda was all emotional because of the news. She was taking it out on Georgia. Maybe it was a little extreme to think of getting her fired for acting snippy.

Georgia just needed to talk to Krystal.

The interior of her Civic was filled with the delicious humidity rising up from the food hampers. When she thought of the hours of chopping, mincing, and stirring, it made her want to weep. She put the car in gear, drove past the Kwik-M Mart, up Forrest Street to the little city park on the hill.

Krystal's forest-green Subaru wagon sat at the curb, sporting a faded Gore/Lieberman sticker and her GRRL MYR vanity plate.

The slam of Georgia's car door seemed loud enough to carry all the way to Montgomery. It was so quiet even the birds seemed to be waiting for someone to speak.

Georgia set off silently walking up the grassy slope, then realized that might not be the best idea, with Krystal armed and dangerous at the top.

"Hey Krystal!" she cried. "It's me, don't shoot, I'm coming up there!" She whooped and hollered, raising such a racket that Krystal finally yelled at her to keep it down.

Bathed in perspiration, snagging her panty hose on a blackberry bush, Georgia thrashed through the last stretch of steep woods. She popped through a wall of bushes to find Krystal in a webbed lawn chair, one foot propped against a concrete culvert at the foremost leg of the great silver water tower. She had come wearing one of her woolen mayoral suits, a maroon number that must have been unbearable in the heat. She'd hung the jacket on the stub of a pine branch and was airing out the sweat circles on her blouse. In the crook of her arm she cradled a double-barreled shotgun that looked taller than she was. "Damn, George, you trying to wake up all the babies from their naps?"

"I didn't want you to shoot me," said Georgia. "I didn't even know you could shoot a gun."

"I can if I have to," said Krystal. "You didn't bring a chair with you? Where you gonna sit?"

"Nobody told me to bring any chair." The word "Rhonda" was right there on Georgia's tongue. It was hard not to say it.

"Well I ain't giving you my chair."

"I'll stand," Georgia said. "How long you planning to stay up here?"

As long as necessary, Krystal said. Until Sheriff Allred sent somebody to relieve her. The portable radio at her feet emitted a low mutter of news, accompanied by the squawk of a police-band walkie-talkie.

Georgia said, "Are you hungry at all?"

"Only starving," Krystal said. "I didn't even get a cup of coffee this morning…it happened so fast. And then it just kept on happening."

"I can fix that. You wait right here."

On her way down the hill Georgia muttered curses against whoever invented the mid-heel pump. At the car she changed into an old pair of sneakers that had lived in the hatchback since she took that aerobics class.

It's a good thing she sprang for the pricey paper plates. Lesser plates would have wilted under the load she piled on. In the center of the food she wedged a pair of Lobster Scallion Shooters, still chilled from their ice bath.

She stuffed plastic flatware and napkins in her purse, and headed up the slope with a plate awkwardly balanced in each hand. It didn't exactly make her Mother Teresa, but she was glad some of her food would be eaten and appreciated by someone she loved.

"Dear God," Krystal said when she saw the heaped-up plate, "I thought you was bringing a pack of crackers. What is this, *Gourmet* magazine?"

Georgia described how she had driven all over Six Points trying to give the food away. She left out the part about hateful Rhonda, but otherwise gave as objective an account as she could, considering it had happened to her. She told about Sharon Overby at the nursing home and Madeline Roudy at Hull's Market.

Krystal laid the shotgun on the cement slab, and dug into the Fresh Mountain Apple Jell-O Compote. They ate standing up with the chair between them as a picnic table. "Now that is good eatin'," Krystal said. "Maybe Madeline didn't understand what you were trying to do. Maybe she thought you were trying to give her charity or something."

Mark Childress

"I distinctly told her it wasn't. I explained the whole thing."

"But you didn't invite her to the lunch, so maybe that's how it felt—to her, I mean. Can't you see where it might?"

"Oh now, you're not going to take her side?" Georgia cried. "Please don't. I can't stand it if you do."

"Hey, you asked my honest opinion," said Krystal. "If you want bullshit, you better talk to somebody else."

True enough. "So what should I have said?"

"George, you're upset. Tomorrow, you call her and tell her you didn't mean anything."

"*Me* apologize to her?" Georgia shook her head. "I'm not the one who was incredibly rude!"

"Maybe she was upset too. We're all upset today, Georgia. It's a bad day."

"Oh shut up!" Georgia cried. "I don't care about that. I'm already sick to death of it! It didn't happen to anybody we know. It doesn't have anything to *do* with us! But now everything's ruined, and I swear I could just—God *damn* it!" A wave of frustration crashed over her. She hurled the plate with all her strength, spattering food on the bushes. The votive candleholders caromed across the gravel, spitting lobster and red sauce.

Krystal put her plate out of Georgia's reach, and turned with open arms. "Come give us a hug."

Georgia said, "I don't want a hug."

"Sure you do. Everybody wants a hug."

"Not me," said Georgia. She didn't want to be comforted. She wanted to feel just this bad.

"Fine." Krystal turned up her hands. "No hug for you then. Go pick up your goddamn plate. That's littering."

"Oh would you shut up!" Georgia burst into tears.

Krystal kept eating, watching Georgia out of the corner of her eye. At last she said, "I only tried to hug you. Jeez."

"I know," Georgia said. "I appreciate it, I really do."

"Why are you crying?"

"I don't know," Georgia said. "Just let me be. I'm almost done."

"Okay," said Krystal. "I swear to God. You are such a mess."

7

After a long afternoon standing guard with Krystal, Georgia arrived home to find the house peaceful, quiet, and clean, the last load of dishes sloshing and clanking in the dishwasher, all the platters washed, dried, and stacked on the counters to be put away. Someone had swooped in to perform this magic while Georgia was gone, like Snow White cleaning up for the dwarfs. She understood why the dwarfs were not all that happy about it: it's alarming to come home and find your house has been cleaned by invisible hands.

She found Little Mama tucked in bed, working the same old crossword puzzle.

"Mama, what did you do? I was going to clean up but you've done it all."

"Don't look at me," said Little Mama. "That was your brother."

After all these years of being waited on hand and foot, Brother apparently had been inspired by the news on TV to try to make all his amends in one afternoon. Mama said his conversion was something to see. Georgia wished she'd been there to see it. He had washed dishes, mopped floors, moved furniture, rolled out the rugs, vacuumed, and dusted until the whole downstairs was shiny clean.

Every once in a while Brother experienced one of these bursts of contrition, usually after a worse-than-usual hangover, his bad acts crashing down around him in a wave. Brother meant well, in short stretches. He didn't seem capable of meaning well for more than two days in a row.

The AA people told him not to bother coming to meetings if he was only going to go out afterward and get drunk.

His parole officer sent him back to jail for a month to put the fear of God into him, but all it did was make him mad and a little crazier. The first thing he did when they let him out was cut off his hair—he shaved his head with a dog clipper he borrowed from his girlfriend Trish (whose name, Georgia thought, was off by one letter). Without hair, Brother announced that he was a punk rocker, then a cancer patient, then Lex Luthor in *Superman*. A neo-Nazi. A Jew in a concentration camp. He "tattooed" a number on his arm with a Sharpie. He drew zigzag hair on his naked skull. When his real hair grew in, he dyed stripes in it and announced that he was an artist.

For a while he spent his afternoons on the washing-machine porch making crazy oil paintings with too much color dripping off the sides. Georgia actually encouraged that phase. Oil paint was messy and expensive, but much less flammable than whiskey. For a few weeks, painting seemed to keep Brother out of trouble.

Just when he seemed to be getting better, he fell into an obsession with Roy Moore, a judge in Montgomery who was engaged in a noisy battle over his God-given constitutional right to display the Ten Commandments in the headquarters building of the Alabama Supreme Court. Moore had his eye on the governor's mansion; he thought he could become the next George

Wallace by riding the Ten Commandments to the statehouse, as Wallace had ridden segregation.

Like all true fanatics, Roy Moore had the courage of his convictions. He raised funds for a block of marble the size of a Hammond organ, engraved the Ten Commandments on its face, had it installed in the lobby of the supreme court under cover of darkness, and dared anyone to remove it. Then he went on a speechmaking tour, trying to stir up the old Wallace magic among the God-fearing citizens of rural Alabama.

Brother taped newspaper clippings about the case all over the walls of his room. He stayed up all night recording long anti-Moore manifestos into a cassette recorder. The next day he would listen back to the tape on his earphones, furiously taking notes, as if he was learning important things from himself.

It got worse after Sims Bailey drove him to Evergreen to see Roy Moore give a speech. Brother came back convinced that Roy Moore was the literal Antichrist. "He's doing the work of Satan by claiming to represent God's will in court," Brother said. "He has built a graven idol and placed it in the public square to be worshipped. Don't you see, it's straight out of the Old Testament! Do you know what 'graven' means?—engraved! He's got people all over the country worshipping a piece of marble. Somebody's got to stop him."

"You don't seriously think that means you," Georgia said, but yes, he did think that. Brother, who had never had a religious bone in his body.

Georgia didn't know what to do. If she ignored what was happening, it would get worse—and she would still have to clean it up later.

She sat Brother down for a talk. They both cried. Little Mama came in and cried too. Brother declared he would move out and get his own place, a job, a new start, really try to make a go of it this time. He talked like that for a couple of days, then let it drop.

Georgia spent the next weeks organizing a change of opinion among the leaders of Six Points. She treated Sheriff Allred to an extra-special Friday night as a thank-you for telling Jimmy Lee Newton he now favored Krystal's annexation plan. His department already spent so much of its resources in East Over, the sheriff said, might as well annex them and let the city help pay for it.

Jimmy Lee Newton reported this change of heart on the front page of the *Light-Pilot*. He didn't realize that's why he got a long, luxurious head-to-toe rubdown the following Thursday.

The fact that Jimmy Lee had come out for annexation did not go unnoticed by Lon Chapman at the bank, once Georgia put the paper in his hand and pointed it out.

A few weeks after that, Lon told her he would be glad to try to talk Jackson Barnett out of his opposition. Georgia could barely contain her smile of triumph. Judge Barnett didn't realize he was outnumbered until annexation passed the town council by a vote of six to two. The subsequent ballot issue carried by a wide margin, thanks to heavy black turnout. Krystal was the hero of the day. Six Points and East Over were peacefully integrated—thirty years after the rest of Alabama, okay, but justice doesn't run to the farthest corners first. Georgia was proud that she had helped make it happen after all this time.

She never told Krystal who had pulled the strings. Better to let her think it was all her own mayoral doing. Krystal knew just enough of Georgia's private life to deflect her suspicion. As far as she was aware, Georgia was carrying on an affair with the married Eugene while seeing another mysterious man whose identity she refused to divulge. The fact that this shadowy man was actually five other men was the kind of detail Krystal did not need to know. They were best friends but even that had limits, if you were living Georgia's life.

She'd been hoping to occupy her empty Saturday night with Eugene Hendrix's replacement in the First Baptist pulpit, if only for the sake of history and symmetry. For months there had been a succession of guest pastors and lay ministers, then finally a new preacher, a harmless old coot named Josiah Barker, with a plain old wife to whom he was plainly devoted.

Barker's unadorned style was better suited to the First Baptist congregation than poor Eugene's tortured, searching explorations. Barker specialized in homilies about huntin' dogs and Mama's biscuits.

It wasn't absolutely necessary for Georgia to have the First Baptist preacher on her client list. Yet it had always brought a certain balance to affairs of church and state.

The first man who ever offered her a gift was the Rev. Onus L. Satterfield, father of Billy, Krystal's onetime high-school boyfriend (and a side interest of Georgia's, although Krystal never knew that). Onus was in his midforties at the time, very good-looking for such an old guy—and jealous of his son Billy getting to slip around with the lovely Georgia, who was seventeen. One night after a Campus Life meeting, the randy preacher waylaid her and led her down the path to Satan's door. He was a horny bastard. He breathed insinuations into her ear, flattered her, promised her things.

Georgia could hardly pretend to be pure, especially when he told her in exact detail everything she'd done with Billy.

Even as a girl, Georgia had a practical bent. She made sure Onus kept his promises before he ever laid a hand on her. Nobody knew but the two of them. Over time, Onus gave her quite a lot of cash. When he had his stroke and was forced to retire, it seemed natural that Georgia would dedicate her Saturday nights to his young, handsome replacement.

But now that was history too. Eugene was gone for good. Georgia felt pure and chaste as a Puritan wife, at least on Saturday night.

Sunday mornings in the tranquilizing presence of Preacher Barker made her wonder why she even bothered going to church anymore. To maintain appearances, of course, and how bad was it to sit there for an hour inspecting her manicure?

Still, she began drinking a second cup of coffee before church, just to stay awake.

She was amazed how easily Little Mama had given up religion after she broke the hip. Every Sunday for months, Georgia offered to take her to church. No, she would say, it ain't worth it.

"What ain't worth it?" Georgia said after hearing this a few dozen times.

"Dragging myself all the way over there," she said, "just to get up and drag myself home."

"Well, if that's all it means to you," Georgia said. "Don't you enjoy seeing the folks? Visiting with your friends?"

"Not especially," Mama said. "If they want to see me, they know where I am."

That was that. After a lifetime of faithful attendance, Little Mama gave up on God because her hip hurt. Personally, Georgia didn't think anyone as old as Little Mama should run the risk of getting shut out of heaven at the last minute. It was left to Georgia, the nonbeliever, to carry the flag for the whole Bottoms clan. Otherwise they couldn't hold up their heads in town.

In April she drove across Alabama to the little village at Catfish Bend, for her annual carload of quilts.

No matter how high Alma Pickett raised the price at Treasures n' Stuff, Georgia couldn't keep up with the demand. "I've only got two hands," she told Alma, without actually saying she used those hands to make the quilts.

This year she called ahead to reserve every quilt in the old ladies' inventory. Those gals were mighty impressed when she whipped out a bankroll and counted off twenty-two hundred-dollar bills. Nobody asked Georgia what she needed with twenty-two quilts. If they'd asked, she would gladly have told them she was marking up their $100 quilts to $500 at Treasures n' Stuff, and splitting the profit with Alma Pickett.

"Can't y'all make 'em any faster?" she said. "I can use all you can make."

The head woman said they'd been thinking of bringing in some nieces to increase production. Meanwhile, one Civic hatchback full of quilts per year was enough to maintain Georgia's cover.

Georgia was always scanning *Cosmopolitan* for 99 ways to be more attractive and 40 ways to satisfy your man. For a while she took to jogging around the track at the high school, ten circuits every morning, until it got so boring she had to quit. No denying that certain areas were beginning to jiggle.

Thank God the men in her life were aging even faster. She

looked better than all of them put together. As long as she maintained that gap, all would be well.

As the year rolled toward September, Georgia thought hard about canceling the luncheon. Who would miss it? she thought. After last year's disaster it might just be best to let it go.

But then—wouldn't that be letting the terrorists win?

Damn right. She couldn't do that. Perhaps her congealed salads did not matter much in the grand scheme of world events, but the least she could do was throw a luncheon to help raise morale in the homeland.

In the weeks immediately after the attacks, that was all anybody could talk about. By the time of the first anniversary, it was considered bad taste to bring it up.

Besides: the luncheon was the high point of the Six Points social calendar. It wasn't even summer yet when people began asking Georgia for the date, saying how much they were looking forward to it.

The television in September was full of solemn memorials. Nobody at the luncheon even mentioned it. Krystal re-created the foresty tabletop scenes no one had gotten to see. Everyone said the food and decorations were better than ever.

Everything was quiet on the Roy Moore front until the *Montgomery Advertiser* reported a rumor that Moore was planning to run for governor of Alabama. Brother's obsession bobbed back to the surface. He painted a sign that said "Ask Me about the 11th Commandment" and got Sims Bailey to drive him up to Montgomery. He showed up on the Channel 12 news that night, standing on the steps of the supreme court with his sign. The red-haired girl reporter said she'd asked him about the eleventh commandment but his answer was "meandering."

Sims Bailey called Georgia shortly after the broadcast to report that he was driving back to Six Points alone. "You know your brother as well as I do," he said. "He wouldn't get back in the car. I begged him, I swear to God, Miss Georgia, I did. There was all these reporters there. He told 'em he was going on a hunger strike."

"You have got to be kidding," said Georgia.

"No ma'am," said Sims.

"He won't last ten minutes!"

"I thought so too. I hung around a couple hours, but he won't budge. Said he's gonna set right there until they take them commandments out of that place. You know he feels real strong about that."

When Georgia reported this news, Little Mama said, "Oh honey, go up there and get him. He's lost his mind."

"It's always my job, isn't it," Georgia said.

"Who else do you suggest?"

"How about that no-count girlfriend of his?"

"I wouldn't trust her to find Montgomery in the broad daylight," Mama said. "Much less at night."

Georgia got in the car and drove straight up there. She arrived at the supreme court building a little after nine p.m. to find Brother at the top of a wide flight of marble steps, resting his face against his "11th Commandment" placard. A lone Alabama state trooper sat watching him from a car at the curb.

Georgia had stopped at the Krystal drive-thru on the Southern Bypass to buy a sack of the square steamed burgers she knew would put an end to Brother's hunger strike. He dove into the sack. "Did you get me a shake?"

"We can stop on the way out of town," she said. "Come on, Brother, get in the car."

"No way," he said around a mouthful of burger. "I ain't breaking no law sitting here."

"That's not the point. Mama sent me up here to bring you home."

"Whoopee for Mama. I am finally doing something for the good of the universe, and she's not gonna stop me." He wasn't drunk, not even drinking. Just sitting there, crazy as a moth attacking a lightbulb.

Georgia said, "What exactly do you think you're doing?"

"We gotta get rid of these commandments, Georgie. For the sake of all of us. It's imperative. Don't you understand?"

"I really don't. Why don't you come get in the car and explain it to me."

"Tonight I started the process of getting the message out through the media," said Brother. "That's the key to starting a movement, working through the mass media."

"I did see you on Channel 12," said Georgia. "Did anybody come out to support you?"

He shrugged. "Rome wasn't built in a day."

"Come on, Brother. Look at that poor state trooper. I bet he has to sit in his car as long as you're here. He's been there all day, hasn't he?"

"Yeah."

"Be a sport, Brother. Let him go home to his wife and his supper. Let him go sit in his recliner, and pet his little dog."

Brother stared at her for a long minute. "Nobody's stopping him," he said. "I'm on a mission from God."

"Yeah, you were on a hunger strike too." She rattled the bag of Krystal boxes. "Don't make me waste a whole trip up here."

"That's your call." Brother blew out a sigh. "I promise I'll respect you, whatever you decide. I wish you would stay and support me in this thing."

"Oh for God's sake! Don't you know how busy I am? Now get in that car and let's go!"

She took that sharp tone with him—Mama's tone—to get him up on his feet and moving. She was astounded when it actually worked: meekly he followed her down the steps. She sweet-talked him the rest of the way to the car. "I want to hear all about this movement of yours." She got him in the car, got behind the wheel, and started driving. She did not slow down until the bypass, where she stopped to get him a milk shake.

"What the hell is the eleventh commandment, anyway?" she said.

"Be sweet," he said.

"You're kidding," she said. "That's it?"

"Harder to do than it sounds," he said.

By the time they reached Six Points and turned onto Magnolia Street, she had him laughing about the whole thing. "His damn *recliner*," Brother said. "That was the thing that got me, when you started talking about his recliner, and his little dog."

"I had to get you in the car somehow, didn't I?"

This episode seemed to get the Ten Commandments out of his system. Things evened out. Brother slowed up on the drinking, even convinced AA to let him come back to meetings. The parole officer said he seemed a little more serious this time. Georgia tried to be optimistic.

8

Little Mama's mind was slipping so gradually you could almost talk yourself out of noticing. The first luncheon after the disaster, she was well enough to participate. The next year she stayed up in her room.

Georgia got better at ignoring birthdays…thirty-five, thirty-six…but then suddenly it was 2005 and that big round number was barreling down the road toward her. Don't say the number don't say it *don't!*

It didn't really bother her, really. She chose not to think about it. If you have spent thirty-eight years toiling on the anthill, you earn the right not to think about anything you want. Once you get over your youthful self and stop all that blue-sky dreaming, you are freer to settle down and enjoy life. Stop striving so damn hard. You have time, a few dollars in your purse. You don't have to eat hamburger unless that's what you want.

Personally, Georgia preferred a rib eye and champagne. Tonight she would be having a ham sandwich and the last piece of chess pie. It was Friday night, Bill Allred's night, but he had canceled because of sheriff business. Georgia was feeling generous and moved him to Saturday, just this once.

She liked to look after Bill's sweet tooth so she drove out to Hull's for the ingredients to make his favorite Lemon Freeze.

Pulling back into the driveway she saw Hazel Vickrey's mail truck approaching. She parked and walked to the mailbox, said hey to Hazel, handed her the stack of bills she was mailing, and took from her one piece of mail.

A small white envelope.

The mail truck puttered away.

Georgia did not recognize the shaky hand that had written her name, "Miss Ga. Bottoms," and her address, "15 Magnolia St., Six Points, Ala." No return address. The stamp was crooked. Someone at the post office had written the zip code in blue ink.

For some reason the envelope filled Georgia with dread. A handwritten letter from a stranger. Was that ever good news?

At any rate she did not want to open it with Mrs. Pinson watching from amidst her petunias.

She waved hi and carried the envelope up the steps, inside. She slit the envelope with her thumbnail.

Dear Georgia,

Forgive me writing this, would call you on the phone but I cannot pay the L.D. Maybe you know my daughter Ree has been sick & now in State Prison at St Gabriel 3 yr. She say not guilty but who knows. The boy Nathan is come to live with me here in N.O. I have just my disability and SSI for 1, it take mos. to get the new papers. You been good to send some $ to Ree, now is very hard. Can you send some more please my name, same place W. Union I make the pick up now. You out to see the boy, big & fine but eats very much! Please let me know what you can. Or if you cannot send $ let

me know I will send you the boy by bus or train. Not want-
ing to trouble you, still I am old and cannot do this myself
hartly no help from anybody. Please call me 586-0645.

Sincerely, Mrs. Eugenia Jordan

By the time she finished reading, Georgia's hands were shaking. Her arrangement with Ree called for one-way communication only. That's what she paid for, month after month, all these
years—to be left out of it. The fourth Saturday of every month,
she went to Western Union and wired as much as she could
afford. In return, no contact. That was the deal.

This letter came from a new direction. To Georgia, it felt like
a threat.

The boy could not come to Six Points. His daddy was in
prison, now his great-aunt Ree too. This would be the boy's
great-grandmother, Eugenia, who must be at least eighty by
now—bless her heart having to handle a big hungry boy...

But the "boy" was almost twenty, wasn't he? Plenty old enough
to help bring some "$" into the house. If not, why not? If
he'd been in Georgia's house, she'd have him out looking for a
job in five minutes. But he wasn't coming here. He was going to
stay right where he belonged, with Eugenia Jordan in New
Orleans.

Nathan.

She didn't let his name enter her mind very often.

She wanted only to send money and forget it. She'd been thinking now that he was growing up, he should be able to take care of
himself and she could ease up on the amount—of course she
would send birthdays, and Christmas, but there comes a time
when everyone has to pull his own weight...then this letter.

There are some debts you never finish paying.

Georgia read the letter three times. Gradually it came to seem less a threat than a plea. She copied Eugenia's phone number, tucked it in her pocket, and carried the letter up to her room.

From the back of her bra drawer, she brought out the green felted box.

Her high-school diary was the usual brown square thing with a loop of leather and a tiny brass lock, long since sprung. Tucked in front was a letter she wrote to herself at eighteen—wrote it on separate notepaper because it was too dangerous to commit to the diary. A trace of Giorgio perfume still rose from the pages, all these years later.

Dear Dairy,

Today something weird. I went to cheerleading and we did the 2-side pyramid and for the 1st time nobody fell. I was top on the right. After practice I was SO wiped out, went over to set on the bleachers & catch my breath. The sun was this big red ball floating, I couldnt stop looking at it. I heard this little like a baby crying, went around back of the bleachers and up under where everybody drops their bottles & stuff.

In the weeds a little kittie, black and white spots, about a week old, maybe 2 or 3 weeks, Real little, crying and its mama left or run over by a car. So, trying to get this scared kittie to stop crying, after awhile it does. So soft like mohair. I carried her back of the bleachers and this boy come up, Clarence Blanchard but is called Skiff, not sneaky but quiet like, "What do you have there." I showed him and he was not like a regular boy, "oh stupid kittie" or something, he was gentle took the kittie in his hand and rubbed her head like a baby. I reached out

just to pet her back, didnt mean to touch his hand but I did &
then he kissed me. (!!!!!!!)

    He was such a good kisser I couldn't stop, I know I should
push him away. Anyway HUH????? BIG SECRET! When we
finished he said he will take the kitten to his house to look after.
So he is a nice person too. But still I have a <u>BIG PROBLEM</u>. I
like Skiff, <u>crazy</u> about him I think, but <u>OF COURSE</u> can't see
him again!!!

    So there it is, what to do? Don't tell anybody not even
Krystal.

—G.

She always signed her entries that way—"G."—trying so hard
to be cool. Like addressing the diary as "Dairy," an eighteen-
year-old's idea of hilarious.

She hadn't been able to bring herself to state in writing the
nature of the BIG PROBLEM: Skiff was black.

Now she tucked that letter with Eugenia's letter into the front
of the diary. She flipped through the pages, breathing in the shallow girl she used to be. She thought there might have been other
coded entries about Skiff, but she couldn't find even one hint
that he existed. She had set down in detail every party, every gos-
sipy phone call, 4-H club meeting, and book report. Not a word
about Skiff. Except in that secret letter to herself the day they
met, Georgia hid what was happening, even from herself.

She remembered how horny they got for each other—meeting
under the bleachers at dusk to play with their kitten ("Rags")
and make out. Not just kissing—some pretty heavy petting, her
hand rubbing on him although she had not opened his pants
yet, his hand rubbing hard against her underwear, making her

feel sexy and overheated. But if he tried to touch her nipple, or tugged at the edge of her underwear, she batted him away. That's exactly how much virginity she had left.

She started sneaking out late at night to meet him. You could only put in so much time in the scratchy weeds under the bleachers before you found your way to the cushy backseat of Skiff's daddy's brown LTD, with things going a little further each time.

Then one time you went ahead and said yes. Well, not really *said* it, hardly a word was spoken. But everything about you cried, *Yes.*

Come on admit it, Skiff was not even the first. First was Denny Ray Patterson in his father's blue Nova. Until she did it with Skiff she thought Denny Ray was good, but then she found out he was nothing at all. He never made her feel all sexy wild the way Skiff did. Skiff's fat sexy lips kissed all over her face. Skiff's fat tongue was a living thing, jumpy squishy sexy hot-blooded animal with a mind of its own. That tongue and those lips kissed her right off her feet into the back of the LTD, where on a certain Friday night Skiff and Georgia sailed past their previous limits.

When they did it, they went on and did it. So much hotter and better than Denny Ray. This was definitely what all the fuss was about—three wild animals in the backseat: Georgia, Skiff's tongue, and Skiff.

Make that four.

There was one huge surprise, then, and one <u>BIG PROBLEM</u>. The problem, of course, was that Georgia and Skiff could not be seen in public. They could not go on a date, in daylight or in darkness. Because Skiff was black and Georgia was white and this was Six Points, 1985.

Georgia sometimes wondered if she went for Skiff as a secret revenge upon her mother. She had rebelled all through her teen years. Little Mama hated black people so much, maybe that's what made Georgia so hungry to have one, to taste one, to feel her lips pressing against the lips of one. It made her feel wild. Naughtier than any girl in town. Skiff liked it too, what a little firecat she became when he touched her. He loved how he could get her motor running using only his pillowy lips, and that smoldering look in his eyes.

Her white boyfriends were boring: Ernie Woolard, Jeff Bright, Denny Ray. Silly uninteresting boys, cars and football and cars. Whereas Skiff was moody and mysterious, deep into Georgia, her mouth, her lips. Her legs. Her breasts. Every square inch of her. His warm brown fingers touching her white skin. She loved sneaking around with him, almost getting caught—by his father, her mother, random people in the outer reaches of Hull's parking lot, once a farmer in their secret spot by the catfish hatchery. They drove the LTD up in the deep shade of three enormous oak trees, hidden from the road by a tangle of blackberry bushes. Through the windshield, they had a nice view of a pond and the spray of cattails at its marshy edge. They listened to Duran Duran and Air Supply, and French-kissed until their jaws ached.

Mama knew there was a boy, but not who. Georgia wasn't brave enough to tell her. She enjoyed the knowledge of how hysterical Mama would be if she ever found out.

One time "all the way" was all it took. You can't get much more fertile than a horny boy and girl of eighteen. Five weeks later, out of the blue in second-period American history, Georgia felt a startling urge to throw up. Bent over the toilet in the girls' room she had a deadly moment of realization.

She was two weeks late but tried to put it out of her mind. She almost managed to forget it for a day or two. She thought Skiff had used a rubber but she wasn't sure, being so wonderfully distracted at the time.

Krystal was her best friend on earth, but this was so serious Georgia couldn't tell even her. Getting pregnant was a hell of a lot more rebellious than she meant to be.

Knowing whose baby it was, she saw only two options: get rid of it now, or run away somewhere and hide until she had it. The only thing that stopped her from running away immediately was knowing how worried Mama would be if she vanished without a word. She didn't mind appalling Little Mama, but she didn't want to scare her to death.

Finally she screwed up the courage to tell Skiff. His eyes got so big she couldn't help laughing. That made him mad—he thought she was making fun of the situation.

She couldn't believe he had the nerve to get mad at her, when he was the one who knocked her up. "I'm gonna get rid of it," she snapped, although she didn't really think she could do that. "I can get it done in Mobile. I need four hundred dollars."

"You can't be doing that," Skiff said. "It ain't only your baby, remember."

"Oh, I do remember," she said. "But it happens to be inside of me, not you. And if you think I'm gonna have it, you're out of your mind."

"Why not?"

"Why do you think? Look at yourself. Look in a mirror." Maybe that was mean, but Georgia wasn't in any mood to be nice.

"You got to have it," said Skiff. "God put it in there. Nothing we can do about that."

"God didn't do it, Skiff. This one was all you."

His face stiffened. For a moment she was almost scared of him. At last he said, "Are you sure?"

It took her a moment to realize what he meant. "Am I *sure?*" she erupted. "What are you trying to say? Come on and say it, I dare you."

"Aw shut up," he muttered. "You know what I mean."

"You think I'm a slut," she said, "because of what I did with you?"

"Not what I said."

"But it is what you think."

"Naw it ain't."

"You were the first, Skiff," she lied. "You were the only boy I've ever been with."

"We could go somewhere and get married," Skiff said. "We could go up north. There's a lot of people up there like that."

"Like what?"

"Where the white go with the black, and get married."

"How do you know?"

"I heard about it," he said. "It's all right if you in Chicago, or Detroit."

"You really want to marry me, Skiff?"

He got real quiet. Even though he was the one who'd said the word "married" first, hearing the word from her mouth shut him up.

"I didn't think so," she said. "Don't worry. I don't want to marry you either."

He frowned. "I will, if that's what you want."

She thought: Hell, that's more than Denny Ray would have said.

Skiff didn't want a baby any more than Georgia did—he was clear about that—but it sure looked like they'd made one, he said, no matter what either one thought about it. Did she really want to kill it? After a lot of arguing in the LTD they decided to find somewhere for Georgia to hide out until she had it, then give it up for adoption.

Luckily graduation was only three weeks away. The gown hid Georgia's thickening middle. The other kids went off to summer jobs and vacations. Georgia told everybody she was going to stay with a cousin in North Carolina. Krystal was not so nosy back then. She was so excited about going off to Auburn in the fall she didn't even notice her best friend lying to her face.

The day before Georgia was to leave, she went to the front of the house, where Little Mama was working the switchboard. This was the eighties, and by this time all of Six Points had direct-dial telephone service, so Little Mama's formerly buzzing central switchboard had dwindled to an answering service with five clients: two doctors, the funeral home, the drugstore, and the ambulance service.

Mama never glanced up from the switchboard. She kept right on taking messages while Georgia explained she was nine weeks pregnant by a boy she did not intend to name. She was going to North Carolina to stay with the boy's aunt. She intended to have the baby and give it away.

"And then what?" Little Mama said.

"Come back here, I guess. If it's all right with you."

"You're always welcome." That's all Mama said. She didn't want to know any details.

When she drove Georgia to meet the bus at the Texaco station, she handed over two hundred dollars and said it was a good thing Daddy was dead, because this surely would have killed him.

Georgia put on a solemn face but she was thinking, oh lady, if you only knew what I did, and who with—if you knew what color your grandbaby is going to come out—you'd be a hell of a lot madder than this.

She fought the impulse to blurt out the truth. She couldn't bring herself to hurt Little Mama that much. She put the money in her purse and kept quiet.

Little Mama didn't even notice the bus was headed toward HATTIESBURG, the opposite direction from North Carolina. Georgia was proud to have pulled off the deception. In fact she was headed west, to stay with Skiff's Aunt Ree in Laurel, Mississippi.

Ree turned out to be Eureka Blanchard, a fat jolly mama with a taste for Riunite pink wine and men recently out of jail. Georgia feared for her life the whole time she lived in Ree's house. She wrote Krystal saying how nice and peaceful it was in North Carolina, what a lovely lady the cousin was, taking her to socials and teas at the best houses in town.

Ree's house was set on an isolated cul-de-sac among gloomy sweet-gum trees at the back of a neighborhood where people threw trash on the ground and nobody picked it up. You never knew whose car would come rumbling and booming down the street at eleven o'clock on a Friday night. Often it was some big tough brother looking for Ree. Georgia cowered in her room, cradling her big belly in her arms, entertaining lurid ideas of what went on in the living room while she was trying to sleep: dope smoking, for sure—she could smell it under the door— and a lot of humping, and a boatload of malt liquor along with the Riunite, to judge from the bottles standing around in the morning. Al Green and the Staple Singers on the stereo, loud. Always, always the TV. For Georgia, it was a real education in how people live.

But Ree was good to take her in. Never asked for anything in return, not a dime. Didn't seem to disapprove of Georgia's looming belly. When Georgia's back hurt, Ree gave her a back rub. When the stretch marks appeared, Ree bought a special cream she said would make them go away. It didn't work, but it was nice of her to try.

Georgia gave birth two weeks before Christmas at the county hospital, in the dead of night. Everyone was very kind until the baby came out. Georgia saw one of the nurses make a face. Maybe the woman hadn't been prepared for the sight of a black baby—although he was not really black, but a halfway shade, the color of golden oak.

The look of distaste on the face of that nurse haunted Georgia. As if she had suddenly become a lesser human because of what came out of her.

The way black people must feel every day.

All along she'd known it would be a boy, and it was. The nurse asked if she wanted to hold him. Georgia was crying and so was the baby, a raggedy pip-squeak sound. She was afraid to hold him. If she ever put her hands on him, she might not let go. So she said no, thank you.

In all the years since, that was her main regret. She wished she had held him for just a minute before they took him away. She thought she might get another chance, but she never saw him again.

Two days later, she took the bus back to Six Points. All the way to Alabama, she stared at the rising and falling power lines tracking her mood like a graph. She made elaborate plans about how to stay out of trouble in the future.

She rolled her suitcase from the bus stop to the house on Magnolia Street. She was so plump from the baby that no one recognized her on the street.

Little Mama was glad to see her, which surprised both of them. Georgia hung around the house until she had starved off the baby weight. She answered the pile of letters from Krystal, who was living with an aunt in Birmingham, working at the Pizitz cosmetics counter.

"Everybody says I look so well rested," Georgia wrote. "Must be that Carolina mountain air."

A couple of years later, Skiff's mother and father ran up under a log truck out on State Road 47. Not long after that, Skiff got arrested the first time. Georgia couldn't tell a soul how much these things bothered her. It wasn't that she imagined being with Skiff again, but she had loved him more than any boyfriend she'd had. He belonged to a warm and loving family when they met— now they were gone. Was it Georgia's fault? Was she the bad luck charm?

Ree wrote to say that no one would adopt the baby because of how he came out—big surprise—so Ree had decided to keep him. She named him Nathan, after Georgia's favorite song that summer. Ree said she was moving to New Orleans to live with her mother, who promised to help with the baby.

Ree never asked for money, but Georgia knew her responsibility. The day she got that letter, she walked downtown and found her first job, ringing a register at Planters' Mercantile, so she could send money every month.

That was twenty years ago. The fourth Saturday of every month she wired as much as she could to New Orleans. In return, all she asked was no contact.

Sad to think of Ree in prison. She wasn't a bad woman but she did have a thing for bad men. And now her poor old mother needs help. I will just have to find a way to send more.

Lord, why is it always up to me?

Call the old lady tonight. She needs to understand there is no reason to think of sending the boy here. That will never work— not for him, not for me or anybody.

You have to draw the line somewhere.

9

The ring of the phone had an odd submerged quality, a froggy nostalgic ring, as if New Orleans was not just another place but another time, as well. That ring stirred Georgia's longing to discover the place for real and not just from movies and books, to breathe the exotic smells and absorb the thump of music on the air. Everything she'd read about New Orleans mentioned the smell of the river, the spicy food, and the music—just walk down any street, they say, and you will hear raucous music pouring from every direction. Sometimes when a yearning swept over her, Georgia would drag down her Chef K-Paul Louisiana cookbook and cook up some mouth-searing dish that called for a pound of butter and one quarter teaspoon of twenty-seven different kinds of pepper. The first bite of Creole Shrimp Jambalaya was enough to transport her imagination to a white-draped table overlooking Jackson Square.

Someone picked up the phone and fumbled it. There were several seconds of bumpety-bumping, then a quavery old-lady drawl: "Hello?"

"Hey, this is Georgia Bottoms, may I speak with Miz Eugenia Jordan, please?"

Of course she knew she was speaking with Eugenia, but with

old folks you can't take shortcuts on the courtesy. All they have is time to sit around reflecting on the miserable failings of youth.

"This is Eugenia," said the quavery lady. You-JIN-ya. "Who is it again?"

"It's Georgia Bottoms. In Six Points."

"I'm sorry, baby, I can't hear you. Let me turn down this noise."

Eugenia set the phone down. The TV was so loud Georgia could hear Regis Philbin saying "That's ridiculous!" and the audience laughing. The sound switched off. Georgia was thinking how long it had been since she knew anyone with a TV you had to get out of a chair to turn off.

"Now!" the lady said. "Who did you say it was?"

Patiently Georgia explained, and this time Mrs. Jordan said, "Oh hello there, how are you, baby? How you doin'? I can't believe you got my letter that quick."

"It came today," Georgia said. "I'm calling you as soon as I got it."

Eugenia said, "You know, I hear people complain about the post office, but honestly I don't know how they do it. I only put it in the box down by the corner here in Na'walyins the day before yesterday. And they done already carried it all the way up to you?"

"Yes, that is good service, all right," said Georgia.

"How y'all folks doing up there, y'all got you some hot weather like we got 'round here?"

Georgia settled in for a few minutes of howdying and weather comparing. After a while she saw an opening and squeezed through it: "Now Miz Jordan, reason I'm calling is, well I'm just so sorry to hear about Ree. What happened? What did she do to get put in jail?"

"I don't rightly know. They tried to tell me what it was, but I couldn't ever get clear on it."

"How long is she in for?"

"Two years, they said, but might not be that long. My grandson Larue say she be out by next Easter if she don't do nothing wrong while she in there."

"Because I'm just one person up here, you know," Georgia said. "I'm a single woman, pretty much unemployed at the moment," which was technically true, "up here in Six Points looking after my mama and my brother, they're both disabled"—Brother might as well be, for all the good he did anybody—"and I want you to know I will try to send you more money, but things are a little tough for me too at the moment." This was a tactic she had planned in advance, the lowering of expectations.

"I understand," said Eugenia. "I'd be mighty grateful for whatever help you could give."

"That's fine," Georgia said. "Now, I did send a wire to Ree two weeks ago. Fourth Saturday of the month. Did you pick that up?"

"I went down there, had to wait a long time for the second bus...but when I got there, they said it has to be my name on the wire, not hers," Eugenia said. "They wouldn't give me any of it 'less you send it again with my name."

"I will go to Western Union tomorrow and straighten that out. How long has Ree been...away?"

Eugenia didn't know exactly. Three or four weeks.

"And how is the boy?" Georgia said.

"Beg pardon?"

"The boy," she repeated. She had never spoken his name aloud, but that was no reason not to. "Nathan. How is he doing?"

"Aw he's a good boy but he sho do like to eat," Eugenia said with a chuckle.

"Yeah, you said. Is he smart, is he good in school?" Georgia was hoping he took after her in at least one respect.

"I don't know about that," said Eugenia. "I don't think he been, lately."

"He didn't graduate?"

"Not that boy. He like to fool around too much. I told him he better straighten up and fly right or I'm gone send him up to Alabama, let you handle him. That seemed to scare him pretty good."

"Yeah, listen, Miss Eugenia, about that . . . I'm not really set up to handle a boy here, what with my mother who's disabled—and my brother is handicapped too," Georgia said, "so whatever we do, we need to keep him living down there with you."

"I hear you," Eugenia said. "You don't want him coming to town and everybody find out you got a black son, I imagine."

"Well, that's part of it too," said Georgia. "I mean, it's not like we know each other. I've never even seen him. Since he was born."

"You ought to come down and visit," said Eugenia. "He would like to meet his mama."

"Is that what he said?"

"No, but if you had a mama, wouldn't you want to meet her?"

"I've got one," said Georgia, "and in retrospect, no."

Whizzy jumped up in the chair beside her. Georgia stroked her ears with two fingers. Talking with Eugenia was easy. There was no judgment in her tone. Georgia couldn't remember speaking this comfortably to a black person before. Except for Skiff, of course—which was what got her into this situation.

"You could just come for a visit," Eugenia said. "I wouldn't try to stick you with the boy."

"That's very kind of you. I've always dreamed about visiting New Orleans."

"Well then you just come on down, baby," Eugenia said. "We'll show you how to eat. I know you gotta be skinny, Ree said you's always a little bitty thing even when you was pregnant."

Georgia was delighted to hear that someone described her as little bitty. "Are you kidding? I have to starve myself to keep from blowing up like a balloon."

Eugenia laughed. "I'm more like the Goodyear blimp but who cares? My mama was big, too. Nothin' wrong with some meat on the bone."

By the time Georgia hung up, she was certain the boy was much better off with Eugenia than he had ever been with Ree. It felt like the lifting of a load, just to know he was in better hands. Whatever extra money Georgia could send would be put to good use.

10

It took most of an hour for Shelley Grinnell at the Wee-Pak-N-Ship to straighten out the Western Union confusion and resend the money to Eugenia Jordan, with an extra fifty dollars thrown in as a sign of Georgia's goodwill.

"What happened to the one we usually send to?" said nosy Shelley.

"That was Cousin Ree," Georgia said, and to make her feel bad: "She passed away."

"Oh my gosh, I'm sorry for your loss," Shelley said. "What happened?"

"They think it was pneumonia but don't quote me." When lying, it's always best to keep the details vague so you don't get crossed up trying to remember. "This is her mama, poor old Aunt Eugenia. I do what I can to help her get by."

"That is so good of you, Georgia," said Shelley.

Stepping out into the creamy April sunlight, Georgia decided to walk the long way around the square. The air was delicious, a promise of better things to come. Sometimes Belk's changed its window displays on Tuesdays, and Hello who is this getting out of a beat-up blue Chrysler in front of Skinner Furniture?

Shiny blond movie-star hair combed up off his forehead in an old-fashioned Cary Grant wave. Pale green double-breasted suit, gorgeous emerald tie, the same expensive green as his eyes. An honest to God dimple in his chin, a face chiseled like the men in those old-fashioned ads for Arrow shirts.

He was young and strong, maybe thirty. If she hadn't seen him getting out of that battered K car, Georgia might have suspected him of being an actual movie star on the streets of Six Points.

She had a good ten seconds to look him over while he was closing his car door and stepping up to the sidewalk. Big rangy rack of a guy. Great big hands. Wide linebacker shoulders, tapering down to slim hips. That was not an expensive suit but he filled it out nicely.

Oh dear, what is that glint on the left hand? Is that a simple band of gold? Yes indeed.

Georgia sucked in her tummy and walked by. She could feel his eyes raking her over. She hadn't been so effectively felt up by a pair of eyes in a while. At the last possible moment, she turned to confront him in the act of watching her. His eyes gleamed— something animal there. "Morning," she sang, sailing past.

She sashayed all the way down the block into Ryan's Drugs without looking back. She knew he was watching her—she could feel his hot gaze on her rear end—but she would not give him the satisfaction of turning around.

The bell jingled on the door. Here was Sally Cranford with her bright smile and elegant, prematurely white hair. Sally had worked at Ryan's since she and Georgia were girls. She knew how to treat her best cosmetics customer; she always called Georgia to let her know when the new lipsticks came in.

"Look behind me and see if you see a good-looking man," said Georgia.

"I sure do, the new preacher, and he's coming on a beeline for you."

"What new preacher?"

"*Our* new preacher—didn't you hear? And here he is now!" she said, as the bell jingled. "Hey, Reverend, my name is Sally, this here is Georgia. We're members at your new church. Welcome to Six Points."

"Why thank you, Miss Sally, it's a real pleasure...And Miss Georgia, how do you do? I've heard about you." His voice was thrillingly deep. It went well with that statuesque chin. Georgia felt a little light-headed, a high-pitched hiss in her ears. She shook his hand but didn't feel a thing.

He said his name was Brent Colgate, and he was really going to enjoy ministering in a town with such pretty ladies. That sounded like something a used-car dealer might say, not the new preacher. Georgia was thinking "Brent Colgate" had the ring of a made-up name.

Preacher Eugene was never all that attractive, although Georgia had talked herself into being attracted to him. This man was almost too handsome. It was like standing next to one of those revolving spotlights at the county fair—you couldn't look directly at it without hurting your eyes.

Brent Colgate said his last church was in a much smaller town, a wide spot in the road called Schuyler's Creek near the Tennessee line. "Daphne and I are excited to be here in the big city, 'cause that's how Six Points feels to us," he said.

He seemed nice—overdressed in his green suit, perhaps, a bit floppy and eager, like a big happy puppy. His manner was endearing, slightly goofy. He said the First Baptist would be "the biggest church family we've ever had." He told Sally he had come for a tube of Pepsodent, but Georgia knew the real reason he came in: to have a look at Georgia.

Sometimes a seduction required an elaborate plan. This one appeared to be only a matter of waiting.

She pretended to study the *Ladies' Home Journal* while he paid for his toothpaste. She wondered why someone named Brent Colgate would choose Pepsodent.

She ignored him the whole time he was in the store. She knew that would drive him crazy. A man that handsome is not used to being ignored. Sure enough, he turned around at the door and came back to the magazine rack. "So nice to meet you, Miss Georgia. Hope I'll see you in church Sunday?"

"I hope so too." She granted him a mysterious smile, and returned to her magazine. She didn't glance up again until the bell ushered him out.

Sally was impressed. "Did you see how he came all the way back to say goodbye to you?"

"Did he?" Georgia shrugged. "I didn't notice."

"Oh, come on. You certainly did."

"That man is too good-looking to be a preacher," Georgia said. "Anyway, he's way too married for me."

Sally said he was not her cup of tea but she could see how some people might like him.

"Sally, what happened to Preacher Barker?"

"You're slipping, you're the one who always knows everything," Sally said. "Heart attack. He was watching *Wheel of Fortune*. They did a quadruple bypass up at the Baptist hospital. I don't think he'll be back."

Georgia chose a tube of Bright Passion lipstick, a compact of Tawny Gold face powder. When she stepped outside, the K car was nowhere to be seen. She was relieved. If Brent Colgate had been standing by his car watching her with those animal eyes, she might have had to go directly to bed with him. Nothing wrong with that—he definitely deserved consideration for her to-do list—but it would happen at a time and place of her choosing, not because she got all worked up just by laying eyes on him.

She stood back from her car door, letting out the heat. She saw Krystal hastening down the steps of city hall. She thought it was a normal hello, but the look on Krystal's face stopped her.

"You can't go home right now," Krystal said. "Come to my office."

"What is the matter?"

"The Alabama Bureau of Investigation has gone to your house to arrest your brother."

"Oh, God. For what?"

"It's complicated. He won't cooperate. He's locked himself in your mother's room and says he won't come out."

"I'd better go over there." Georgia started for her car.

"No, Georgia—he's threatened to blow up the house if they don't go away and leave him alone."

"That's ridiculous," Georgia said. "He can't blow up a balloon without my help. Are you coming? Get in the car."

Krystal got in. Georgia drove. Krystal revealed that the ABI had opened a file on Brother three years ago, at the time of his supreme court demonstration. Agents had observed him and Sims Bailey purchasing a quantity of explosive material, placing it in a drive-up storage locker in Alexander City. The ABI believed Brother and Sims were planning to blow up the Ten Commandments and the Supreme Court of Alabama.

"Oh for God's sake," said Georgia. "Like I don't have enough on my plate? When did you hear this?"

"They called me a week ago," Krystal said. "I was not allowed to say a word, Georgia, I'm sorry. I hope you understand."

"Did you call Bill Allred?" The sheriff and his deputies had known Brother since he was a kid. They had seen him at his worst, plenty of times. They knew how to calm him down and get him in the back of a patrol car.

"I was trying not to make it into a big thing," Krystal said. "I told them he's harmless, but this ABI guy is a bit of a dick."

"I swear to God, Krystal, I leave home for one hour and look what happens!"

"It won't help for you to get all upset."

"I'm gonna kill that boy," said Georgia. "And you know Sims Bailey was right there, egging him on. I'm gonna kill both of them."

The driveway was blocked by a conspicuously unmarked Ford Crown Victoria in a fecal shade of brown. Georgia had half expected a SWAT team surrounding the house, but there was no sign of any confrontation. Krystal lagged behind; Georgia hurried onto the porch and opened the door. "Anybody home?"

She strode down the center hall to the kitchen, where she found Brother sitting with three men who had come to arrest him. Brother was drinking a can of Bud, holding a bloody wad of Kleenex to his nose. The agents were laughing at something he'd said. Georgia's sudden appearance caused them to turn. Their laughter trailed off as they checked her out.

She said, "What the hell is this?"

The skinny man on the left got to his feet. "Alabama Bureau

of Investigation, ma'am, I'm Agent Lathem. We're serving a warrant on this man."

Georgia said, "I ran over here at the speed of light because somebody said this was a hostage situation."

"Yeah," Brother said, "I was trying to stage a nonviolent resistance."

The agents laughed. "That didn't work out so well," said Lathem.

Krystal came in, breathing hard. "I'm Mayor—Lambert, I— spoke with one of you men?"

The older agent seated at the table identified himself as Agent Poole. He cast a skeptical eye over Krystal. "Mr. Bottoms was just as cooperative as you said he would be. Once we figured out we had something that he wanted."

Georgia asked what that might have been. The men chuckled.

"Basically, he surrendered in exchange for a beer," said Lathem.

"They had me barricaded in Mama's den and they wouldn't give me a goddamn thing," Brother said. "They didn't care if I died of thirst in there."

If ever a cause was lost, it was Brother. Still, Georgia felt she had to make an effort. "Officer, whatever plan he was trying to hatch, surely you can see he was never in danger of being able to pull it off. I suggest you talk to Sheriff Allred. He knows all about the history here."

"Aw hush, Georgia! You're only making it worse." Brother sipped his beer. Georgia saw his hand trembling, holding the can. His bravado was all for show.

Her heart went out to him.

"I'm trying to keep you out of jail," she said.

"That's not going to be possible," Agent Poole said. "I suppose a judge might let him have bond. Not if it was me."

"On behalf of the city of Six Points, I can assure you this man is absolutely harmless," said Krystal. "I've known him most of his life. The things he says often have no relationship to reality. I suggest you come down to city hall and look at his record."

"We're not gonna do that today," said Lathem.

"You're making a big thing out of nothing."

"We've got a warrant and we're sworn to serve it," said Poole. "If you want to help him, get him a lawyer. Come on, fellas, we don't need a lecture from Mr.—I mean Miz Mayor, excuse me."

There was no mistaking the slant of his remark. He winked at his buddies when he said it. Agent Lathem laughed in surprise, as in, *I can't believe you said that!* Krystal's jaw tightened.

The third agent at the table looked about nineteen years old. He carried a dot of shaving cream on his left earlobe. He hadn't said a word until now. "He's far from harmless," he said. "He's a domestic terrorist, he belongs to a radical group. He's in violation of at least nine Alabama statutes and a bunch of federal ones too. He'll be in prison till he's old."

"God, what an asshole you are," said Brother. "I come out of that room of my own free will—in a show of cooperation, you know, fuckin' peace on earth and everything. And that's the kind of bullshit you lay on me? No way, man. I call bullshit on your bullshit."

The other agents laughed at the spectacle of their shaving-cream newbie put in his place by a loser like Brother. Usually, where Brother was concerned, Georgia tended to side with the law. But these officious clowns had driven down from Montgomery in their crap-brown Crown Victoria just to ruin her day.

"What group?" Georgia said.

"Ma'am?"

"You said he belonged to a radical group."

"AA," Brother said.

"He goes to AA meetings, you call that a radical group?"

"He belongs to a gang that calls itself the Alabama Anarchists," said Junior Detective.

"AA," Brother said.

"Oh for God's sake!"

"I told y'all, they ain't no 'group,' it's just me and Sims," Brother said.

"Now fellas," said Georgia, "if I can prove to you that my brother never intended to blow up anything, can we get you some lunch and put you back on the road?"

"We've had lunch." Agent Poole stood from his chair. "We'll be taking him now."

"But if I can demonstrate to you—"

"Ma'am," Agent Poole said, "don't try to interfere with our duty." He went behind Brother and stood him up roughly, cuffed his wrists behind his back.

"Dang, man, no need to hurt me," said Brother. "I ain't resisting you at all."

Poole said shut up. He didn't like the interference from Georgia—his scowl stretched all the way over to Krystal—ah okay, maybe that was it. He took one look at Krystal and maybe made some assumption about her and Georgia.

"Society always persecutes the visionary," Brother was saying. "I've tried to warn you people that leaving that man in his office is exactly the same as worshipping a false god."

Agent Lathem snorted.

"Get him out of here," Poole said.

Georgia moved to block the door. "Where are you taking him?"

"Stand aside, please," he said.

"Don't I have a right to know where to go bail him out?"

"The ABI office in Montgomery can give you that information." He steered her out of his path, making way for Lathem and Junior to hustle Brother out of the kitchen. Brother put up no fight at all but they wouldn't just let him walk out like a normal person. They had to drag him down the hall, out the door.

Georgia followed them onto the porch. "I can report you for police brutality!"

"Go right ahead," said Agent Poole.

Brother yelled, "You'll never take me alive, copper!"

Lathem said, "We just did." The others laughed like a gang of frat boys.

Poole put his hand on Brother's head and ducked him into the backseat, then went around and got behind the wheel. Lathem climbed in beside Brother. Junior rode shotgun. The Ford backed into the street, and drove off.

When Georgia realized Krystal was beside her, she said, "I've got half a mind to just leave him in this time."

"No one would blame you."

"God, I wish I still smoked. You want a cup of coffee or something?"

"I have to get back to work," said Krystal. "You gonna make me walk?"

"Just let me look in on Mama and I'll drive you down."

Little Mama was in her den watching Martha Stewart make a piecrust. She had already forgotten whatever part she might have played in Brother's hostage drama. She didn't know anything about any police. Sometimes Mama's affliction was almost a blessing. Georgia found herself wishing she could catch a mild case of it, just for one afternoon.

Driving by the First Baptist parsonage she pointed out Brent Colgate in the driveway, still sporting his pale green suit. He was lifting a carton from the trunk of his K car. "Wow, look at that," Krystal said. "I may have to become a Baptist."

"I want to thank the search committee from the bottom of my heart," Georgia said. "Listen, Krystal—do you think you could make a call to Montgomery? You know I hate to ask, I never ask you to get involved in Brother's messes. But this is state level. I've got no connections at all."

"I was trying to figure out who I could call," Krystal said. "I do know the director of public safety. He's not exactly the boss of these guys, but he'll know who we can talk to."

"That would be so great," said Georgia. "How lucky am I to have a best friend who's also the mayor?"

After a pregnant pause Krystal said, "Might not be for long."

"What's that supposed to mean?"

"You know I'm up for reelection in September."

"Of course. Unopposed as usual."

"Filing deadline was five p.m. yesterday. Turns out I'm going to have an opponent." Krystal smiled out the window, enjoying her air of mystery.

"You're kidding me. Who?"

"Madeline Roudy," said Krystal.

Georgia's mouth dropped open.

"Watch that car—" Krystal grabbed the wheel and deftly steered them around a Cadillac pulling out of the diner.

"Thanks... Madeline Roudy is running against you? Can she do that?"

"Of course she can." Krystal's smile tightened. "I annexed them into the city. Which gives them enough votes to elect her, if they all stick together—and why wouldn't they? I knew it would happen eventually, but I was hoping they might at least give me a term or two as thanks, before they booted me out."

"Krystal, you're the best friend they've ever had in this town. Who else stuck their neck out for annexation?"

"They don't think they owe me a thing, and you know what? They're right. Anyway, you're preaching to the choir. Whyn't you let me out here. Gotta do the people's work while I've still got the job."

Krystal was amazingly cheerful. Georgia knew she must be crushed. Being mayor of Six Points was the only thing Krystal had ever wanted. In the hubbub over annexation, Georgia had never realized Krystal was knowingly setting up the means to put herself out of a job.

Madeline Roudy?

An impressive woman. A pediatrician. Taking care of poor sick kids. Just the kind of person you would want to be the First Black Mayor of Six Points.

Krystal didn't stand a chance.

Just as Brother didn't stand a chance.

Just like that new preacher, Brent Colgate? He didn't stand a chance either.

Survival of the fittest, that's the law. Don't blame me, Georgia thought. The world was this way when I got here.

11

Riding back from the prison in the dark, she turns on the radio and listen what song's coming on: that beat starts up, *whick-it whick-it* strummed on electric-guitar strings, a dirty horn section, phasey electronic mixer sound taking us straight into The Girls, only the girls ain't backing Diana anymore, Diana done left and gone solo on their ass, left them behind in a movie-star cloud of gold dust, leaving Mary and Cindy to try and replace her with another thin trembly soprano, Jean Terrell . . . The song is "Nathan Jones" and maybe because Georgia is hearing it for the first time in years, through a good car stereo, it's absolutely transcendent—the best thing the Supremes ever did. Is that possible? The Supremes got better *after* Diana?

You can hear The Girls trying to erase all memory of Diana, who thought she was better than the others, always parading out in front, and now! We are The Supremes! We sing as one! Equal parts! No lead!

For a moment Cindy takes the melody, for a moment Jean takes it, then they stand aside and let Mary holler it out. A rhythm shake a shake it just keep rolling down the road like a big old Greyhound bus, *You never wrote me (ooh ooh) You never*

called! The heat of three voices fused into the sound of one abandoned woman, beaten down though she never admits it, the way
she clings to the pain of his memory you just know he had to be
hitting her…The sound was relentless, unstoppable, rolling
down the big old highway. A handclap—or is it a whipcrack?
Doin' it without you, Diana, strutting it proudly on Better-
Than-*Ever* Street!

Mama in the passenger seat: "What are you going on about? I
don't understand a word."

"The Supremes," Georgia said, "without Diana Ross."

Bringing Mama along was the last thing Georgia wanted to
do, but it was getting harder to leave her home alone now.

"Nathan Jones" put Georgia in high spirits considering they'd
just come from that horrible prison where they were not even
allowed to see Brother. The man at the front desk said he was in
solitary, the next "visitation window" was a week from Wednesday. After successive rings of concertina wire, chain-link fence,
electric-lock doors, thick greasy glass reinforced with steel mesh…
coming out to the car, breathing free air, and finding "Nathan
Jones" on the radio seemed like a gift from God.

Of course Georgia didn't believe in God, but a gift like that
song helped her understand why some people do.

She loved that song, and that's why Ree had named the boy
Nathan.

"I told you to keep him away from Sims Bailey," Mama said,
helpfully.

"Yes you sure did," Georgia said. "You are so much smarter
than I am. I don't know why I never noticed it before."

Turns out that having a couple barrels of ammonium nitrate
fertilizer in proximity to some barrels of fuel oil gets you in the

kind of trouble you can't grin your way out of. As far as Georgia could tell, Brother was screwed. He wasn't Timothy McVeigh, but try telling that to the Alabama Bureau of Investigation.

Solitary confinement his second week in state prison was not a good sign.

Georgia could sell all her jewelry, the house, the family silver, put every dime into Brother's defense, throw everything onto the fire knowing he would be found guilty in any event.

Or: Let him get a public defender. Handle this one himself, without the assist from Big Sister who is called in to save his sorry rear end every time.

Georgia had a feeling that would be dooming him to jail for a goodly portion of his life. But hadn't he doomed himself? How was that in any way her fault?

She had tried to be Brother's keeper all his life. Time to admit she had failed. Every time she told him to go right, he went left. Now let him fend for himself.

...But that didn't feel right. She couldn't shake the image of four-year-old Brother with that headful of soft white curls. She couldn't believe that lovely child, that spirit was entirely gone from the earth.

At the prison she'd seen only two actual prisoners, black guys in dark-blue prison clothes at the end of a hallway glassed off from the visitors' lounge. Looking at those men, she found herself thinking: If that was me, if someone told me I had to spend the night in this place, I'd find a way to hang myself.

There was also the lingering disturbance from *NOVA* last night. She had looked forward to the show all week, after spotting the listing in the Sunday *Light-Pilot*. She was a sucker for ant documentaries, always glad for any chance to embroider her grand theory of the Ant Connection. Ten minutes into the program, the camera focused on a mob of particularly murderous ants digging a pale wriggling white worm out of the earth.

The ants swarmed over the blind, defenseless worm, testing its worm skin with their cruel jaws, finding the soft places between its segments. Georgia emitted little cries of "Oh! Poor worm! Poor worm!"

The worm writhed, trying to throw off its torturers, but soon they were clamping their hideous mandibles, slicing into the worm so as to eat it from the soft jelly outward. That was when Georgia felt the rising surge in her throat, a mad scramble for the remote control turn it off!

She sat in darkness for a while, breathing, trying not to throw up.

It took half a bottle of Chardonnay and three Excedrin PMs to knock her out that night. Then it was the kind of restless sleep that leaves you more exhausted in the morning.

"I watched a terrible show about ants last night," she said, just to hear a live voice in the car.

"Why did you watch it, then?" Mama said.

"Normally I like ants," Georgia said. "Not these ants."

"Why not?"

"They were vicious," said Georgia. "They all ganged up on this one worm."

"You ought not to watch it if it bothers you," Mama said.

"But I love ants," said Georgia. "Normally."

After a long pause Mama said, "Where are we going?"

"Home."

"Can't we go any faster?"

"No, Mama. This is the legal limit."

"What were we talking about before?"

"The song on the radio," Georgia said. "The Supremes."

Little Mama said, "I always liked the Supremes."

If it hadn't been nighttime on a curvy stretch of road, Georgia would have pulled to the shoulder just to get a good look at her. "You *what?*"

"I said, I like the Supremes."

"The singing group," said Georgia. "Diana Ross and the Supremes."

"Uh-huh," Mama said. "I like their songs."

"Oh Mama, you don't," Georgia half scolded her. "You know the Supremes are colored girls."

"So what?" said Little Mama.

"So *what?* You don't like colored people, that's all." For as long as Georgia could remember, the appearance of any black enter-tainer on TV was Little Mama's cue to change channels with a muttered curse.

"Don't tell me what I like and don't like," Mama said.

Georgia was astounded. Not liking colored people was Little Mama's big thing. It cut to the heart of who she was.

For the moment, at least, she seemed to have forgotten entirely.

Georgia said, "What about Nat King Cole?"

"What about him?"

"You like him too?"

"I do. That song about sailboats, in the sunset." She even hummed a bit of the tune.

"Oh Mama, you're pulling my leg now."

"I hate to disappoint you," Mama said, "but I am not your mother." She spoke in a kindly voice, as if gently breaking the news. "I never had any children of my own."

Georgia said, "Are you all right?"

"I'm fine. How are you?"

"Do we need to go to the hospital?"

"I don't think so," Mama said. "Where are you taking me?"

"Home."

12

Georgia changed clothes three times before settling on the textured knit jacket and skirt by St. John in an especially hot pink called peony. The jacket was sharply tailored to show off her figure. The straight skirt cut a sexy line above the knee. There was no way Brent Colgate could look out over his new congregation and fail to notice her.

She hadn't counted on word of the handsome new preacher racing through Six Points like a wildfire, bringing forth the biggest one-week rise in attendance in the non-Easter history of the First Baptist. The new worshippers were almost all female, and sat near the front. Each, in her own way, seemed to have dressed to attract the attention of Brent Colgate. Within Georgia's field of vision were three other women in hot pink—none quite as hot as peony, but still it embarrassed Georgia to be in any respect like those women, to have had the same idea. She considered bolting out the door to go change—into what? There wasn't a color in the rainbow that someone was not already wearing in an effort to be seen by the new preacher.

With all the buildup, you might expect the sight of Brent Colgate himself to come as a letdown. It was just the opposite. The members of the pastoral committee lined up in front of the pulpit to emphasize that it was they who had gone forth into a world full of ugly preachers and brought back this dreamboat reverend, this vision in a velvet black robe with regal blond mane and gleaming smile, making his way up the center aisle, kissing and blessing, embracing his new flock as if he'd been among them all his life—a favorite who had been away too long, returning now in triumph.

It seemed a bit much. Georgia made a skeptical face to the back of the pew.

Colgate hugged a few of the front-pew ladies, shook hands with the committee, and ascended his pulpit in a cloud of mass approval. "What a kind welcome, friends," he said. "Thank you so much, thank you."

Brent's voice came from deep, deep down in his chest. Georgia found herself drifting off before a word ever registered in her brain. His voice cast such a spell that she was able to perceive the essence of what he was saying without even listening to the words. He spoke about goodness and welcome and solid and fine... She was happy just drifting along gazing up at his face, feeling the rumble of his voice to her toes.

Then suddenly it was over, they were on their feet singing a hymn. That had to be the fastest sermon in history. Georgia looked at her watch. A full forty-five minutes had passed. Had she fallen asleep? Or been hypnotized?

She noticed several other women in a similar daze.

Reverend Colgate and his wife went to the main entrance to greet the departing congregation. Mrs. Colgate positioned herself so that you had to greet her first, then she would present you to her husband. On the surface this seemed gracious; to Georgia it gave a strong hint as to who ran the Colgate household. This wife would be a tricky proposition. This was no Brenda Hendrix or Mrs. Judge Barnett, this put-together brunette still in her twenties with the beauty-queen violet eyes and a stylish sloping haircut straight out of *Vogue*.

Young Mrs. Colgate placed herself astride the approach lane to her great-looking husband, as if to say, "I'm as good-looking as he is, so unless you can compete with me, don't even try." Brent Colgate looked pleased to be standing beside her, radiating pastorly good cheer.

"Do they have children?" murmured Stephanie Durant, at Georgia's elbow.

"Not that I've heard of," said Georgia. "She doesn't really look like the type."

"No," Stephanie said, "but those kids would be freaking gorgeous."

"Hello, I'm Daphne Colgate!" The wife trapped Georgia's hand between her own two in a graspy overfamiliar way that made Georgia's skin crawl.

"Georgia Bottoms," said Georgia. "That suit is so attractive— where on earth did you find it?"

"Why thank you! How nice of you to notice. I think it was Macy's in Birmingham. Have you met my husband, Brent?"

Brent smiled. "Oh, sure. Miss Georgia and I are old friends from the drugstore."

"He was downtown trying to drum up church attendance," said Georgia. "I'm only here because he ordered me to come."

"Just like the passage in Brent's sermon," said Daphne, "when every lamb was redeemed with a firstborn donkey."

"Exactly." Georgia smiled as if she had some inkling of what

Daphne meant. If Georgia had just been insulted, her insulter gave no outward sign.

Brent's eyes gleamed. "Daphne's the only one who really listens to my sermons."

Old Mrs. Haworth took Daphne's arm and turned her away. Brent used the moment of distraction to pounce. "Miss Georgia, I think your idea for a church-wide garage sale is absolute genius. Would you mind sticking around after I finish greeting the folks, so we can discuss it some more?"

Georgia did not miss a beat. "Of course," she said. "I'll just wait in the sanctuary for you."

She ducked her head into the foyer and swam back upstream through the crowd. She sat down in her pew.

She felt her heart thumping. She had not given Brent Colgate any idea about a garage sale. By tossing out a blatant lie, forcing her to go along with it, Brent had made her complicit in whatever game he was wanting to play. It was, to say the least, an unusual beginning to the minister-parishioner relationship.

Georgia ran her hand along the silky wood of the pew, worn smooth by generations of Bottoms. She would tell the reverend she hadn't wanted to seem rude, but it was not she who had mentioned the garage sale to him. Shake his hand and walk away. If the vibe didn't feel right.

But she was fairly sure they were on their way to a satisfactory resolution. They had already cheated a little: a small made-up cheat between the two of them. It was not very far from there to the place Georgia wanted to go.

As a matter of fact, the shortest way there might be the long way around. Get out of here now. Let him come looking for you, and not find you.

Georgia walked quickly to the side door of the church, and out.

Sink the hook. Make sure it's in deep.

Then give a little tug. That fish will land itself.

13

In the first place Ted Horn was a medical doctor so whoda thunk it? In the second place Ted always had been an ol' horndog, so much so that "Ol' Horndog" was Georgia's pet name for him. He liked her to use the nickname at certain crucial moments on a Wednesday evening. Add in the fact that on this hot July Wednesday Ted had had more than his usual glass or two of red wine. He and the missus had laid it on beforehand at the Hopalong Steak House BYOB Early Bird Special. Then when he arrived at Georgia's, he insisted she make a pitcher of her famous Cajun martinis. This put him in a festive and rambunctious mood, and also served to open up his blood vessels, in combination with the self-prescribed pharmaceutical.

Ted liked martinis and black leather. He liked to wear the zippered hood. He liked the silk handkerchiefs with which Georgia fastened him to the four-poster bed. Of all her clients, Ted was easily the most exotic in his tastes. Georgia looked forward to Wednesday—a bit of variety in the middle of the week, when one's energy naturally tends to flag.

Adjusting her approach to the peccadilloes of each man was what kept the game interesting. As much of a pain as it was to launder, starch, and iron the layers of petticoats needed to turn herself and Judge Barnett into Scarlett and Rhett once a week—not to mention the French maid getup she wore for Jimmy Lee Newton—all that effort had paid off in years of customer satisfaction. Jimmy Lee fancied himself a sophisticated gentleman being naughty with his maid. At times he put on a French accent that wavered between Maurice Chevalier and Pepé Le Pew.

Lon Chapman liked her to dress as a shit-kickin' country gal, in cowboy boots, frayed Levi's cutoffs, and a Daisy Duke tight white T-shirt. Georgia ordered those T-shirts by the dozen so Lon could rip them off as he pleased.

Then there was Sheriff Bill, who preferred his Friday night loving as bland and flavorless as grocery-store pound cake. For one night of the week, Georgia got to experience married life, as she imagined it: lights off, radio on low, no sound of any kind save for his muffled grunting. They had to be quiet, as if there were children in the next room. Sheriff Bill was always on top, never took off his V-neck undershirt, kissed her dryly as he finished, climbed off and immediately started putting on his pants.

Sheriff Bill was crucial to her business plan, or she'd have eased him out of the schedule long ago. Ted Horn was so much more fun: Mr. Take Your Time, Mr. Tie Me Up and Make Me Pay the Price, Mister Ol' Horny Horndog himself. Ted encouraged her imagination. She got to apply a variety of implements—a feather duster, a spatula, an old silver fork with rounded-off tines. She approached the problem like a scientist in a laboratory: a Slinky, an egg timer, a series of battery-powered appliances from the Adult Superstore in Mobile...

Ted was exceedingly sensitive. And he liked to be surprised. Once she got him spread-eagle and tied to the bed with the hood zipped shut, surprising him was easy.

The hard part, of course, was that Georgia had to do all the work. Ted just lay there and thrashed and groaned over the strains of Def Leppard, Van Halen, whatever eighties hair band she put on for him. Then there was the time they got frisky with the candle wax and glitter. Tiny sparkles kept showing up in the most unexpected places for months.

At some point Ted would decide to throw aside the toys and get down to business—but not right away. He liked for Georgia to take him right up to the edge, and keep him there—

—and hold him there...

—and hold it...

Personally, Georgia thought that level of tension would drive her mad. But Wednesday night was Ted's night, and Ted liked it tense. Sometimes his face got so red it concerned her, but he rattled off this long Latin name for the underlying medical condition and told her not to worry.

Tonight all the wine and martinis made him redder and more vocal than usual. Double-glazed windows could only do so much. Georgia cranked up Bon Jovi, "Livin' on a Prayer."

Ted was one of those Southern straight men who seems kind of gay when you meet him—a mama's boy, slightly effeminate in his speech, with a flair for dramatic expression. Ted wasn't as gay acting as Tommy the Dixie Florist, but then, who was? Around town there were whispers about Ted, a kind of don't-ask-don't-tell attitude that even if he was "that way," he was a good doctor, kept his private life to himself, and did whatever he did out of town. That's all Six Points asked of people like that. *You can do what you want,* as the saying went, *just don't shove it in my face.* Ted had never married; he was never seen to go on a date; Georgia was the only one in town who knew that behind closed doors, Ted Horn was a raving heterosexual.

At the moment, he was rattling the windowpanes. Georgia stuffed a handkerchief in his mouth. That struck him as funny and he started chuckling. She slapped him lightly on the cheek and told him to hush. He laughed harder.

Ted was naturally ginger all over. Every part of him flushed where she pressed a finger. Any investigator would be able to lift her fingerprints off that skin, pale and translucent as a slice of lunch-meat turkey.

He was laughing so hard she thought he might choke on the handkerchief. She yanked it out.

"Ahrrr." Now he was a pirate. "Ya naughty wicked hoor!"

"Aw now, don't you go starting again! Look at you still poking up. You are so bad, Ted. So bad."

"Yeah I know, it's kinda getting—what is it now, three times tonight?"

"Four," she said.

He laughed. "But who's counting?"

"I am. It's four." She folded her arms. "It's enough. Tell that thing to go down."

"I don't have much influence, apparently." Ted bobbed his head up from the table to have a look. His range of motion was limited by the hood and the chain.

Georgia sighed. "Sorry, Horndog. I can't believe I'm going to have to send you home with a boner, but I am all out of tricks." She unzipped his hood and slid it off.

He blinked up at her, his sweaty red hair plastered to his skull. "I'm not trying to do this, I swear."

"I believe you," she said. "Do you think—I hate to even say it."

"What?"

"Well, you're the doctor. The four-hour thing. You know."

"No way it's been four hours," he said.

She glanced to the digital clock in its discreet niche behind the bowl and pitcher. "Almost," she said. "Time flies when you're having a good time."

Ted moved to sit up but got pronged in the stomach, and lay back down.

His problem wasn't that thick, but it was long and skinny, bright red, throbbing and bobbing like an angry buoy on a pale-ginger sea.

"Think about baseball," she said.

"For some reason that never works for me."

"What if you stand up," she said. "And let the blood run down to your feet."

That made them both laugh, but not for long. It was becoming apparent that Ted's condition had nothing to do with anything going on in his head. That thing was standing tall and proud on its own. Ted's face gradually changed from half-drunken glee to a kind of bemusement, then a puzzled expression that evolved into real concern.

He went into the bathroom, bearing his extremity before him. He spent quite a while in there, doing whatever men do to make the thing go down. But when he came back it was the same.

Georgia tightened the sash on her robe. "Should I look for that sheet of paper with the side effects? I'm sure I've got one around here somewhere."

"I don't need that, I prescribe it every day," said Ted. "You have no idea how many of your friends and neighbors..." He didn't finish the thought.

She said, "You've seen this before?"

"No. It's a fairly rare condition. Despite all the advertising."

"How do you treat it?"

He winced. "You don't want to know. Hell—*I* know, and I don't want to know."

"It's that bad?"

"All options involve either a needle or a scalpel. You have to drain the blood, is the idea."

"Dear God." Georgia clasped her hands together.

He rolled onto his side. Man-o'-War thudded against the mattress. "What time is it?"

"Ten minutes to twelve."

"Oh Jesus, that's *more* than four hours. I took that pill just after seven, before I left the house."

Anxious minutes of deliberation while Ted waited for the thing to unhappen. He described the permanent damage that could result from ignoring the condition. You could damage blood vessels, ruin the tiny valves that control the hydraulics, leaving yourself unable to . . . If there was anybody who treasured that ability, it was Ted.

Georgia went to the bathroom for aspirin. Ted crushed two and put them under his tongue. He didn't think it would work. The problem wasn't that the blood needed thinning, but that the tiny valves had stuck shut, trapping the blood where it was no longer required.

Ted considered going to his office. He had all the tools to do the job on himself. But he was afraid that no matter how deftly he administered the anesthetic, the pain would be so bad he might pass out with the ultrasharp blade in his hand, and do irreversible damage.

Georgia offered to stand beside him and steady his hand, but Ted said he didn't think he could do it.

He wanted to call the hospital to see who was on night duty in the ER. There was no phone in the apartment, and Georgia couldn't very well send him to the house wagging his tail in front of him. She got dressed and went to make the call herself.

She didn't give her name, just said she was trying to reach Dr. Horn. The nurse said Dr. Horn was not on duty tonight, Dr. Have-a-Cherry was.

"Doctor who?" Georgia said.

"Have-a-Cherry," the nurse said.

"Is that someone's name?"

"Close as I'm gonna get," said the nurse. Georgia recognized the voice of Susan DeShields, who'd been working in the emergency room the night Daddy died. It was all she could do to keep from saying, "Hey Susan!"

Susan said, "Would you like to speak to the doctor?"

Georgia said yes. Before he came to the phone, she hung up.

Climbing the steps to the apartment, she thought about her one inviolate rule, the rule that had allowed her to maintain perfect secrecy through the years. Never, ever did she meet a man anywhere but in the apartment, at the appointed hour, after dark. Never did she allow one of them to take her anywhere—no romantic drives in the country, no midnight suppers at the all-night diner in Butler, no innocent strolls at the state park boat landing. If she ran into one of the men on the street, or at a social function, fine. He'd be with his wife, and Georgia would chat them up like the casual acquaintances they were supposed to be.

She returned to find Ted scooched forward on the velvet armchair, frowning down. Georgia relayed what the nurse had said.

"That's the new resident, the young Indian guy from UAB," Ted said. "He does seem very sharp." He forced a grin. "Better sharp than dull, anyway."

"Oh Ted, isn't there any other way?"

"Believe me, honey, if there was, I wouldn't be considering this." His laugh contained a note of real fear. "You gotta drive me there, and he's gotta lance this thing."

"I'm sorry. I can't do that. You'll have to drive yourself."

He frowned. "I don't think I can get behind the wheel."

"You're going to have to figure out a way."

"Aw come on, sugar," he said. "You don't have to go in. Just drop me off. I can find my own way home from there."

There had to be some other option. Georgia couldn't think of one. Six Points hadn't had taxi service since Bobby Higginbotham went to jail for DUI. "What if somebody sees us?" she said.

"Oh for God's sake, Georgia, don't you think this qualifies as an emergency? We're single, we're grown-ups, I don't see what the—"

"No, Ted." She folded her arms. "Absolutely not."

"Why not?"

"Ambulance service is not a part of our arrangement. We cannot be seen in public together—especially you in this condition. You're not the only one with a reputation."

"You're the one responsible for this *condition*," he snapped. "The least you could do is drive me to the goddamn hospital."

His face was getting redder. Rule Number One had just run head-on into Rule Number Two: Never get into a disagreement with a client.

"You took that pill before you came over, Ted," she said calmly. "Is it really fair to blame me?"

He stared down at his predicament. "You're right, honey, it's not your fault. If you could give me a towel or something I could wrap around me...I don't think I can get those pants on."

Georgia felt her determination fading. "I thought all you men went around like this all the time anyway."

A wan smile came to his face.

"Sorry," she said. "It's not all that funny, is it?"

"Actually it's kind of starting to ache," he said.

"Poor baby," said Georgia. "I don't think a towel's gonna work. Let's just take this sheet here—" She whipped the flat sheet off the bed, draped it around his shoulders, and stood him up. By draping and tucking, she managed to arrange a kind of toga, loosely hanging so as to conceal the protuberance.

She disguised herself with sunglasses and a fringed brown silk scarf from the seven-drawer highboy. In the mirror she looked like a sixties Italian movie star trying to avoid the paparazzi.

She stuffed Ted's clothes in a Hull's Market sack and hurried him down to his car, checking both ways before waving him into the alley.

He tried, he really did try to get behind the wheel, to spare her having to go. The steering wheel of his Hyundai was adjustable up and down, but he couldn't reach the pedals without causing unbearable pressure.

Finally Georgia ordered him to move his butt over and slid behind the wheel.

He was pleased. In the last analysis she'd had to admit this *was* partly her fault—she had been encouraging that erection for hours.

Her job now was to stay vigilant and avoid making eye contact with anybody. Drop Ted, park his car in the hospital lot, and walk home. If anyone saw her, she would raise her arms and pump her elbows like a fitness walker.

The hospital was on Catawba Street, which went one way south from the courthouse. There was no way to get there without going through the square. Just after midnight, there were still dog walkers strolling, a Mexican boy hosing the sidewalk in front of the diner, a crowd of teenagers loitering at the video arcade.

Ted sank down in the passenger seat and pulled the sheet over his head. Probably he thought he was doing Georgia a favor. He didn't notice the sheriff's car tucked into the dark alley beyond the hardware store. A deputy sat watching the teenagers for signs of dope smoking.

Before Georgia knew what was happening, blue lights filled her rearview, a siren *bloo-woop!* The deputy must have seen the flash of white in the passenger side. He flipped on his lights and whipped around in a U-turn to zoom up behind Georgia with flashers and super–high beams glaring.

"Oh Jesus," she said, "don't you stop me. Ted. He's stopping me."

"Did you run the stop sign?"

"No!"

"Well what did you do?"

"Nothing!" Georgia flipped on her blinker to indicate her willingness to pull over, but she didn't pull over quite yet, she kept coasting along until she was well out of the lights of the square. The deputy hit his siren again, an impatient *brooop!* Georgia pulled to a stop beside the dark stretch of woods backing up to Swaney Johnson's place.

When she saw who it was in the rearview mirror, she said, "Let me do the talking." Leon Bulmer was the man Sheriff Bill Allred had hired to satisfy the affirmative action laws of the state of Alabama. After years of litigation, the state had finally ordered Bill to round out his force with at least one African-American deputy. Bill went out and found the whitest Negro he could find, Leon Bulmer of Geneva, whose father was pure redneck Caucasian and whose mother couldn't have been more than cream-colored. Leon was lighter than most white people—a bit chalky, even. If not for his slightly flat nose and the kink in his hair, you would never guess he was black.

He was kind of a goof, too.

"Hey Leon," she sang. "It's Georgia Bottoms."

"Miss Georgia? What in the world?" Leon played his flashlight over the sheet from which Ted Horn was peeking. "What's going on here?"

"Don't you recognize Dr. Horn? We were over at the mayor's house at a costume party." Georgia hated to drag Krystal's name into it, but the story needed a shot of authority just then.

"A party? At this time of night?"

"Well sure," Georgia said. "A midnight costume supper. In honor of Bastille Day." Leon would never realize Bastille Day was weeks ago, mid-July. Georgia could have been a great actress, she thought. She believed the story, even as she was making it up.

"I saw that white sheet and you know what my first thought was," said Deputy Bulmer. "I didn't want to believe it. Not in this town."

"Oh, no no no," Georgia said. "He's a Roman senator, see? And I'm his Italian movie-star date."

"Leon," said Ted, "you didn't really think I was a Ku Klucker, did you?"

"For a minute there, I sure did, Dr. Horn," Leon said, chuckling.

"Leon, we have to go," Georgia said. "Dr. Horn was having chest pains at the party and I'm driving him to the hospital."

Leon's eyes widened. "Okay, now stay calm, now, you gonna need an escort, let me get some backup—"

"No, we do *not* need an escort, Leon, thank you very much. Just let us go, so they can see about him."

Ted leaned over. "I'm fine, I just need them to refill my cardiac meds."

"I will escort you," Leon said firmly. "Fall in behind me."

What choice did they have? Leon got back in his sheriff's car and blooped the siren and led them two blocks to the former Callum's Nursing Home, which had been the Cotton County Medical Center since the old hospital burned. (Quantities of pharmaceuticals disappeared in the fire. Brother and Sims Bailey were never charged.) The emergency bay glowed brightly at the far end of the long, low building. Georgia did not want to drive Ted's car into all that bright light, but how could she avoid it with Deputy Bulmer leading the way?

The brown scarf and Sophia Loren shades did not hide the plain facts: her cover was blown, Rule Number One lay shattered in pieces on the ground, Deputy Leon had more than enough information to spread around, not to mention possibly dragging Krystal's name into it. Amazing how quickly a minor mess can turn into total disaster.

Georgia turned to Ted. "You still got a problem?"

"Oh yes. Worse than ever." You would think the element of

danger, the sudden appearance of flashing blue lights might help, but it had the opposite effect.

"I am not going in that hospital with you, Ted."

"That's fine, honey. I really do appreciate you driving me here."

"Just get out and go in. I'll park your car over yonder. Go."

She didn't sound very sympathetic but so what? She was mad at Ted for getting them into this, furious with herself for going soft and forgetting her most important rule. That was a sloppy move, putting her entire lifestyle at risk.

Ted got out with his sack of clothes and began hobbling toward the double doors. Deputy Bulmer jumped out of his car to help. He shot a look at Georgia that said what he thought of letting a man with chest pains hobble by himself into the ER.

Georgia drove toward the parking lot.

Deputy Bulmer helped Ted through the door with a modified fireman's carry. They were facing the other way; Georgia could not see if Ted's dilemma was still in evidence. She hoped the deputy did not notice it and get the wrong impression.

She tucked Ted's keys over the visor and stepped out of the car. Through the glass of the emergency entrance she saw Ted immediately place himself in a wheelchair. Good thinking!

Georgia's job was done. She whipped off the scarf and sunglasses and set out at a fitness-walking pace across the parking lot, trying to decide which street to take home so as to meet the fewest people.

A deep voice came from the darkness: "Miss Georgia? Do you need a ride?"

She couldn't make out the face. He sounded familiar but who among her male friends had that deep, almost radio voice?

He stepped into the light and oh yes of course, the new preacher, Mr. Wavy Blond Hair, the Reverend Brent Colgate. Standing beside his beat-up K car with the Jesus-fish license plate. Had he been there the whole time, watching her?

"Well, hello," Georgia said, and, since the best defense is a good offense, "What are you doing here?"

"Visiting our infirm brothers and sisters," he said. "I'd be happy to give you a lift."

"No thanks, I like to walk. I enjoy the exercise." Of course she wanted to get to know the reverend better, but things were complicated enough for one night. To accept a ride now would be asking for trouble.

On the other hand.

Brent had already seen her. Perhaps by engaging him she could deflect his attention from whatever else he had seen. And riding home in his car would lessen the chance that she would be spotted by anyone else.

Once you stopped to think about it, Georgia really had no choice but to go with him. She sent him a mind signal: *Ask me again.*

"Are you sure?" he said. "I'm headed home now. I'll be glad to drop you."

"Well...if you really don't mind." She gave him a grateful smile. "It is kind of late. Six Points is totally safe, of course, but still, to be walking around this time of night..."

"It will be my pleasure, Miss Georgia," he said in that thrilling rumble, deep enough to produce its own pleasure. It wasn't just his voice, but his manner. He was so courtly. You didn't find that quality much in young men these days. Georgia remembered her father's friends speaking with that kind of elaborate courtesy when a lady was present. Colgate swept open the passenger door as if his K car were a chauffeured limo.

"Poor Ted," she said, getting in. "We're old friends, all the way back to high school . . . Whenever he gets these heart palpitations he calls me. I drive him down here and they do some kind of procedure, I don't know what you call it. In an hour he'll be all better, and he'll drive himself home."

"Very kind of you to help him out." Brent Colgate started the engine.

Georgia buckled her seat belt. Colgate's car smelled of old french fries.

"Ted's a nice man," she said. "Kind of sad when you think about it. He's the doctor, keeping everybody else healthy, but when he gets sick, who can he call?"

"I've enjoyed getting to know Dr. Horn," Brent said. "For a medical man he has a good sense of humor."

She wondered if that was some kind of subtle dig. She turned to give him the once-over, found him gazing placidly at the road ahead with those glowing green eyes. He didn't seem all that subtle. For a preacher, he was a sharp dresser. Tonight he had tried for casual, but the sleeves of his green plaid shirt were rolled up just so, khakis pressed to a crisp edge. Georgia could not quite identify the scent rising off him—woodsy like Old Spice, but muskier.

"I'm sure you need a sense of humor in your line of work, too," she said, steering the conversation away from Ted.

"Oh yes," said the reverend. "I was just visiting a certain parishioner who shall remain nameless. He's had some surgery on his, well, how can I put this—on his rear end. And he was dying to show me his scar!"

Georgia laughed. "I hope you declined."

"As emphatically as I could." Colgate flashed that creamy white smile. "But thinking about it, I wonder if that was the right thing to do. I doubt Christ would have turned away. I think he would have been willing to face the sight of the poor man's suffering."

"You always try to do what Christ would do?" Georgia said.

"'Try' is the operative word," said Colgate. "I fail a lot more than I succeed."

"Don't we all," Georgia said.

One thing she always liked about Preacher Eugene was that he never brought Jesus into the conversation. When he was with Georgia he was definitely off the clock.

This fellow Brent seemed to carry his job around with him. Georgia would have to work on that. There are plenty of nice things you can say about Jesus, but frequent mentions of his name do not help a romantic mood.

14

It was a quick drive to Georgia's house on Magnolia Street—too quick to establish any real connection, but long enough to confirm that Brent Colgate was as polite as he was handsome, and, thank God, not at all nosy. He didn't question why Georgia had brought Ted Horn to the ER wearing only a bedsheet. They chatted about small things. Brent said he and Daphne loved living in a town where everybody knows everybody. "Such a sense of community," he said.

"Yeah, we've got community coming out our ears," Georgia said. "Sometimes I go to Mobile just to get away from it."

He smiled. "What's in Mobile?"

"A stoplight," she said. "A store that sells more than one kind of panty hose."

She wondered if the mention of panty hose was too forward for their first time alone in a car. Brent just smiled.

"Did you know they have cell phones in Mobile?" she said. "We're still waiting for a tower. The rest of the world has call-waiting, too. And cable TV. And high-speed Internet."

"But that's the charm of Six Points," he said. "Y'all don't need those things to be happy."

"I've spent my whole life in this town," she said, "and don't get me wrong, I love it—but sometimes I think I was born to be a city girl."

At first she asked him to drop her in front of the house. At the last minute she directed him around back, to the alley—to make it seem slightly illicit, just as he had involved her in his little white lie after church.

Brent cast a glance sideways. "You're not like the other ladies in Six Points, are you?"

"How do you mean?"

"You speak your mind. You don't care what anybody thinks."

"I care," she said. "I just don't let it show."

His teeth flashed in the darkness. "Good for you."

"See there, under that streetlight?" she said. "That's our slave quarters. Let me out there."

"We never did discuss your idea about the garage sale."

Georgia looked at him. He was smiling, maintaining that innocent expression.

"Yeah, well, you made that up," she said. "Or else you have me confused with somebody else."

"No, you're right, I made it up." A quiet admission. He pulled the car to a stop. "I just wanted an excuse to talk to you alone."

"Well, you got what you wanted. Thanks for the ride!" She gave his wrist a friendly squeeze—could have been thank you, or possibly more—and hopped out of the car.

He leaned across the seat. "Wait, I want to—"

"Thanks again! Bye!" Georgia slammed the door and hurried around the garage without looking back.

She released the breath she'd been holding. The man had an effect on her, no denying it. Georgia got carried away just being in his vicinity. She felt breathless from the torrent of ridiculous ideas rushing through her—she found herself reimagining her name, as if he were a junior-high crush: "Mrs. Brent Colgate..." "Mrs. Georgia Colgate..." "The Rev. and Mrs. Colgate..."

Georgia was no longer sure if she was the fisherman, or the fish.

Anyway. There already *was* a Mrs. Brent Colgate, and that woman was nobody's pushover.

Whizzy came scampering over the yard. Georgia remembered the load of towels she'd washed before Ted came over. "Come on, Whiz, if we leave 'em in the washer all night they'll sour." He trotted along after her, happy for the mission.

With both hands Georgia dragged the heavy towels out from around the agitator and shoved them into the open maw of the dryer. She tossed in an antistatic sheet to perfume the air in the apartment, and twisted ON.

In the great Ant Connection it didn't matter much that Georgia stopped to put towels in the dryer. She was just another dutiful citizen doing her work for the colony. But the delay meant that by the time she and Whizzy reached the house, there was only a vague disquiet, a disturbance of air, the dying ember of a sound: a telephone that had just left off ringing.

Georgia sensed something, she didn't know what. She went upstairs to peek into Little Mama's room—Mama's death being the foremost possible calamity in her mind. She found Mama snoring happily under quilts.

Then of course there was Brother in jail. Georgia liked to pretend he was safe in there, but in jail there are shivs, gangs, stabbings.

She hurried to her room. The red light blinked on the answering machine.

Oh God. She dreaded news of any kind. Her life was perfect just now.

She pressed PLAY. The click of the machine, hesitation as someone decided whether to speak. A human sound, not exactly a word—a sigh?—then whoever it was hung up.

Georgia pushed REPEAT to hear it again.

The person took in a breath—trying to decide, should I speak?—then that small sound, an exhalation or the beginning of a word—then *click*.

She played it a third time, a fourth, a fifth.

It might be Ted Horn, starting to leave a message and thinking better of it. But it didn't sound like Ted.

It couldn't be Brent Colgate. He'd have had to drive directly to his house, call her number, and hang up without leaving a message. Which made no sense at all.

She had a feeling the call was important. But then why not leave a message?

Maybe it was something too important to leave on a machine.

The next morning she replayed the message three times without hearing anything new. Finally she hit ERASE and instructed herself to forget it.

She had a full list of errands before the League of Women Voters at noon, where Krystal was to face off against her opponent, Dr. Madeline Roudy. It wasn't organized as a debate, but since Roudy was scheduled to speak first, Krystal had decided to use her time to destroy her challenger. No more Madame Nice Guy! None of Madeline Roudy's supporters seemed to realize she had no governmental experience, in fact had never showed the slightest interest in civic affairs. Krystal told Georgia that all she had to do was point this out in a public forum, and Roudy would fold like a tent.

Krystal had phoned first thing this morning for an anxious fashion consultation. Her nerves had been causing her to pig out a lot recently, so she couldn't get into her nicest mayoral outfits. She was trying to choose between the navy wool suit, which was really too heavy for all but the coldest days in Six Points, or the khaki pantsuit from Lane Bryant, which was "on the snug side."

Georgia proposed they meet at Belk's, pick out something nice in the right size so Krystal would feel attractive, but no, Krystal was too busy running from garden club to church supper to VFW begging for votes.

Entering the meeting room at the community center, Georgia was dismayed to see that Krystal had settled on the khaki pant-suit, which you would only call "snug" if you avoided looking in a mirror. The buttons of the jacket did not even meet the buttonholes.

Krystal, who never used makeup—she didn't "believe" in it—that same Krystal had slapped on peachy lipstick and a layer of foundation, and rubbed some kind of product into her hair that made it look sticky and strange.

Madeline Roudy, on the other hand, wore a crisp white cotton sleeveless shirt dress, cool and elegant against her lovely brown skin, also subtly emphasizing her role as doctor, medicine woman, healer of the poor.

Dr. Roudy didn't wait for chapter secretary Irma Winograial to call the meeting to order. She walked to the front of the room and took charge. "Hello, everyone," she said. "I'm not going to be able to stay, but I took a few minutes away from the clinic to come say hello."

Her bullhorn voice was now carefully modulated, silky in tone.

"Most of you ladies know me, or at least you know who I am. You know I'm a person who gets things done. I really appreciate the mayor we have now. I can only hope to improve upon the excellent job she has done."

Improve? Was that a dig at Krystal? Of course it was.

Roudy smiled. "Anybody have any questions?"

Georgia looked around at all the silent ladies, so dazzled they could not think of one thing to ask.

Georgia had hoped not to be the one to have to do this, but what are friends for? She raised her hand. "Dr. Roudy, can you please tell us what experience you have in city government?"

Roudy maintained her gracious smile. It was the first time Georgia had noticed her slightly buck teeth, which detracted only slightly from her resemblance to Diahann Carroll. No one could say she was not an attractive woman.

Krystal, on the other hand, looked like Kathy Bates in that movie where she bashed James Caan's ankles with the sledgehammer.

"Thank you for the question, Georgia," Roudy said pleasantly. "While it's true I haven't had experience in governing a town per se, I was president of my junior and senior class at Auburn. I've been vice president of the Alabama Federation of Pediatric Physicians twice, and of course y'all know me as the founder and CEO of the Six Points Wellness Center."

Georgia wondered when the free clinic became the "Wellness Center," and how you could call yourself "CEO" of a county-funded clinic. Little Mama had an expression for people like this: *Her dog's named Brag.*

Roudy said, "Now, do you need some form of executive experience to do as good a job as our current mayor is doing? Of course you do. But do you have to have *been* mayor in order to *run* for mayor? I don't think so."

Georgia hadn't said a word about having to have been mayor. Her question was about experience. See how Roudy danced out of harm's way, pirouetting to re-ask the question with her own slant, delivering her answer as a slam dunk. She turned back to Georgia with a pretty smile. "Anything else?"

Georgia smiled too, and shook her head no.

"Okay, well, I hope y'all will excuse me, I've got appointments all through the noon hour." Madeline Roudy edged toward the door. A ripple of appreciation traveled through the ladies. They could only dream of a schedule as busy as hers.

To Georgia it seemed obvious that Roudy was far too busy to be mayor. How could she ever squeeze in city business between all those important appointments? Roudy shook hands with Maribeth Parker, president of the LWV, then made her exit to a smattering of applause.

Georgia was amazed at all these white women in awe of the doctor. Even the Junior League types acted as though they liked her. Georgia knew in her heart that if Roudy had won over the Junior Leaguers, Krystal was finished.

Never mind that Krystal had been the best mayor ever— annexing East Over without a hint of racial upset, landing a fat state grant she used to resurface every street in town, breaking ground for a new office park on the Andalusia Highway. If the people of Six Points wanted the hardest-working, most compe- tent mayor, they would vote for Krystal. If they wanted a glam- orous lady doctor who looked like a slightly bucktoothed movie star . . .

Krystal was watching Roudy's protracted departure with a predatory smile, like one of those hard-eyed lady tennis players when the ball is coming down and she's planning an overhead smash. Georgia tried to send a mind signal: *Go easy on Roudy. She went easy on you. These ladies like her, or at least the idea of her. Nobody wants to hear you trash Madeline Roudy.*

The air in the community center must have been too cool and dry to conduct mind signals. Krystal tugged her lapels, stepped to the podium, and spread out a speech of many pages. The ladies around Georgia wilted. Punch and cookies were the chief attraction at an event like this, and it was awful to think of that much speech before the first bite of anything.

Georgia gave up trying to be subtle. She waved a hand at Krystal, made a clownish face, and drew a finger across her throat.

Krystal was looking straight at her but didn't appear to notice. She focused her gaze on the pages on the lectern. "Good morning, ladies, and thank you for inviting me," she said. "Let me first say that I always thought 'ABC' was a hit record by the Jackson 5. But now, from what I understand, in some corners of Six Points it has come to mean 'Anybody but Crystal.' I'd like to remind you that I spell my name with a *K*."

She looked up for a laugh that never came. A lady coughed, way in back.

What a lame opening line! Georgia marveled—and she was Krystal's best friend. Imagine what was going through the other women's heads!

Krystal was headed for disaster. Georgia could not just sit there and let it happen. She hadn't felt an urge this urgent since the day she rose from her pew to stop Preacher Eugene from blurting the truth.

She raised her hand. "Excuse me, Krystal, can I ask you the same question I asked Dr. Roudy? Tell us about your experience in city government."

Krystal frowned. "Yes, Georgia, I plan to get to that. If you let me. If you could, please, hold your questions till I'm through."

That was a bit rude. Some ladies sucked in air. Everyone knew Georgia was Krystal's best friend. Georgia thought most of them recognized she was only trying to save Krystal.

Krystal wouldn't take well to further interruption. But if Georgia didn't stop her, she was going to ruin herself.

Georgia said, "I don't think we want to hear some long speech, do we? Just tell us what you've done, and what you plan to do."

A murmur spread through the audience, a positive hum of agreement.

"Do you want to come up here and do this for me?" Now Krystal was pissed. She seemed to have no idea why Georgia might be trying to stop her. Georgia couldn't think of a way to explain in front of everyone without causing her even more embarrassment.

Maribeth Parker cleared her throat. "If the mayor's gone to all the trouble to prepare a speech," she said archly, "I for one would love to hear it."

Oh drop dead, Maribeth Parker, Georgia thought. She was just like that in tenth-grade biology, too. A monumental suck-up.

"Sorry, Maribeth," she murmured, "of course you're right, never mind—please go ahead, Miz Mayor."

Smoothing her skirt, Georgia fixed her eyes on a place where the floor tiles were laid slightly crooked. She was thinking what a burden it is to be right all the time—right, yet unable to convince anybody. Doesn't that indicate a failure of character? What good is it to be right if you have no influence? If everyone ignores you? You might as well be wrong.

Also she thought: I love Krystal as much as anybody on earth. But to love Krystal is to know that sometimes she can be a pig-headed fool. Now that Georgia had failed to stop her, her job as a best friend was to sit quietly and let Krystal make an ass of herself. And still be her friend when it was over.

"Sometimes you think you know a person," Krystal began. "Someone who's lived among you all their lives, you've said hello to as you passed in the street, and thought, hey, isn't she nice. Then come to find out there's a side of her you didn't really know at all. Folks, I wish Madeline Roudy had stayed around to face the music, but I imagine she left because she knew what was coming. Frankly, I don't think she had the courage to stick around. Because I'm here to tell you honestly that Madeline Roudy is not quite the person you think you know."

That's how it started. It went downhill from there.

Every now and then Krystal would veer close to a specific accusation—for a moment it seemed she was about to reveal a criminal past, or at least a nasty divorce—but then she would veer off again, leaving only a mist of innuendo. Without quite saying it, she implied that Madeline Roudy was nefarious in some way, a liar who had misrepresented herself.

Nervous tics were breaking out in the seats all around Georgia. Evelyn Manning propped her head against her index finger as if it were a gun she would like to use. No one wanted to hear the mayor ragging on the nice black lady doctor. For Krystal to roll on with her assault as if Roudy were still there to defend herself? Huge mistake.

Georgia closed her ears. She couldn't listen to one more word. A true friend would tune out the other friend now.

The speech went on for about a month. A couple of phrases floated into Georgia's ears, despite her efforts to block them: "Brought down shame on the whole community," and later, "Without a shred of evidence to the contrary!"

Poor Krystal. Bless your heart, you won't be mayor anymore. That's okay. We'll find you a nice job, a better job, where you won't be slaving away nights and weekends for an ungrateful citizenry. *And good luck to you, Madeline Roudy!* Georgia thought bitterly. *You'll be wishing for something as easy as a clinic full of sick kids!*

By the time Krystal's speech was over, even the ladies with good posture had slumped in their seats. The cookies slumped against the glass of the plate. The bubbles went out of the punch.

No one clapped, or asked any questions. No one wanted to prolong it by even one second. Krystal thanked them all for coming. The ladies smiled tight smiles and mobbed the door trying to get out. Several of them sidled up to Georgia to murmur "She should have listened to you" and the like, but this was just irritating. Where were they when she stuck her neck out?

From the visual darts Krystal was flinging at her, Georgia knew she was still mad. Not surprising. Krystal had failed, and she needed someone to blame. What a best friend does in this situation is hang around until everyone else is gone, so Krystal can rant and rave and blame it all on you. That's why Georgia hung around, anyway—to get what she knew was coming to her. Certainly she did not expect to get thanked.

Krystal walked across the indoor-outdoor carpet and stuck

out her hand like a politician introducing herself. "I want to thank you," she said, with a firm grip on Georgia's hand. "Thanks for showing me who you really are. I never would have believed it. Now I do."

Georgia was stunned. "Come on, Krys, don't say that. I'm sorry."

"You can't put the genie back in the bottle," Krystal said.

"Me and my big mouth," said Georgia. "I regretted it the instant the words were out of my—"

Krystal exploded. "Get the hell out of my face! I'm not interested in your apology!"

Georgia backed up a step. My God—Krystal was livid! Face all twisted to one side. Her eyes shining with anger.

"I know I should have kept my mouth shut," Georgia stammered, "but I was only trying to keep you from—"

"You sabotaged me on purpose! Of course they hated me, they would have hated anybody after you did that. 'Please not another one of your long-ass speeches, Krystal, can you spare us the long-ass speech?'"

"I did not say that!" Georgia was beginning to get her back up. "Not exactly. I was trying to stop you from making a fool of yourself."

"Oh no. Quite the opposite."

"Hey, you know what? This is really inappropriate, for *you* to be mad at *me!*" Georgia's voice pitched way up high—it surprised her, how panicky she sounded. She would never have opened her mouth if she'd suspected Krystal would misunderstand this badly. "I tried to warn you before you started, I gave you all the high signs in the world. You saw me but you ignored me. I was trying to tell you, those women did not want to hear you tearing down Madeline Roudy. They *loved* her. Did you even notice that? No."

"Last night you said it was a good idea to go on the offense."

"Last night it *was* a good idea," said Georgia. "Then Roudy came in and charmed the pants off everybody. Were you completely oblivious?"

"I've had it with you!" Krystal stormed. "Damn it! It's your fault she's running against me in the first place!"

"*My* fault?" Georgia was mystified. "What the hell?"

"Because you made her mad—you know what I'm talking about! That time at Hull's Market. She's only running against me to get back at you!"

"God, that is so junior high school," said Georgia. "You're trying to put this whole thing on me? Because that's just not fair."

Krystal said, "Oh why don't you just *fuck off!*"

Krystal said that.

The word echoed and rang off the cinder block walls and the flat carpet.

Georgia had never heard that word out of Krystal's mouth. Even quoting someone, she always substituted "the *F* word."

But she said it now. Then turned on her heel and rushed from the room.

The outer door slammed so hard Georgia thought the glass would surely shatter.

For a moment the room went pale. Georgia thought she was going to faint for real. Blood drummed in her ears. She sank down in a folding chair.

The right side of her face stung. As if she'd been slapped. *Fuck off.* Her best friend had said that to her. Good Lord. This was a new day. A territory she never expected to enter.

*　　*　　*

Georgia got up from the chair and went outside. Krystal's car was gone, the parking lot deserted. Irma Winogrand stood under the eave, smoking, staring out at the pine woods. "Did your mother find you?" Irma said.

Georgia turned. "I'm sorry?"

"She was looking for you. Seemed kind of upset. I told her you were in there. Didn't she come inside?"

"You sure it was my mother?"

"Georgia." Irma took a drag on her cig. "I've only known Little Mama my whole life. She looks pretty good, too. 'Cept she forgot to change out of her bedroom slippers."

"The pink ones?"

Irma nodded. "Bunny rabbits."

Georgia's heart filled with dread. Mama had been out of the house exactly twice in a year—once to accompany Georgia to the prison, and once to the doctor. She made Georgia handle all interaction with the world. That way nobody noticed her "memory problem," which she still insisted was mostly in Georgia's mind.

Irma said, "Poor old Krystal. You tried to save her from herself. But she wouldn't listen."

"I know," Georgia said. She could think of lots of other things to say, but not to Irma Winogrand.

"Nobody's gonna vote for her now," Irma said. "That was just...ungracious." She shook her head in disgust, as if *ungracious* was the worst thing you could be.

Georgia found herself springing to Krystal's defense—never mind that Krystal had just attacked her. "Aw, she didn't mean it that way. Krystal gets frustrated because she's worked so hard, and done such a good job as mayor. And nobody seems to notice."

"Maybe so," Irma said, "but that ain't the way to go about it."

"When was Mama here?"

"Not five minutes ago," said Irma. "I thought she went in there with you. Is she all right, Georgia?"

Georgia worked to keep her voice light. "Oh, she's fine. She just forgets."

Irma blew out a cloud of blue smoke. "Hell, I wish *I* could forget."

Georgia cruised the streets near the community center, looking for Little Mama. She swung by the Pik-N-Pay. Frances hadn't seen her. She looped back by the house, parked in the alley. She found the back door standing open, all that expensive A/C pouring out into the hot afternoon.

She made a quick check of the rooms. No sign of Little Mama.

A truly caring daughter would be getting hysterical by now. Georgia was not that worried; her heart was still racing from the confrontation with Krystal.

There was something so awful and definitive in the way Krystal had slammed that door.

Georgia didn't even want to think what it could mean. She could not imagine a world in which Krystal was no longer her best friend.

She went to her car, drove out of the alley to the front of the house. Here came Little Mama shuffling up the sidewalk as if wandering the streets was her daily routine.

Georgia rolled down her window. "Mama, what in the world?"

Mama leveled her finger at Georgia's nose. "I been looking for you."

"What for?"

Mama indicated the house with a flourish. "A nigger tried to break into the house," she said.

"Say what?"

"Big tall one. He was trying to come in the front door. He saw me through the glass and got to bangin' and whalin' on the door. I thought he was going to bust it down."

"You are making this up," Georgia said. "Get in, I'll drive you up the hill."

"I'm not going back up there," Mama said. "He might still be there."

"I said *get in the car.*" Georgia didn't often order her mother around. Little Mama came meekly around the front bumper and got in.

Georgia had learned to deal with extreme forgetfulness. She wasn't sure she was ready for full-blown delusions. "If you thought somebody was trying to break in, why'd you go off and leave the back door wide open?" She looked over her shoulder to execute the three-point turn.

"That nig must have seen me leave, and broke in again."

"Why did you leave?"

"I don't remember," Mama said.

"Think about it. You left home because . . . you were looking for me?"

"For somebody. Maybe it was you. But why would I be looking for you?"

"To tell me somebody was trying to break in?"

Mama said, "Could you give it a rest with all these questions? I'm exhausted."

"Okay, but—"

"*Georgia!* That's enough!"

Georgia drove up the hill thinking the whole thing was just another load of hooey from the dump truck that never stopped giving. But when she glanced at the front door she saw a young black man leaning against it.

She hit the brakes so hard her tires chirped.

He stood with arms folded, as if he was waiting for her. She was struck by the casual insolence of his pose. He wasn't trying not to be seen.

He must have been standing there when Georgia was around back, looking through the house.

"Is that the guy, Mama?"

"Lord, he's come back!" Mama cried. "Back up! Back up! Get away! Go!"

"Would you be quiet? He can hear you."

He refolded his arms and cocked one foot against the other ankle. He was a tall, good-looking young man—awfully young, she saw, as she got a closer look. A boy with a pretty face.

Georgia rolled down her window. "Can I help you?"

He just stared at her.

"Hello?" Georgia said. "Were you trying to break into our house?"

He didn't say a word. He wore his oversized black windbreaker zipped up to the neck (in this heat!), baggy oversized basketball shorts of shiny polyester, and the largest sneakers Georgia had ever seen, huge black boats with a white stripe to match the stripe on the jacket sleeves. The boy's legs tapered like skinny brown pipes into those shoes. On one shoulder he carried a black nylon backpack.

Georgia had just about decided to be scared after all when he said "No" in a soft dry voice that wasn't the least bit scary.

She got out of the car. "How can we help you?"

"Omnay," he said.

"What?"

"Omnay. F'na'walyins."

After a few more exchanges like this, she told him to stop talking like he had marbles in his mouth. He tried again. This time she made out, "I'm Nate from New Orleans."

"Nate?" she said. "I don't know any Nate."

The boy said, "Nathan."

"Nathan? You mean . . . you're . . ."

She felt as if she'd fallen over backward. But she was still standing upright.

No wonder she thought he was pretty. Look at that face! That was Georgia's face, blended with Skiff's face.

It was the weirdest sensation, like looking into a mirror and seeing two faces overlapping.

Dear God, this was Georgia's son.

Her own flesh and blood—*her own black son* standing there with his arms crossed, mouth turned up skeptically at one corner.

A huge smile opened up on her face. "Well hey, Nathan!" She should open her arms and embrace him—but how could she, with Little Mama watching from the car?

Inside, Georgia was dying. Inside, she was crying out, *No!* But she did not want him to think she was not glad to see him.

"You must be hungry," she said.

His eyes came to life.

"Lucky for you I can cook," said Georgia. "Come on in this house."

For a minute, she had been too shocked to know what to do. But now she knew: feed him, give him a bed for the night, then put him on the next bus to New Orleans. Little Mama wouldn't remember him for long, and no one else would ever have to know.

15

It took ten minutes to coax Little Mama out of the car into the house. Casting a baleful glance at the tall black boy hunched over the kitchen table, she muttered "Never in all my born days!" and fled to her room.

Nathan barely glanced up. He was fully engaged in his first round of eating. Georgia remembered Eugenia complaining about his appetite. If anything the old lady had understated it.

Georgia went up to tell Little Mama about her old high-school chum Dorothy Blanchard, a person she invented on her way up the stairs. Poor Dorothy had recently died, she explained, of very sad natural causes, and this was her son Nathan come to Six Points to look for a job.

"I can't believe you letting some nigger sit at my table," Little Mama said. "You must have forgot whose table that is."

"Hush your mouth with that word," Georgia shot. "If you can't keep a civil tongue in your head, just stay in your room till he's gone."

That's exactly what Mama used to say if Georgia said "damn" or "shit." *If you can't keep a civil tongue in your head...* Saying it back to her mother now made Georgia feel sad. And tired. Somehow, without noticing, or wanting to, she had turned into her mother.

No. Worse. Into her mother's *mother.*

"Hmp!" Little Mama folded her arms. "You can't wait till I'm dead so you can let niggers run wild all over the house. You'll probably throw parties for 'em and let 'em sleep in my bed."

"That's true," Georgia said. "That is actually my secret master plan. I'm surprised it took you this long to catch on."

Little Mama said, "Did you know Rosa Parks is running for mayor now? They got her damn picture up all over town."

Georgia had to smile. "That's not Rosa Parks, Mama. That's Madeline Roudy. The pediatrician at the clinic. She's running against Krystal."

"I know Rosa Parks when I see her," said Mama.

Georgia went downstairs to find that Nathan had consumed a whole jar of Skippy with a loaf of Holsum bread, half a roasted chicken, a bag of Doritos, and a quart of milk. Georgia cleaned out the fridge and moved on to the pantry. Good thing she always kept tons of canned and frozen food in case of tornado, power failure, or famine. From the freezer she brought out Colonial "heat-n-serve" rolls, a spaghetti Stroganoff casserole, and a spiral-sliced honey-baked ham.

Nathan ate silently and fast, as if he'd never been allowed to eat before and this might be his only chance. Georgia was tentatively impressed with his manners. He didn't gobble. He used the correct implements correctly. Only once did he rest his elbows on the table, and he moved them the moment she pointed it out.

She stood by the stove, watching him eat. "You like peach pie?"

He nodded. She put the pie plate in front of him. He assumed the whole thing was for him, and ate it all.

Georgia was beginning to like this boy.

Liking him was the last thing she needed to do. The situation was absurd. First thing in the morning she would drive him to the Texaco station and put him on the bus.

She still felt a trace of shame from her very first thought upon seeing him, which was what a pretty face he had, and how much she might like to... It was wrong even to remember thinking that. Of course she hadn't known who he was, but still.

Until today, Nathan had been an abstraction, a kind of make-believe boy. At some level Georgia hadn't quite believed in him. Now here he was, so real she could smell him—the pungent smell of a man, not a boy, who badly needs a bath and a change of socks.

Nathan ran his finger around the pie plate to get the last crumbs.

"You still hungry?"

He hesitated, then shook his head.

"Well, hallelujah." She intended it as a joke but Nathan didn't smile. "What I mean is, I'm glad we finally got you enough to eat. You were so hungry when you got here."

That was so inane Nathan didn't bother answering. He trained those big, brown, unblinking eyes on Georgia. She didn't need a birth certificate to know whose eyes those were—Skiff's, just as luminous and bottomless.

She was surprised how dark-skinned Nathan had turned out. From that glimpse in the delivery room she thought he would be lighter. It didn't matter to her, but she had heard that lighter-skinned blacks were treated better by their peers.

She saw a reflection of herself in the shape of his face, the curve of his mouth. But she doubted anyone would ever guess their relationship just by looking.

"So, Nathan. What brings you to Six Points?"

"The bus," he said.

Oh no. Was he stupid, too? "I mean, what made you decide to get on the bus?"

"Mamaw," he said.

"Mamaw. That's Eugenia?"

He nodded.

"Something wrong with her? Is she ill or something?"

He shook his head.

"Come on, Nathan, you can tell me. Whatever it is. Surely you know this comes as a pretty big surprise for me."

"I try to call you," he said.

"You did? When?"

"Last night."

"I didn't get any—wait...Did you start to leave a message then hang up?"

He nodded.

"I wondered who that was." If only she'd gotten to the phone in time, she might have headed this off. "Why did you hang up?"

He shrugged.

"Well, what were you planning to say?"

The boy stared for a long time. Evaluating her trustworthiness, she thought. He glanced at his plate. She could almost hear him thinking: *At least the food is good.*

"Mamaw say you rich and she ain't got nothin', if I ain't do zackly what she say every got-damn minute of my life, I just as well carry my sorry ass on up here and let you look after me," he said in a rush. "That's all she been say since Aunt Ree gone to jail." He pronounced it "awnt" in that old-fashioned colored-folks way.

"What did you do to make your Mamaw mad?" Georgia said.

He cut his eyes at her—she was sharper than he had suspected. "Nothin'."

"Nothin'? Aw now, come on, Nathan, she didn't throw you out for *nothin'*. What did you do?"

Nathan studied her. His brow wrinkled up in a frown. "I smoke some a her weed."

Georgia sighed. "Sorry I asked." She had no idea what might be an appropriate punishment...Go get Mamaw some more weed?

"Well she done smoke up all of mine," Nathan said. "I just took some back, no need for her to get all riled up like 'at."

"You and Mamaw smoke each other's weed all the time?" Georgia said with a tone she thought sounded lighthearted.

Nathan glared at her. *"Sheeeit."*

"What?"

"What you mean with that bullshit, 'You and Mamaw smoke each other'—yeah we smoke each other weed, what the hell you got to say about it?"

"Nathan, all I was saying was—"

"Look, you ax me what I done," he said. "I told you the truth. You want me to lie?"

"Don't say 'ax,'" Georgia said. "The word is 'ask.'"

"Aw fuck off, lady, damn," Nathan said.

Twice! In one day! Georgia had now been told to *fuck off* by her best friend and her half-black offspring.

"I beg your pardon?" she said stiffly.

"Why the fuck you want to say some like that for," he said. "Ain't nothin' wrong the way I talk! Just cause e'body in the world don't talk like you."

"Oh I get it, you can talk just fine when you want to," she said. "When you want to be understood you have no problem. Now Nathan, listen to me. This is my home, mine and Mama's. And you are welcome here. But not that gutter language. I won't have it. Understand? I don't care if you're twenty years old or two thousand, I do not allow that word in my house. You got that?"

He gaped at her.

"I said, do you *got* that?"

He tried to hold his mouth still, but a little grin leaked out.

"What are you grinning at?"

"Do you *have* that," he said. "If you gonna bitch me out, at least get it right your own damn self."

My God, the balls on this kid! He got those directly from Georgia. She struggled to hide how much his cockiness pleased her.

"Well okay, smarty-pants. And don't say 'bitch.' "

He rolled his eyes. "Ah-ight, bitch."

She was on him in a flash—towering over him, her hand raised to slap his face—and it was going to hurt, too. "Call me that again," she urged. "Go on. I dare you. I'll slap you from here to the middle of next week. Go ahead. I'm waiting."

This was not the reaction Nathan had expected. His eyes loomed large. "Jokin'," he said.

"No. A joke is funny and that was not funny." She lowered her hand. "You watch that mouth, young man."

He squinted his eyes. "You really gonna hit me?"

She raised the hand again. "Try it and see."

"Dayum," he said.

"You probably thought I was some little shrinking violet," she said, "some little Southern belle you could come up here and push around. Well, I am not afraid of you."

"Ain't you rich?" he said.

"Hell no I'm not rich! I work hard for every penny I make."

"What kinda job you do?"

That's for me to know, Mr. Smelly Socks. "I make quilts. Collectible quilts. I make them, and I sell them in a gift shop in town."

From the expression on his face she might have said she was a part-time whale hunter.

"This look like rich people's house," Nathan said.

"My great-grandfather had money," said Georgia. "By the time it got down to me, there was nothing left but the bills. Sorry, maybe you were thinking you'd come up here and inherit the family fortune, but there ain't one."

"Don't say 'ain't,'" Nathan said.

She laughed at his display of brass. "Isn't," she said.

Nathan said, "I didn't come up here for money."

"Well, then? Why did you?"

He shrugged again.

"I mean, I'm sure you had some reason in mind when you got on the bus."

He shook his head. "See what you look like."

"Okay well, you've seen me. What do you think?"

His eyes flashed. "Nothin'."

"What does that mean?"

"I thought maybe you'd like me or something," he said. "But you don't. I'm just like a stranger to you."

"You think I don't like you? It's too soon to say that. We're just getting to know each other."

"I guess," he said.

"Well? Better late than never," she replied. "You're still hungry, aren't you?"

He nodded.

She couldn't help it: she did like this kid. He reminded her of herself at that age—headstrong, fearless, immortal. Hungry all the time. Although in her case that meant hungry for boys.

She went to the oven for the Stroganoff casserole. Nathan went back to being a bottomless eating machine. The more he ate, the more relaxed and happy he became, until he was slouched over in his chair humming a soft little tune, forking in his third plateful.

Georgia tried not to hover. She came and went, performing her regular late-afternoon chores while he ate. She'd gotten an early start on the day, so the apartment was ready for Jimmy Lee Newton.

Whenever Georgia had let herself think about Nathan, she had always pictured a kid like the young Michael Jackson—a snub-nosed charmer, winning smile, ingratiating talents. She wasn't prepared for this raw-boned young black man. Obviously there was nothing special about him, nothing prodigious except his appetite.

And so? Whose fault was that? Who abandoned whom? Who gave up her baby to a woman with a taste for Riunite and convicted felons? It was ridiculous of Georgia to blame anyone for how he turned out. If she'd wanted something better for him, she could have raised him herself.

"You can stay here tonight," she said. "But then I'm gonna have to put you on the bus back to Mamaw."

He regarded her with a plain expression, almost blank. But there was something in his eyes, a little touch of disappointment that pricked Georgia to keep talking.

"No offense," she said. "You seem like a nice enough guy. I'm sure we would like each other if we got to know each other. But as you may have noticed, I've got a lot on my plate here. Mama's not all there, mentally, and I have a—my brother's in jail."

"Really?" Nathan sat up, his first show of real interest. "For what?"

"Nothing," she said. "Conspiracy to commit a terroristic act. And an explosives charge."

He did an exaggerated double take and said, "*Dayum.*"

"It's all a misunderstanding. But like I said, my hands are full right now."

"Mamaw didn't say nothin' about all that," said Nathan. "She said you was a straight-up white lady."

"I am," Georgia said. "At least, I think I am."

16

Little Mama spent a restful night, thanks to the Ambien that Georgia added to her evening pills. With Nathan camping out in the guest room, Georgia didn't want any incidents.

Jimmy Lee Newton got stomach flu and canceled at the last minute, so Georgia's night was peaceful too.

The next morning she fed Nathan a big breakfast, put him in the car, and drove him to the Texaco. Bennie Fisher said there was only one bus going south these days. It didn't run Fridays or Saturdays. The next one was Sunday, at one fifteen in the afternoon.

Georgia tried to think of someplace she could stash Nathan until then. Too bad the LaSalle Hotel on the courthouse square disappeared years ago, with the last of the traveling salesmen.

In normal times Georgia would phone Krystal and explain without having to explain, and Krystal would say, "Hell, bring him over here," and that's what she would do. But too much time had elapsed since the disaster at the League of Women Voters. By now Georgia should have called Krystal and apologized at length. Instead she had let the rift stretch out, unmended, over a whole day. Normally she and Krystal would have exchanged five or six phone calls in that time. The phone hadn't rung once.

That meant Krystal was still mad. Nothing to do but leave her alone until she got over it. Georgia didn't dare ask a favor.

She took a swing by Hull's Market to refill the fridge. She made Nathan wait in the car while she went in. She drove him the long way home, around the bypass and in from the north, to show him more of Six Points. On the way by the No-Tell Motel she took particular note of whose beat-up Chrysler was parked next to whose red pickup in the middle of the day.

She took Nathan home and installed him in Mama's TV den. All afternoon she left him in there eating chips, watching in silence, flipping between the channels.

"Listen, Nathan, I've got a prior engagement this evening," she said. "I have to go out for a couple of hours. Just stay out of Little Mama's way, all right?" If he got hungry again, she told him, he was welcome to anything in the fridge. If he wanted to take a shower, *hint hint*, she'd put soap and shampoo and fresh towels in the downstairs back bathroom. She would also be very happy to wash any clothes that were dirty. Anything else would have to wait until she returned.

He agreed about washing clothes. Together they started a load, and she showed him how to work the dryer.

She hurried to her room to freshen up. She put on a yellow polka-dot sundress and tied her hair back in a ponytail for Sheriff Bill. She stopped by Little Mama's room to issue a stern warning, which she hoped would penetrate the fog of cranky forgetfulness that had been hanging over her all day. Mama scowled the whole time Georgia was talking, waved her away like a gnat.

Georgia went downstairs. "Okay, Nathan, I'm going now," she chimed from the hall.

He didn't answer. She poked her head into the den. All that

comfort food had finally kicked in. He lay sprawled across Little Mama's recliner, asleep, head tucked into the crook of his arm. Behind him, a car chase roared softly on TV.

He looked almost sweet in that pose. She picked up his baseball cap from the floor and placed it on his knee.

Whizzy snoozed on the rug beside him. That was a sign. Whizzy always had been a good judge of character.

Georgia forced herself to stop standing there, staring at him.

Half an hour later she was stretched out beside Sheriff Bill, breathing his whiskey breath, as the recording of the old-timey *Grand Ole Opry* broadcast played on the CD player concealed within the antique radio. The Opry at very low volume helped set the right mood for the sheriff. He was a man of famously few words; it took years of careful prodding for Georgia to tease out such basic information as what kind of music he liked. Gradually she realized that their Friday nights were a re-creation of a specific scene from the sheriff's adolescence. It wasn't clear if it was something that had actually happened to him or a fantasy he had carried with him all this time. Really it didn't matter. Georgia was the stand-in for a specific young woman in a yellow dress. The first time she wore yellow, Bill complimented her so lavishly she'd worn yellow for him ever since.

The low whine of the Opry fiddlers was another part of the scene, and the lights off, the sheriff in his white V-neck undershirt wiggling his skinny butt on the bed, shucking off his Fruit of the Looms...They had done this exact thing the same way dozens of times. To Georgia it felt furtive and stale and a bit deadly, but Sheriff Bill found endless reward in replaying the scene. Sometimes he got to breathing so hard he was positively wheezing with pleasure.

Tonight he was in a lazy mood. He wanted to cuddle, to cradle her head on his chest and stroke the hair of that girl from long ago. On a normal Friday, Georgia would be glad to take time for this kind of thing, but she could not quite relax knowing Nathan was in the house, snoozing in front of Little Mama's TV. At least she hoped he was snoozing.

Bill murmured some little endearment. Ten to one they were re-creating the night he lost his virginity. Men are so fascinated by their own navels, and nearby organs. They spend the first part of their lives trying to lose their virginity, the rest of their lives trying to get it back.

Georgia felt like a girl in an Opry song—caught between the sheets with Sheriff Bill and his old friend Jack Daniel's. What is it about sex that makes a man want to drink? And what about drinking makes a man so horny? Why does he have to forget himself, lose all thought of who he is, in order to become the wild thing the occasion demands? Are we all so stuck in the rut of our little ant lives, our notion of ourselves as upright purposeful creatures engaging in useful endeavor—gathering crumbs for the anthill—that we can't enjoy ourselves unless we get drunk?

If Georgia took a drink every time she poured one for her gentleman friends, she would be a hopeless alcoholic. She only pretended to drink, because men don't like to drink alone. Also they don't like women who drink. Georgia's usual practice was to pour a neat whiskey, take one sip to get the taste on her lips, then after the man leaves, use the little funnel from the seven-drawer highboy to pour it back in the bottle. That stuff was too expensive to waste.

"Oh goodness," the sheriff sighed into her hair. "Oh me."

"What's wrong, Bill?"

"Naw, nothing." He patted her cheek clumsily, pat pat.

"Something on your mind?"

"Aw, not really," he said. "It's just...nothing."

She lifted up, resting her chin on the bone in his shoulder. Usually the only way to get him to talk was to wait.

Finally he said, "Maybe best not to talk about it."

Georgia squeezed his arm. "You can tell me, or not. I don't care."

"Oh, I was just...daydreaming."

"Mmmm," she said, to coax it out of him.

"Like, if I could get free," he said. "We could go off somewhere. I could get another job."

Dear God. These were the most words Sheriff Bill had strung together in a long time. She wished he hadn't done it. Of all her clients, she would have picked Bill as the *least* likely to fall into this kind of longing.

Georgia's usual reaction was to thank the man for such a sweet thought, then invent some reason she couldn't keep their next date. Usually a week off was enough time for him to come to his senses.

"That's a sweet thing to say, Bill," she said. "Is something wrong at home?"

"Just—"

She waited.

He got started again: "Hate to think I might lose you 'cause I never said nothing to you."

"Aw now, Billy, you're not gonna lose me. Not a chance," she said lightly. "What on earth makes you think that? I'm not going anywhere."

"But—I'd like to..."

"What, marry me? No you wouldn't. Think about it. You've been with Raynelle how long? Thirty years?"

"Thirty-four," he said, like a man serving a life sentence who knows exactly how many days remain.

Almost as long as I've been alive, Georgia thought. "Remember how in love with her you were, until you married her?" she said. "That's what would happen with us."

"It's different," he said. "You're different."

"After a while, I'd be the same." She put her feet on the floor. "Same old Georgia, just like she's the same old Raynelle to you now. She's a good lady, Bill. You don't want to mess that up."

A flicker of lightning etched the lacy pattern of the sheer curtains on the opposite wall.

Bill sat up.

Another flicker, and another. The bluish flash was too rhythmic to be lightning.

"That's a squad car," Bill said. "What the hell?"

Georgia rushed to the window to see a pair of squad cars splashing blue light all over the side of her house.

"Oh *God!*" She grabbed up the sundress. "I've got to get down there."

The sheriff was down on all fours groping for his underwear, showing his skinny white butt.

Georgia wrestled the dress over her head. "Bill, do *not* come down there, you hear me? Let me handle this." She hurried out the door, down the stairs, through the backyard, toward the house. Here came Nathan out the side door with his hands cuffed behind him, hustled along by a deputy on either side. Little Mama watched in triumph from the front porch, brandishing the pellet gun she used to chase squirrels from her bird feeder. There were two cops on the porch with her to protect her from the dangerous Negro.

In a flash Georgia saw one possible future, in which she gazed coolly at Nathan in the arms of the law and said, *I've never seen him before in my life.*

Easiest thing in the world. No action required—just stand back and watch them take him away. He would never come nosing around her house again.

But she did not think she could do that.

It wasn't that Nathan was her own flesh and blood—hell, they carted Brother off to jail all the time, and Georgia barely roused herself to protest.

The truth was, she already cared about Nathan. She knew that watching him sleep had been a big mistake. In just those few moments, she had formed an attachment. He started to matter to her.

This went against her long-standing rules against emotional engagement, but what can you do? It's not every day your own *issue* shows up at your house.

And not every day the armed forces of Cotton County join with the city of Six Points to arrest him. Georgia knew these men—those were the Six Points cops, Jimmy Wagner and Jack Logan on the porch with Mama, sheriff's deputies Clay Ford and Lester Pine frog-marching Nathan toward their blue-flashing car. Georgia had gone to high school with Lester. He dated Eileen Simmons the summer of their junior year.

"Hey Lester," she sang. "It's Georgia Bottoms, how you?"

He stopped to give her the once-over. "Well fine, Georgie—damn, don't you still look good!"

"Why thank you. What's going on here?"

"Your mother called 911, said a black male broke into y'all's house," Lester Pine said. "We got him right here."

"Well, I sure do appreciate it, Lester, but Mama made a mistake," said Georgia. "This is Nathan. A friend of our family. You can let him go."

"We had a complaint of breaking and entering," said Lester, "and we caught this subject inside the residence. We have to take him in and write up a report, at least."

"Lester, mind stepping over here a minute? Nathan, you stay right there with Officer Ford. That's right, just—I need to—if I could, just a minute—" She got Deputy Pine off to the side, laid an imploring hand on his elbow. "Lester, don't make me say this too loud, okay? My mother is not of sound mind. She's confused. Whatever she told you is all in her head. That boy's a friend of ours. Now you just let him go and we'll forget this ever happened, all right?"

Right in the middle of saying this, she realized Lester Pine was gazing at her mouth, dying to kiss her. Georgia did not think she'd done anything to encourage him, but sometimes these things happened without her doing anything at all. She let the notion dangle in midair, a promise she might keep one of these days.

Just that hint was enough to soften him up: "Aw, I don't know…"

Georgia heard the fatal waver in his voice. "Let him go, Lester. I promise, this is all a big mistake."

"Well, maybe if you was willing to—"

"Absolutely, I take full responsibility." Georgia squeezed his arm to reinforce the promise. "He'll stay right here with me till he goes back to New Orleans tomorrow. Will that be okay?"

Nathan stared at the ground, silent as a tree, his face devoid of expression. Looking at him, you would never be able to guess whether he was innocent or guilty. His face was just that blank.

He's been arrested before, Georgia thought. He knows exactly how to behave.

Lester Pine turned to Clay Ford. "Gotta let him go."

"Well damn it," said Clay, "catch 'em inside somebody's durn *house* and they still want to turn 'em loose. Hell if you ask me—how is that not interfering with the conduct of our duty?"

"It's a false alarm," Lester said. "She knows him. He was in the house by permission. Don't ask me why."

Georgia had been waiting for the implication, and there it was. It was unusual in Six Points for an African-American male to be in a white lady's house by permission, except to do some kind of labor.

"False alarm? It ain't no damn false alarm!" Little Mama turned on the nearest cop, big old Jack Logan, and smacked him—hard!—on the forearm. "Don't you dare let him go! That boy broke into my house!"

"Now Miz Bottoms, ma'am," said the bemused Logan, "you can't hit me, I can't allow that, I'm an officer of the law."

"Shut up!" Little Mama smacked his arm a second time. "You get off my property!"

"Mama, stop that!" cried Georgia.

Jack Logan removed the pellet gun from Mama's hand, and propped it against the porch rail. Stepping behind her he gently wrapped one beefy arm around her, pinning her hands to her sides. "Miz Bottoms, cut that out, hear? Don't make me put cuffs on you."

"Mama, for God's sake," said Georgia.

Little Mama struggled, trying to kick him. Logan gave a grim smile at the humor of this little old lady resisting him. He lifted her in a one-armed hug—like Popeye with that bulging forearm.

Little Mama screeched and kicked at him. Logan winced—she had landed a good one.

Georgia had been wondering how to convince them of Little Mama's infirmity. Little Mama had handled that all by herself.

Suddenly Georgia felt foolish about the whole situation—she must be especially slow-witted this evening, or maybe the rush of circumstances had dulled her into letting this happen. How could she have left Mama alone with the boy, knowing her slippery grip on reality? The minute Georgia realized Nathan was going to spend another night, she should have canceled Sheriff Bill—but she did not want her regularly scheduled life interrupted by something as inconvenient as *the fruit of her womb.*

Little Mama worked one foot loose and tried for one last kick at Officer Logan. Her heel struck the porch rail. Georgia watched the barrel of the pellet gun slide along the rail. Time slowed down, as it does when a disaster is unfolding in front of your eyes.

The gun went into free fall, smacking down *crack!* on the floor.

That crack was the gun going off.

Pellets blew through the seat of Jimmy Wagner's khaki uniform trousers. To hear him howl you would think it had blown him in two. "I'm hit! I'm hit!"

Clay Ford scrambled for the squad car, the radio. "Officer down!" he hollered. "Shots fired! Officer down! Get me backup!"

"Oh for God's sake, it's a pellet gun," said Georgia. "Would you please calm down?" No one listened. The radio squawked. Clay Ford bellowed for backup.

Georgia cried, "Nobody fired! The durn thing fell over 'cause he had it propped on the rail!"

"Stand back and be quiet!" Officer Ford pulled his pistol from its holster and began waving it wildly. Georgia ducked.

Jack Logan one-arm-carried Little Mama down the driveway toward the second squad car. Jimmy Wagner groaned, twisting his head around to see where he'd been hit.

Lester pushed Nathan's head down and shoved him into the backseat of the first car.

It went against Georgia's nature to stand in silence, but she was the only one not getting arrested. If she stood quietly, she thought, they would turn off their flashers and go away.

Eventually they did. The yard got dark again, quiet enough to think.

17

Georgia walked around the house to the backyard.

"Georgia." A whisper from the camellia bush by the back porch.

"Bill?"

"Shhhh—"

"Oh, come out of there. They're gone," she said. "Were you hiding in there the whole time? While your stupid boys arrested my mother and—that boy?"

Hearing him rustle the branches, trying to find his way out of the bush, Georgia realized that she was surrounded on all sides by idiots. Her well-stitched life was showing definite signs of fraying.

She glanced to the alley. The sheriff's brown Chevrolet was gone.

The branches parted, ripping open a whole new seam in her life. It was not Sheriff Bill who stepped out of the camellia bush. It was the Reverend Brent Colgate.

Gleamingly handsome and tan, in creased khakis and a burgundy polo shirt, he might have stepped out of a Sunday-supplement ad.

God he's gorgeous, was Georgia's first thought. Maybe she said it out loud. Thinking back, she was never quite sure.

"Well, hello, Miss Georgia!" he said, as if they had just happened into each other on the street.

"My, my," said Georgia. "You sure do tend to turn up."

He smiled. "I do, don't I?"

"At the most inopportune moments," Georgia said. "What the hell are you doing in my bushes? Spying on me?"

"Not spying," he said. "I was waiting."

"For what?"

"For you to be done with the police. So we could talk."

How could his teeth be so white, in the shadows of the side yard? The streetlight fell through the branches at just the right angle to glint off his smile.

"It's like you're following me around," she said.

"Really?" said Brent. "What if it turned out I am?"

Georgia said, "Then I'd want to know why."

Brent Colgate said, "You fascinate me, by God. You are the most interesting person in this town."

"It's a small town," said Georgia.

Sometimes life comes stealing up like a little kid who sneaks up behind you and yells so loud it stops your heart.

This was different: something new announcing itself, like the pealing of a bell, right there in Georgia's side yard.

A moment after Brent stepped out of that bush, Georgia zoomed up and up to a great altitude from which she could survey their future: first the passionate kiss, the coming together, the weeks, months, years of sexy sneaking around, followed by the difficult period while he extricates himself from his marriage, the surge of happiness when he's finally free and then...a quiet little wedding in Biloxi, or Vegas, or—hey, why not New Orleans?

And then *look out, world*—Georgia Bottoms will be the last thing anyone ever expected: a preacher's wife, perfectly happy!

Thank God she had maintained her church attendance all these years.

She could even give him kids—she wasn't too old yet, although her clock was ticking pretty loud. She could give him beautiful blond children. And she would do it, too. Raise his kids. Keep his house. Have his supper ready at the end of the day. Georgia had spent her life looking down on women with no more ambition than that—and now, for the first time, she knew it was something she could do. No. Something she *wanted*.

She could give up the life she had built for herself. The clients. Independence. Easy money.

Gladly. The whole pancake. For him.

If only Brent Colgate would love her, would fall deeply in love with her and swear *until death do us part*.

Floating way up over herself, seeing the map of their happiness stretching out into the future, Georgia also realized that tonight, for the first time in years, she had the big house to herself.

Mama was behind bars. Nathan too. You couldn't count on them staying there for long, but for now that's where they were. She thought of that old Elvis song: "It's Now or Never."

There stood Georgia and Brent in the side yard like two magnets placed near each other—neither one of them actually moved, but suddenly both found themselves in motion, unable to resist the gravitational attraction of two bodies in space.

Brent grabbed her.

Georgia fell into his arms.

He was kissing her.

Oh, it was good.

18

Ella Fitzgerald singing: *Spring can really hang you up the most...*

Waking up from a hard sleep, a fleeting moment when Georgia didn't know who she was. Then something pierced the dream world and drew her down toward the light of day. On this morning, it was Ella. The CD had been playing softly all night.

Georgia struggled to open her eyes. The right eye was glued shut. She ran a finger along the eyelid to unglue it.

She saw her foot poking out of the sheet. She ran her hand all the way to the other side of the mattress. Brent was gone. Of course he was gone, it was morning, and not early, either, to judge from the hot yellow sunlight pouring in through the sheers.

Good God—had she really fallen sound asleep with a man in her bed?

She might have been sleeping for days. A crusty rim had built up inside her lower lip. The mattress was damp where her mouth had been, the coverlet wadded in the corner, top sheet flung over the chair. The fitted sheet had come half off the bed, bringing the mattress cover with it, leaving a stretch of mattress that looked somehow too naked. As if wild animals had been tearing each other apart in this room.

Georgia smiled, padding to the bathroom. She was seated spraddle-legged on the toilet when it dawned on her that she had let Little Mama languish in jail all night.

Oh God, and Nathan too!

Her natural selfishness and lust had overwhelmed her sense of duty. A hundred times last night this knowledge tried to crowd into her mind, and a hundred times she told it to *go away*.

Last night was Georgia's night. A night just for her. She didn't want any nagging sense of duty getting in the way of her after-glow. If she wanted to be Scarlett O'Hara, waking up blissful the morning after Rhett had his way with her, that was her right.

She felt...taken. Ravished.

She would get up, get dressed, go get Mama out of jail, because that's what she had to do. But no one could keep her from exulting in this wonderful feeling, of having been well and truly made love to. By a man who was on fire for her. Her whole body sang a happy song, every finger and toe. That's what sex with a crush can do.

It had been so long since Georgia went to bed with anybody for a reason other than professional duty. It reminded her what she liked about sex in the first place. The stickiness, the humidity of each other, the natural slipperiness...

She needed a shower, clean clothes, then she would go get them out of jail. They'd been in there all night. Another hour wouldn't kill them.

Georgia wasn't quite sure what she would tell them, other than how hard she'd been working to get them out.

Ella Fitzgerald sounded weary, breathy, a little wistful, "I Concentrate on You." Georgia pressed STOP and gave her the rest of the day off.

It happens in the great Ant Connection that sometimes an ant finds another ant. Just like the millions of ants running around—but different, somehow. There's a spark, a connection. Next thing you know...

The comparison founders on the rocks of what actually happens. We are different from ants, Georgia thought. The queen lays her eggs, the drones come along later to fertilize. We humans still like to do it together—we hook up, we connect, to keep the race going. That's the way the Big Joker planned it, and that's the way it's always going to be, no matter how many test tubes and surrogate mothers you have, how many embryos you implant. The old-fashioned way of making a baby is still the most popular.

Of course there won't be any baby with Brent. Georgia took her twenty-eight-day pill yesterday, as she did every day.

Maybe today she wouldn't take it. Hell, maybe she'd stop taking it altogether.

She was wild for this man. In her bed, Jesus H. Christ, he was something else. Oh yes. Here's how good he was: it felt as though they were making a baby, and her only impulse was, Go ahead, make me pregnant. She had *never* felt that way before.

It shook her up a little.

She forced that thought from her mind. Of course there was Brent's pretty face to distract her. She lost herself kissing his mouth.

Her bedroom was a wreck. She would deal with it later. She had to reenter the real world for a couple of hours.

She carried the afterglow with her into a hot shower, steaming and singing the Ella song about praying for snow to hide the clover...

Humming while she toweled off, smiling as she shaved her legs, brushing her teeth, gargling, spitting... Georgia felt like a silly girl completely in love—with Brent Colgate, with herself, with life in all its possibility.

Her mood began to lose altitude when she stepped into her room and saw the blink of the answering machine, the startling number in the MESSAGES window: 23.

Twenty-three messages? She didn't even know the display had double digits. What could have happened? Was the world on fire again, terrorists blowing up things, friends trying to let her know?

The first thing she'd done after bringing Brent to this room was switch off the sound of the answering machine.

She snugged the towel around herself, easing down to the edge of her bed. She made her hand go out, willed her finger to push PLAY.

The first two calls were hang-ups. The third caller hesitated a moment before speaking. "Georgia? Hey, it's Alma Pickett... Listen, I don't know if you're watching TV right now? Anyway, you're going to be *very* interested in the program on Channel 13. Turn it on and then call me, okay? I'm at home."

Odd. Why would Alma want to talk about some show on public TV? She and Georgia were friendly but not friends. Alma never called unless she was running out of quilts.

The machine beeped. "Hey Georgia, it's Alma again, I'm sure you'd pick up if you were there but—my gosh, the nerve of some people! I'm not a lawyer but I think you might have an excellent case here. And I will gladly testify on your behalf. It's outrageous! Call me."

In her first confusion Georgia wondered if some TV reporter had somehow discovered her secret life and aired an undercover exposé—but that was impossible. Only six men on earth knew any part of Georgia's secret. Georgia was the only one who knew everything.

Calls five through eight were hang-ups, probably the same person calling and hanging up over and over. Might be Krystal. Caller nine said, "Hey, it's Krystal," signifying right off that everything was still not okay. Georgia and Krystal never identified themselves. They didn't have to. They knew each other's voices. "I've been trying to get in touch with you since, uhm, since Friday, and it's very frustrating," Krystal said. "If it's not too big an imposition, give me a call when you get this message."

Her voice was frosty. Georgia felt a twinge of guilt about what she was doing last night when Krystal called. A night for yourself is one thing, but Georgia had gone totally AWOL at the moment her best friend was extending this olive branch. And then Krystal waited all night for a call back that never came.

The next message was from Malone's Dry Cleaners. They had managed to get the spot out of the linen jacket, Miss Georgia could pick it up anytime.

Three more hang-ups—Krystal, just checking?—then a familiar deep voice: "Uhm, hello Miz Bottoms, this is the sheriff, Bill Allred," he said, for the benefit of anyone listening in. "Just letting you know, we've straightened out this, ah, misunderstanding...You can come on down, sign these papers, and pick up your mother and this young man whenever you want. It's just past ten o'clock, I'm headed on home. All right then, bye now."

After that, the hum and click of the same person calling again and again, hanging up—it had to be Krystal. Calling all night. She knows I wasn't here, Georgia thought. So what? I'm a grown woman. Free to do what I want. Who got mad in the first place?

Not me. Why should I be in a big rush just because she decides now is the time to make up?

Then another message from Alma, less cheerful: "Georgia? Alma Pickett again, trying to track you down. Listen, I'm getting calls from some of my customers, and I must say I am rather confused. We've all seen the same show, but they came to a different conclusion...I mean, I do not want to believe it, but the designs are so, so similar. I can't imagine how it could be a coincidence. Anyway—I'm reserving judgment till I hear from you. Okay? Call me." Click.

Georgia felt her stomach sinking. The reference to "designs" could only mean one thing—and sure enough here came a message from Myna Louise Myrick: "Georgia, this is Myna Louise, I'm watching Channel 13 right now, and far as I'm concerned you can come get this damn quilt and give me back my money. If you want to support a bunch of freeloading black women, fine. But don't lie and trick *me* into doing it!"

Georgia pressed PAUSE. She hurried to the front porch, flung this morning's *Light-Pilot* aside, and grabbed yesterday's paper. She paged to the TV listings as she climbed the stairs, running her finger down rows of small type:

7 PM (APT) **"The Quilters of Catfish Bend"**—
Documentary—Poor black women, descended from
slaves, decorate their quilts with African tribal motifs
handed down through generations. (CC)

Oh Jesus. Okay. Busted!

Georgia knew it was theoretically possible. She had never seen another white person when she was in Catfish Bend buying the quilts, so she'd hoped her secret was safe. In hindsight, that was naive. The quilts were beautiful, after all, and she had no exclusive. The quilters gladly sold them to whoever showed up with money.

Georgia bought the first one years ago at a fancy gift shop in Fairhope, then decided she wanted to give quilts to Little Mama and Krystal for Christmas. She tracked down the quilters and drove all the way across middle Alabama to buy them. The quilts were so pretty she bought four instead of two. Driving home, pondering how much that gift shop had marked up the first quilt, she realized she could sell two of them for double what she paid, to cover the cost of the two she was giving. And thus was born a business.

Georgia had been careful never to actually claim she made the quilts herself. But she knew that was like some highly sexed president nitpicking the meaning of "is." She had never turned down praise for the quilts. Nor the profit. Marking up merchandise was truly the oldest of all the professions.

Georgia's afterglow was fading fast. She closed her eyes and tried to recover the full shimmer of the Brent Colgate feeling. It was like waking up trying to keep a dream from slipping away— you erase it, trying to remember.

Quilts would have to wait. Georgia could only imagine the conniption fit Little Mama was pitching in her cell.

She changed into a smart white sleeveless top with a skinny black belt, black capri pants, and strappy sandals. She stopped at the hall mirror to check her look.

Here came Whizzy through the doggy door, wagging his tail. Georgia bent down to scratch behind his ears. "Poor Whiz, everybody ignores you, don't they? You okay, buddy?" He waggled and smiled.

She started out to the porch. The door was stuck. She pushed. It gave a little. Something blocking it. She pushed harder. Whatever-it-was slid heavily across the porch, *shhhh*.

Georgia put her head out to see what: a cardboard box, a jumble of items. On top was a plastic replica of a big-mouthed bass on a plaque.

Georgia knew this fish.

If you pushed the red button, the fish would wiggle and sing "Elvira."

Georgia had paid good money for this thing at the Dollar General last year, and presented it with great ceremony, elegantly wrapped, to Krystal for Christmas. Their history of gag gifts stretched all the way back to high school.

Georgia was careful not to touch the red button, but the song started up anyway when she lifted it from the box. The fish writhed and moved its hideous mouth. "Elvi-RA!" There was no stopping it—once it started, it sang the song all the way through before shutting off. That was part of the joke.

Giddyup a-oom papa oom papa mau mau...

Underneath the fish was a monkey that clanged cymbals and turned somersaults. A red-white-and-blue headband with spangly stars on springs. A Pet Rock. A dachshund in a Santa hat that barked "Jingle Bells."

These were Georgia's Christmas gifts to Krystal, each lovingly repacked in its original box with the original gift card and the bow. This box was a museum of their friendship, going back twenty years. The Reagan doll "with articulated limbs!" A Nancy Reagan Halloween mask. A pair of "clackers," acrylic spheres on a string that bounced loudly off each other; they were wildly popular for about ten seconds in the midseventies. A piggy bank with a bent-over hillbilly, a coin slot in his butt crack.

Georgia had also received a gag gift from Krystal each year, but she would be hard-pressed to name a single one. Okay, one, from years ago: a corncob on a stick, labeled "Executive Backscratcher." The gifts were supposed to be jokes, Georgia thought—fun for the moment, then out they went with the wadded-up wrappings, the day after Christmas.

Krystal had hung on to every stupid little gift. As if they were priceless antiques.

And then dropped this box at Georgia's door without a word. What more final a statement could there be?

Georgia went to the kitchen phone and dialed the familiar number. The last four notes of the touch tone always sang a little tune, "Here comes Krystal!," into her ear.

The phone rang and rang. No answer, no machine.

Georgia went to her car. This felt like one of those frustrating dreams where you're trying very hard to perform an important task you can't quite remember, but obstacles keep cropping up. Instead of taking time to back down the driveway, she did what she used to do as a teenager—drove straight across the yard to the alley, and screeched the tires making the turn onto Magnolia.

She hoped she wasn't too late.

Krystal lived in her parents' sprawling old one-story house on Live Oak Street. After her mother died, she spent a fortune gutting the house, redoing plumbing, electrical, kitchen, and bath, fancying up the yard with gazebos, pergolas, trellises, waterfalls, bird feeders, statues of gnomes and elves and classical Greek naked ladies. It was way too cottagey and girly-girl for Georgia's taste, and it didn't resemble Krystal's personality in the slightest, but she poured her heart into it. Once the landscaping grew in, Georgia had to admit the yard was lovely in a tacky kind of way.

What looked wrong was the great white truck parked in front, a crowned man riding a bucking moving van: Charlie Ross Regal Moving.

Georgia's heart sank. It hadn't been forty-eight hours since the League of Women Voters. Could Krystal have made up her mind to leave, and arranged it that fast?

Of course. Georgia knew Charlie Ross would come on short notice. And if there was anyone in Six Points more determined than Georgia, once she made up her mind, it had to be Krystal.

Georgia parked in front of the truck, blocking its path. That's when she noticed that the ReElect Mayor Lambert sign by the mailbox had been replaced by another sign. For Sale.

She looked up to see Krystal on the front porch, lifting a geranium basket off its hook.

Their eyes met.

Georgia knew she could fix this. All she had to do was throw herself on Krystal's mercy. Convince her the whole thing was a huge misunderstanding.

She got out of the car. "What the hell are you doing?" was the first thing out of her mouth. She didn't mean to sound so combative, but it was all too alarming, the moving truck, the For Sale sign.

Krystal turned and went inside, letting the screen door bang behind her.

All right, now who's playing games? Georgia hurried up the sidewalk, under the willow-rush archway, and barged through the door without knocking.

It was startling to see all the way down the shiny dogtrot hallway, long as a bowling alley, without a stick of furniture to stop the eye.

"Krystal?" Her voice echoed.

"Back here."

Two big moving men were wrestling a dresser out of the late Mr. Lambert's room. Georgia ducked around them and hurried back through the house.

In the kitchen, a chaos of boxes and wadded-up paper. Krystal was wrapping a cut-glass goblet in a sheet of blank newsprint. She had on her Saturday clothes, flannel men's work shirt and brown holey corduroy pants. She barely glanced up. "I wondered if you were gonna put in an appearance."

Georgia had practiced her speech on the way over. "Look, Krys. There's just one thing I want to tell you—"

"No, wait. You *always* get to talk first," Krystal said. "Then I'm stuck having to say whatever is left."

A bit bewildered by this accusation, Georgia chose not to respond.

"I'm leaving everything in order," Krystal said. "The city accounts are balanced to the penny. Everything that might need signing has been signed. I've written a formal letter to the city council. The personnel and tax forms are in a box on my desk. In case anyone asks."

"Krystal, you can't just leave," Georgia tried.

"Well, yes, as it turns out, I can," she said. "There's no law against resigning when you've had it up to here."

"Look, if this is because of what I did the other day—I just don't know how to even start telling you how sorry I am."

"Save it for somebody who gives a shit," Krystal said, not unpleasantly. "This time it's not about you, Georgia. Believe it or not, it is not...always...about *you*."

Okay, well, I deserve that, thought Georgia, for not being available when she tried to call me all night. But bringing in a moving van to make me feel bad is a hell of an overreaction! Sometimes Krystal can be such a brat.

I was only trying to save her from herself. But now was not the time for establishing the facts of the case. Now was the time for heartfelt apologies. Georgia tried again. "If you would just—"

Krystal cut her off. "I said *save it.*"

"Okay." Georgia folded her hands.

"Actually you did me a favor," said Krystal. "I didn't realize how stuck I'd gotten in this place. Suffocating. My sorry excuse for a life. And that stupid-ass job."

"Don't say that. You are a great mayor. I was just talking to Irma Winogrand about what a great job you've done."

"I always counted on you not to BS me." Krystal laid a goblet on its side and twisted paper around the bowl. "I've withdrawn from the race, and resigned to Larry Withers on behalf of the council. You really helped me see the truth. I don't need to put myself through all that crap just to lose to Madeline Roudy."

"You might win," Georgia said. "There's still more white people than black in this town, right?"

"Did you forget I annexed them?" Krystal said. "They have two hundred and eighty-three more registered voters than we do. You're looking at the last white mayor Six Points will ever have. And that's a good thing, I'm sure. They'll do a better job for their folks than any of us ever did."

"So you're just going to quit?" Georgia said. "Quit and run away? Honestly, that does surprise me. I never thought of you as a quitter."

"Oh stop it. You know that hokey stuff doesn't work on me." Krystal's eyes shone behind her glasses.

"Krystal, why did you bring back those presents?" Georgia couldn't help that her voice had gone soft and plaintive as a child's. "I gave those things to you. You're not supposed to give back presents just because you get mad at somebody."

"That's not how I meant it," said Krystal.

"Well, that's how it felt." Georgia wanted to say how beautiful it was that Krystal saved all those presents through the years, but she didn't.

"Just, I've got so much crap of my own," Krystal said. "I'll probably be in an apartment at first, I won't have room for half my stuff, much less Mother's . . . I've given away so much in the last two days."

Georgia said, "Please don't do this. I'll pay 'em to put your stuff back."

"Too late now," said Krystal. "You'd better let me go, George. I've got a lot to do and these guys are charging by the hour."

"Don't tell me you're gonna leave mad at me," Georgia cried. "Tell me what to do, tell me what you want me to say."

"Georgia. Please! I could never be mad at you. You just made me take off my rose-colored glasses, that's all. You saw what was what, all along."

"What the hell are you talking about?"

"It was never gonna happen," Krystal said. "I'm a slow learner, that's all."

Ah. Georgia got it. That was one conversation she did not want to have. It could never lead anywhere good. She didn't have those feelings for Krystal, and she never would. "That's not really the reason you're leaving."

Krystal didn't answer. She took a goblet from the shelf and rolled it in the paper.

Georgia said, "Where are you going, anyway?"

"Atlanta. Try my luck in the big city. I know a couple of women I can stay with till I find a place."

"What about the stuff on the truck?"

"All going to storage," said Krystal. "I'm traveling light this time."

"Krystal, you and I need to talk about this. Finish up here, then come to the house. I've got part of a cake, I'll make coffee. We'll talk. Okay? I've been so crazy lately I haven't even seen you."

Krystal let herself smile. "That sounds good. Okay."

"Just one thing I absolutely have to do first, then I'll be at the house waiting for you."

Krystal's face fell. "Oh, I see."

"See what?"

"Tell you what, Georgia, go on and run your very important errands. If I have time, I'll stop by on my way out of town."

"No. Don't do this. Now listen to me—Mama flipped out and spent the night in jail, it's a long story, all a big mistake but I've got to go get her out of there. Then I'm going straight home to wait for you, hear me? You promise you'll come!"

"Your mother's in *jail?* Georgia, what the hell are you doing talking to me? Go!"

"I thought you might leave without saying goodbye," Georgia said.

Krystal shook her head. "I wouldn't do that."

On her way out the door Georgia remembered the speech she had practiced. "Hey, I love you, Krystal. If that makes any difference."

Krystal didn't look around. She tucked the ends of the paper into the goblet. "I know," she said. "Me too."

19

The courthouse was a Greek Revival palace with huge Ionic columns and a gleaming white dome, built by the wealthy cotton planters who owned the county before the Civil War. Every time Georgia walked up the marble steps, she felt as though she was entering the seat of a much grander county. Amazing to think that in antebellum times Six Points was one of the richest towns in Alabama. Things had been going downhill ever since. The courthouse had not been improved, beyond a fresh coat of white paint on the dome every few years. The clock in the portico hadn't kept time since before Georgia was born.

The excited uproar of a school field trip echoed through the rotunda. Georgia climbed the staircase that curved up the wall. Kids thundered all over the second floor, peering into the glass cases at the same dusty Confederate flags that were on display when Georgia was a child.

She waved hi to the teacher, her old classmate Cindy Helms, and continued up the stairs to the jail. Some of the kids followed her with their eyes. No doubt they still liked to spook one another with stories of prisoners hanging themselves in the cells up there, ghostly images of their faces etched by lightning into the leaded windowpanes.

The third-floor landing opened onto a small lobby with plastic chairs for waiting, as at a dentist's office. In the security glass of the window, Georgia had a dim double vision of a man in uniform.

The speaker crackled. "Can I help you?"

Georgia stated her name and why she was here. The deputy walked his eyes up and down her body while deciding whether to help. She gave him a generous smile.

Soon the deputy was buzzing Nathan into the waiting room. He appeared to be undamaged, still wearing his shiny drapey polyester basketball clothes with the black windbreaker zipped up to his neck.

"Where's Mama?" said Georgia. Nathan shrugged.

She waved to get the attention of the man in the window.

The speaker crackled. "Yeah?"

"What about my mother?"

The deputy swiveled on his chair to talk to someone behind him. He leaned back to his microphone: "She's refusing to come out."

"What? Why?"

"She says she doesn't have a daughter. Her daughter is dead."

"The woman has dementia," Georgia said. "Can you please let me talk to her?"

"No civilians allowed in here. Hang on."

"Dayum," said Nathan, "that ol' lady is *pissed off* at you."

Georgia turned. "Would you please sit down and let me handle this?"

"Say she gone write you out of her will, leavin' us in here all night," Nathan said, and when he saw her face: "Well? That's what she say."

"When did you talk to her?"

"All night long," he said. "She don't ever shut up. Told me all about you—all the trouble you used to get in, you was my age."

Georgia was surprised the sheriff would put them together. Nathan said no, they were in cells facing across the hall. It was a small jail, he said.

"Smaller than the one in New Orleans?" Georgia watched for his reaction.

He started to answer, then cut his eyes at her. "What you think? I been in jail before?"

"Well, haven't you?"

"Just visiting," he said.

"Good. Glad to hear it," said Georgia. "Let's keep it that way."

"Uh-huh."

"But you have been arrested before," she said.

The slouch went out of Nathan's spine. Suddenly he stood about a foot taller. "What?"

"You heard me."

"How you know that? Mamaw told you that?"

"I didn't know for sure." Georgia smiled. "But you just confirmed it."

He narrowed his eyes. "Why you want to trick me for?" He scrunched his mouth into a narrow point and set it over on the side of his face—exactly the way Georgia did when she was vexed.

Until this moment she had never really felt it. She had known it in her head, but had never been physically touched by the idea that Nathan really was *her son.*

She covered her mouth. She had an almost violent urge to throw her arms around him. She realized she'd been with him for two days and had not touched him once.

He stared at her. "What?"

"Oh," she said, "oh God, oh Nathan I am sorry. You're right. I really don't want to trick you. Did they give you something to eat?"

"Yeah."

"I bet you're still hungry."

He nodded.

The door buzzed behind them. Here came Little Mama with a uniformed man leading her by the arm. She brushed his hand off, and turned to Georgia. "It's about goddamn time."

The man said, "Take care, Little Mama," and went back in the buzzing door.

Mama said, "Where the hell have you been?"

"Don't you start on me! Haven't I told you to leave that pellet gun in the closet?"

"I told them I didn't have any damn daughter, my daughter must surely be dead if she'd leave me to rot in this goddamn hell-hole all night."

"Hush your mouth with that cussing," said Georgia. "There's children downstairs that can hear you."

"I don't give a damn if Billy Graham is down there," said Little Mama. "I don't care if the goddamn Pope in Rome is down there—"

"Okay Mama," Georgia said loudly, "I get it."

The speaker made a staticky click. "Miss Georgia, I need you to sign by your name there, if you would please." The deputy slid out the steel drawer, with a clipboard. Georgia signed and put it back in the drawer with a friendly smile. The deputy grinned at her like a fool.

Georgia gathered her parolees and herded them down the stairs.

The schoolchildren were lined up double file along the wall, preparing to depart. They gawked at Nathan, the obvious prisoner in the group. One bratty-looking girl with straight-across bangs was really giving him the evil eye. Georgia fought the temptation to stick out her tongue.

Somehow Little Mama kept quiet until they were outside. Georgia was thinking how unfair it was that Mama never forgot anything you might actually want her to forget, like the fact that she'd spent the whole night in jail. Why couldn't *that* slip her mind?

Nathan slunk along in their wake, bobbing his head to the beat of unheard music, silently declaring that he was not associated with the quarreling old white ladies. He seemed to love it when Little Mama cussed. He snickered at every Goddamn and Bullshit. It blew Georgia's mind to think of the two of them talking all night. The boy must have gotten an earful. Good to see he was still amused by her.

The Honda was blazing hot in the noonday August sun. They groaned and complained even after she got the windows down, motor running, the A/C pumping out as much cool air as it could manage.

"There's too much whining in this car," Georgia said firmly. "I could use a little thanks from you two. You'd still be in there if it wasn't for me."

"I didn't do nothin' to get put in there in the first place," said Nathan.

"Me neither," said Little Mama.

"Mama! You slapped that deputy—twice!—and it was your stupid gun that shot the other one in the butt."

Nathan cackled.

"Don't you laugh, Nathan Blanchard. You'll be lucky if they let you off without a criminal record." In fact no charges had been brought against either of them. Georgia had confirmed that with the deputy before signing the paper.

"Aino Blanchit," said Nathan.

"What?"

He repeated it until she understood, *I ain't no Blanchard.*

Georgia tilted the mirror to see his face. "That was your daddy's name."

"That's what you say," said Nathan. "Ain't never seen him. He ain't never bothered to seen me."

"Well then, what is your name?"

"Nothin', I guess."

She smiled. "Nathan Nothin? Nice to meet you."

His expression was deeply serious. "I used to put Jordan, 'cause that's Mamaw's name." He pronounced it as Eugenia had: *Jerdin.* "But I ain't no Jordan neither."

"You can be Nathan Bottoms if you want," Georgia said.

He met her gaze in the rearview. "I don't think so."

Little Mama laughed. "Why would he want to use our name? He's got a perfectly good name of his own."

"Because," Georgia said.

She felt Nathan's eyes on the back of her neck. The correct answer was "Because he's my son, Mama," but she didn't feel like getting into that right now. She hoped Nathan would understand. Or at least keep his mouth shut about it.

"Nathan's going to have to spend another night with us, Mama. I'll put him in the blue room again. I really need you not to call the police."

"Why would I do that?"

"Beats me," said Georgia, "but you did. That's why the two of you spent the night in jail, remember?"

"I did nothing of the kind," Little Mama said. "Nathan is a good boy."

This announcement was as unexpected as Mama's declaration of love for the Supremes. Georgia glanced at the mirror to find Nathan smirking at her, mocking her look of surprise.

"Yeah, we big friends now," he said. "Ain't we, Mama?"

Georgia turned to look at Little Mama. "Is that so?"

Mama said yes, it was. They had a lot in common. Both liked LSU and hated Tennessee. Both liked cornbread made from white meal, not yellow, with no sugar. Both liked Clint Eastwood movies except the one with the monkey. It was amazing, Mama said, two strangers having so much in common.

"You're just trying to drive me crazy now," Georgia said.

"Nuh-uh," said Nathan. "Her and me *bonded* in there."

"She and I," Georgia said.

Considering Mama's tendency to say "nigger" at the first opportunity, it was hard to imagine their friendship could last. For now, though, this was better than having them hate each other. Mama's dementia was coming in handy after all. She was a little bit less like herself every day. Soon she would be a completely different person. Maybe Georgia would get along with her then.

At home, Georgia cooked up a big lunch of baked chicken, field peas, sliced tomatoes, pop-the-can biscuits with homemade fig preserves. Once Nathan got going on his eating, he had no further comment. Little Mama forgot how mad she had been, and scarfed down three of those biscuits.

While they ate, Georgia ran up to check her machine. No messages. She dialed Krystal to tell her to come on over.

Three rings, then a recording: "The number you have dialed is not in service at this time."

Krystal would come by. She promised.

Georgia didn't believe Krystal was really going to move away forever. Even if her stuff was already on the truck. Trucks can be turned around. Stuff can be put back where it was.

For a while there, it had seemed as though Georgia was headed for disaster on all fronts, but now she could dimly make out a way through this mess. First, convince Krystal to stay, or if need be let her go to Atlanta for a few weeks, get it out of her system, then come back. Next, feed Nathan a good supper and send him home tomorrow with a hug and no hard feelings. Then it was just a matter of simmering Mama down, dealing with the problem of the quilts, and putting her life back on schedule.

Her life.

Suddenly there was more to Georgia's life than just her. There was Nathan—and there was a new man for Saturday night.

Maybe not just for Saturday. That man would be just fine, come to think of it, for every night of the week.

The thought of her night with Brent had been bubbling up inside her all day like the most wonderful crisp champagne. A great night like last night lends a special color to the air of the following day.

Once she got Little Mama down for her nap, the phones unplugged and stashed in the cupboard (in case Mama got another urge to call the cops), and Nathan installed with a vast bowl of chips in front of *Celebrity Deathmatch*, Georgia headed out to the apartment to straighten up after Sheriff Bill.

She found his envelope tucked under the hurricane lamp. She folded the bills away in the pocket of her dress. So sweet of him to remember to leave a gift, amidst all that confusion.

She returned to the big house to clean her own room. She gathered the sheets from the floor and carried them out to the washer. She pressed her face into the sheets to breathe the last traces of Brent Colgate.

Once the washer was going, she filled a bucket with soap and hot water, and carried it back to her bedroom.

She turned on the clock radio—a Madonna dance tune, a thumping beat perfect for swabbing the floor. She mopped and danced, shaking her booty while getting the job done. The mop head swung back and forth, dragging a piece of paper from under the bed.

Bending down she saw it was not a piece of paper but an envelope.

A sealed white envelope with GEORGIA BOTTOMS hand-printed in small precise letters.

Her heart began beating faster. She didn't recognize the handwriting.

What the hell was this doing in her room?

The idea that it was somebody's gift she had accidentally brought back to the house, drop-kicked under the bed or something—that was impossible.

Georgia kept the books in her head. She knew to the penny how much money came in and went out. From each according to his ability to give, that was her pay scale, with adjustments if someone went through a rough patch and needed a discount, or a gift in return...

"Oh hush," Georgia said, and switched off the radio. She knew what was in that envelope: trouble.

She tore off the edge, and drew out a sheet of onionskin paper folded around some bills.

A hundred. A twenty. Three fives.

The message was printed in the same precise hand as the envelope.

> *Dear Georgia,*
> *Surprise!*
> *Bet you didn't expect to find this tucked under your pillow.*

Georgia's eyes raced down the page to the signature. Not a name. Just the inscription,

> *You Know Who*

She went back to the top.

> *By the time you read this letter, we will have spent the night together. A night of great passion, if what I've heard about you is true. I'm really looking forward to it. Deep in the night I will hold you in my arms, and tell you I believe we were meant for each other.*

That's just how it happened. About three o'clock in the morning, Brent woke her up to whisper those words in her ear. Georgia smiled, kissed him, drifted back to sleep.

Never dreaming she was sleeping in the arms of a snake.

> *Since my sister confided her troubles to me, and asked for my help, I've been looking forward to getting to know you. It took a lot of string pulling to get myself assigned to the church her husband had recently left—rather abruptly, as you will remember.*

My friends at the Ala. Baptist Convention were surprised I would request a move from one backwater to another, but finally they approved my request. And here we are!

My original plan was to get to know you, learn all about your evil ways, and expose you to the public for what you are.

When I saw you, I had to abandon my original plan.

You are an exceptionally beautiful woman, charming to a fault. I realized I could accomplish my goals in a way from which everyone would benefit.

Even you, if you play along.

Enclosed you will find $135. I believe that is your going rate, for men of the cloth anyway. I don't know what you charge others. Please accept it with my thanks. I'm sure you were worth every dime.

I have to warn you, though. This will be the only time I pay. From now on I will receive your services free of charge.

Just this once, I wanted to pay you, so you know that I KNOW.

I know about you, Georgia Bottoms.

I don't know all the names yet, but start with a certain Honorable Judge, and a certain MD who shall remain nameless (for now). And of course—my sister's husband. I know there are more. What a naughty, busy girl you have been!

If you follow these instructions exactly, your secret will be safe with me.

If not, you may find my sermons in the coming weeks especially relevant to you personally.

1. *Tell your other "men friends" you have retired from the profession, effective immediately.*
2. *Starting today, you will make yourself available to me <u>anytime I choose</u>, day or night. I will give you one hour's notice by telephone.*
3. *You will <u>tell no one</u> about this letter, or about us.*
4. *I expect to see you in church <u>every Sunday</u>. Listening attentively to the sermon.*

That is the way to heaven, Georgia. Not the path of flesh and the Devil, the path you have chosen.

Do not be angry with me. You knew in your heart you could not walk down this road forever. You knew one day a reckoning would come.

Today is that day.

Together we will find a new life for you—a better life.

You Know Who

P.S. This one's for Brenda

20

Georgia read the letter over and over, thinking she would see the word she had missed, one word that would reveal the whole thing to be some kind of gigantic joke.

She would never forget how sunlight streamed through the wavery glass of her bedroom window. Sparkles of dust danced like tiny diamonds in a column of light. It was a moment of uncanny beauty, little jewels floating and sparkling, here in the middle of the room on this day. In a weird way it made Georgia feel grateful to still be alive.

She knew something drastic had just happened, the equation of her life changed forever. As if she had been in a terrible accident but by some miracle survived. Screeching tires, the airless moment before impact, the smash of metal on metal—all that was over. She was alive. Still breathing. She had no idea how badly she was hurt because it was too soon, she hadn't even crawled out of the wreck.

She folded the bills in the crease of the paper, and slid it back into the envelope. She sat awhile on the edge of the bed, holding the envelope.

Then she finished mopping the floor. She did not turn on the radio.

She went to her bathroom, poured the mop water in the toilet, flushed it, sprayed lemon-scented cleanser, and got down on her knees to scrub the toilet with the brush. Without knowing she was going to, she burst into tears.

She clung bawling to the side of the tub until she was able to stop.

She sat on her knees for a while, collecting herself. Then she washed out the tub, aiming the spray of the showerhead around the shower to hose off the soap.

She splashed her face with water, and blotted it on one of her fancy guest towels.

Georgia knew she was weeping for the sudden death of the crush. That was the truth. If that made her an awful, shallow woman, so be it *amen.*

The worst pain was not that her secret had been discovered, or that Georgia the trickster had been tricked. The worst was knowing she would never be in love with Brent Colgate, and he was never in love with her. She had thrilled at the allover feeling, the breathless, light-headed giddiness. It had been a long time since she'd walked around on a cushion of lighter-than-air.

Now she knew there had never been anything real about it, not one moment. When she was snuggling into the soft blond fur on his chest, breathing his scent of sweat and Old Spice, dreaming of their future together, he had already written the letter.

He knew all about Eugene from Brenda. He found out about Ted the night he ran into Georgia outside the emergency room. But how did he know about the "Honorable Judge"? Last night must not have been his first time hiding in the bushes, spying on her. What else did he know?

Georgia's mind whirled, going back over every encounter they'd ever had since the first time, getting out of his K car in the courthouse square. Now all those seemingly random encounters felt tainted. The night in the hospital parking lot—maybe he wasn't there visiting parishioners, as he'd claimed. Maybe he was following Georgia.

A shiver ran up her spine. For a person who lived a secret life, she had never spent much time looking over her shoulder.

The sensible thing, her first reaction, was to go along with his instructions. How hard would it be?

Think of it as a business proposal.

Number one, tell the other men you're out of business. Well okay, she could do that—or pretend to, until she figured out some way to get rid of Brent. Then she could pick up where she left off.

Item three was easy. To "tell no one" was Georgia's natural inclination in all things, anyway. As for number four, she'd been going to church every Sunday her whole life without any reminders from him.

The sticking point was item number two: make yourself available to him anytime, day or night. Be his slave. His drop-in girl. Always on call. At a 100 percent discount.

Just think—before the mop dragged that envelope out into the daylight, Georgia would have been delighted to give herself completely to Brent Colgate. She'd been trying to think of ways to make herself available to him.

Now the idea of being touched by him, or touching him,

seemed worse than anything she'd ever done in the pursuit of her career.

Worse than sleeping with Rev. Onus L. Satterfield for the money, while doing it with his son Billy for fun.

Worse than enduring Sheriff Bill's grunts and silence, Judge Barnett's garlic breezes, Ted Horn's peccadilloes, Jimmy Lee Newton's casual slaps on the ass.

Through the years Georgia had become very good at doing whatever she had to do. Oh yes. She had learned to grit her teeth, close her eyes, and get through it. She was a strong woman with powerful skills of denial and repression.

Perhaps she could entertain herself with the sight of Brent's pretty face. After a while she might even come to enjoy it, and almost forget he ever wrote that letter.

Georgia heard a car come into the yard. Her first thought was, *He's come back for his first installment.* Panic fluttered up in her heart.

She stole to the French doors, back pressed to the wall. From this angle she could see all the way to the end of the driveway.

A forest-green Subaru wagon, the most practical car in Six Points. GRRL MYR.

Krystal climbed slowly out of the driver's seat, peering up at the house. She had changed into a blue work shirt and jeans. Her hair was wet from the shower.

Georgia's heart was still pounding, residual panic. She wondered how she could possibly summon the strength to talk Krystal out of leaving.

She threw open the window. "Hey, you."

Krystal craned her head around to locate her. "Hey."

"Come on up."

Krystal considered. "Listen, George, I really need to hit the road. I'm driving all the way to Atlanta. I was just going to call you, but they switched off my phone."

"Come in for a minute. I made coffee."

Krystal shook her head. "Thanks, I don't want any long goodbyes."

"Me neither," said Georgia. "At least let me come down and give you a hug."

"Now you're the one who wants a hug." Krystal sighed. "Can't we just do this nice and clean? I know you don't want me to go. I don't either, but I have to."

"But why?"

Krystal hesitated.

"Stay right there," Georgia said. "I'm coming."

She hurried downstairs. She knew what to do: coax Krystal into the kitchen, pour her coffee (black, two sugars), introduce her to Nathan ("Krystal, this is my black son"), then turn on all her powers of friendship and seduction to convince Krystal that no other place was as good as right here, no friend on earth as reliable as Georgia, no lights in any big city shining as warmly as the lights of Six Points.

By the time she got outside Krystal was in the Subaru with the motor running.

"Wait," Georgia said, "there's some things I have to tell you."

"I'll call when I get there." Krystal adjusted the outside mirror. Her eyes came up to Georgia's. "You look great, Georgia. You always look great. I hate you."

"No you don't," Georgia said.

"No I don't," Krystal said. "I'll call you." Her window went up.

"Wait!" said Georgia.

Krystal backed down the drive.

Georgia had the feeling something between them was over. She thought, is it a love affair if only one of the two people knows about it?

Late sunlight glazed the windshield of the Subaru. Krystal disappeared in a rectangle of dazzling light.

The car paused a moment in the street, then pulled away.

Georgia let out the breath she'd been holding.

She stood there in the driveway for five minutes, or an hour. She lost track.

Suddenly Nathan was on the porch. "Ol' Mama done lost it again! Act like she never seen me before! Say nigger get out of my house, and all that!"

"Aw damn it to hell!" Georgia cried. "I'm sorry, Nathan. In case you haven't noticed, Little Mama's got a serious problem upstairs."

"Well come in here and do something!"

"You stay out here and let her cool down," Georgia said. "In five minutes she'll forget all about it."

Nathan said, "She got like the, what they call it, the Allhammer disease?"

"Well...yeah. More or less."

He followed her around to the backyard. "I don't think that's all that's wrong with her. I think she's crazy on top of that."

"That's not exactly breaking news to me," Georgia said. "Don't forget I've known her all my life. If you wonder why I didn't tell her about you, now you know."

They stepped up to the washing-machine porch. Nathan peered down at her. "She don't like black people?"

"Not in the least. Are you just now discovering that?" Georgia led him into the kitchen. "Whatever you do, don't get her started on Rosa Parks."

His face went blank. "Who?"

"Rosa Parks."

He shook his head.

"You never heard of Rosa Parks?" Georgia couldn't believe it. What did they learn in school?

"You ain't tell anybody about me, when you had me, did you," Nathan said.

She'd figured this was coming but still it caught her off guard. "Not really, no. Mama knew I went off to have a baby. She didn't know what color you were."

"You never even want to come down and see what I look like?" he said.

"I sent money, Nathan. Every month, all these years since you were born. That's what I did. It's the best I could do at the time. I thought it might be easier for you if I stayed out of your life."

He stood with his back to the wall. "Easy for *you,* you mean."

"Well—"

"You didn't want me," he said. "Go on and say it."

"I guess that's one way to look at it," she admitted. "Hey listen, you must be starving. I'm going to heat up some Mexican Fiesta Chicken and a blackberry cobbler. I can make you a couple sandwiches until it's ready."

"You think if you stick food in my mouth it'll shut me up."

"Well?" She grinned. "It worked real well yesterday."

He wasn't smiling. "How come you didn't want me?"

"Nathan, please," she said.

"You think you ain't got to answer? You think it's ah-ight just to go off and leave somebody, and never even have to say why?"

"I was eighteen, okay? Younger than you are now. And your father was black. It was a different time."

"You coulda married him."

"He didn't want me," said Georgia. "And I didn't want him either. It would never have worked out."

"You didn't want anybody, did you," said Nathan. "Him or me."

"No, I didn't," said Georgia. "You're right. I like being single. I'm selfish. I like to do what I want without somebody pulling on me all the time. Nathan, listen to me—I honestly thought you'd be better off with your aunt Ree."

"Better off than here in this big-ass house, with all yo fuckin' money?" said Nathan. "Okay okay, sorry, I didn't mean to say that."

At least he was hearing her injunctions. "I told you, I haven't got any money."

Nathan said, "You got a hell of a lot more than Mamaw. You know what I'm sayin'. You didn't want me 'cause I'm black."

Georgia didn't know what to do. As a last resort she told the truth. "That's not it. I would have given you away no matter what. I just didn't want a kid."

His face fell. He didn't appear to have considered this possibility.

Georgia shrugged. "I don't know what you want from me, Nathan. I've had a hard day."

"It's too late for what I want," he said.

The barrel of a gun poked through from the hallway, followed by Little Mama. "You still got that nigger with you?"

Damn it! Georgia had meant to hide the Daisy gun after she locked up the phones.

Nathan ducked under the table.

Georgia snatched the gun, broke it open. "Nathan, she's just trying to scare you." She showed him the empty chamber. "Mama, stop pestering this boy. I have told you fifty times, he's our guest. He's spending the night with us."

"Not in my house he ain't," said Little Mama.

"Hell yes in your house, it's my damn house too," Georgia said, "and if you don't like it, go find somewhere else to sleep."

"What makes you so partial to this ni—"

"Stop it! Do not say that word again!"

"To this *Nigro* is what I was gonna say, thank you very much, Missy Jean!"

Georgia put her hands on her hips. "Mama. Nathan is my son. Okay? There. Are you happy?"

Nathan gawked at her.

Little Mama said, "Don't be ridiculous. How could he be your son? He's colored!"

Georgia said, "So was his daddy."

Mama frowned. You could see the wheels turning. "You give me back that gun," she said. "You're the one I need to shoot."

Georgia exploded. "I've had enough, do you hear? This boy has not done one thing to you! The two of you were best friends when I got you out of jail! Should have left you in there."

Nathan held the smirk at the corner of his mouth. He liked Georgia going at her mother, guns blazing. Or maybe he liked the sound of Georgia finally admitting who he was.

"Well!" Little Mama huffed. "I think I'll go where I will be treated with a little bit of respect!"

"I wish you would," Georgia said. "If you can find a place like that, which I sincerely doubt, I wish you'd go right on over there. I'll be glad to drive you."

"You telling me to leave my own home?"

"If you can't keep a civil tongue in your head, I don't care where you go. Nathan, sit down. You're as welcome in this house as she is. I've got the gun now. Nobody's shooting anybody."

Little Mama stormed to her room. Georgia went to the chest freezer to fetch the Mexican Fiesta Chicken. She put it to warm in a slow oven, then went to hide the pellet gun where it would never be found. (It may still be there.) When she came back, Nathan was in the TV den watching *Who Wants to Be a Millionaire?*

He said, "Don't leave me alone with her again."

"I'm sorry. I thought we were okay. Y'all were such big buddies before. She won't find that gun where I put it."

"She like two different people," he said.

"At least. Did you ever see—no, you wouldn't know *Sybil*."

The phone rang. Georgia hurried upstairs to the answering machine, her heart jumping for joy—then the bitter memory flooded in. Oh, right. We don't love Brent Colgate anymore. We hate him, remember?

Anyway it wasn't him. It was Alma Pickett, calling for—the fourth time? The fifth? You'd think the quilts had all spontaneously caught fire and burned their owners to death. Georgia let Alma tell it to the machine, yak yak, on and on. She had no intention of speaking with Alma Pickett about the quilts, now or at any time in the future. Alma was welcome to think whatever she liked about what she saw on public television. There was nothing illegal or even unethical about reselling a quilt at a better price. Hadn't Alma been making a pretty profit herself all along?

Anyway, those ladies got a very nice quilt for their money. The quilt makers of Catfish Bend were famous now. Those quilts probably quadrupled in value the minute that documentary went on the air.

21

Mama and Nathan were still snoring in their rooms long after Georgia got up and drank coffee, scanned the Sunday *Light-Pilot*, made a pot of grits, rolled and cut a sheet of biscuits for the boy's breakfast. (She would wait to cook the bacon because she knew the smell would wake him.) She was trying to decide about church. Of course she had to go, God knows what kind of sermon *that monster* might preach if she didn't go. But she couldn't leave Nathan at home with Little Mama. She couldn't force Little Mama to go to church with her. She didn't want to take Nathan to church and have to explain him. Maybe he could wait in the car—no, it was the height of August, too hot for that. If only there was someplace she could drop him for an hour . . .

She thought of the video arcade on the courthouse square. It seemed to be always open. She could give him the roll of quarters she kept in her car for parking meters. If Nathan was like most boys, an hour of beeping, buzzing, smacking buttons would be heaven. She could run to church, then hurry him to the Texaco station for the one fifteen bus.

Problem solved. Georgia was glad she had awakened in an optimistic mood. Last night, trying to fall asleep, she found herself entertaining some pretty dark notions.

She actually considered, for the first time ever, what it might be like to gather a bunch of Mama's pills and swallow them all.

She turned that idea over in her mind for a few moments before deciding she just didn't have it in her. All these responsibilities...Besides, she was curious. She wanted to know what would happen tomorrow, and the day after that.

She thought a bit longer and more seriously about another kind of death. Somebody else's death. The kind where if you're caught, you go not to the nice jail at the courthouse, but to Julia Tutwiler Prison for Women for the rest of your life.

It seemed to Georgia that if a man sets off dynamite under somebody's life, he deserves to get hurt in the explosion.

Georgia thought she could kill someone. If she had to. If it came down to kill or be killed. But she was pretty sure she could not plan and commit a murder and get away with it. She would make some fatal mistake, overlook some detail. Or she'd crack under the first line of questioning and confess everything.

One thing for sure: if Brent Colgate happened to get hit by a truck, Georgia would drink a toast to the truck driver.

Turning, tossing, she wished she'd taken one of the sleeping pills she'd given Little Mama. She pictured Brent now in the parsonage on Maple Street, dozing next to Daphne, congratulating himself on his ingenuity.

To Georgia, Brent Colgate seemed like a pretty good argument against the existence of God. A real God would take care of someone like Georgia, who had maybe a few moral blemishes but was basically a good person, never intentionally harmed a soul. A real God would not let a man use his good looks and God's word and God's pulpit to go around playing God in someone's life.

Today, in the brightness of a Sunday morning, things didn't seem quite as drastic as they had last night. She had drifted to sleep full of outrage, determined to find the strength to tell Brent Colgate where to stuff his list of instructions.

In the morning, she found herself slipping back into self-preservation mode.

Perhaps she could do what he demanded, after all.

If she did, Brent would let her carry on with her life. Her reputation would not be destroyed. She would not have to go around town hiding her face in shame. She would simply be adding one more layer of secrecy to all the other layers.

She heard Whizzy scratching at the door. Why didn't he come in the doggy door? She pushed it open. "Come on in, Whiz."

Very softly a voice said, "You alone?"

Georgia fell back with a little scream.

A thin man with close-cropped hair stood in the shadow of the deep freeze. "Georgie?"

"Brother?" Oh my God.

"Hey hey!" He shuffled into the light, trying to put his arms around her. He smelled as though he hadn't bathed in a week.

"Don't!" She pushed him away. "You scared the bejesus out of me! What are you doing here?"

"I got out," Brother said.

"How in the hell...? Your parole hearing is not for six weeks."

Whizzy charged out of the kitchen, barking and licking Brother's ankles. Brother was bone thin, shaven-headed, so hard-looking and muscled that Georgia could have passed him on the street and not recognized him. The only thing familiar was that big gorgeous ear-to-ear grin, wide and shiny as an ear of sweet corn. He wore a fluorescent orange jumpsuit with a ripped-out square on the back.

He knelt down to pet Whizzy. "They put me in this work gang," he said, "and yesterday they had us weed-eatin' along I-65. By the Stuckey's at the Letohatchee exit, you know where that is? All a sudden this eighteen-wheeler runs over this little car, I mean just totally *creams* this poor little Hyundai or whatever it was. *Long* smear down the shoulder. So while everybody was having a good look at that, I walked up to Stuckey's. Met this girl who give me a ride to Montgomery. Cute girl. Then I called Sims Bailey to come get me. And here I am!"

"Glory hallelujah," she said.

"You look good, Georgie. Do I smell coffee?"

Brother was the last thing Georgia needed right now, but what could she do? She let him in.

He towered over the kitchen table in his jumpsuit. "Sit down," she said, pouring him a cup. "You're making me nervous."

He obeyed, with an eye on the stove. "Are you planning to bake them biscuits?"

"You're not supposed to escape, Brother."

"Well, duh," he said. "Think I don't know that?"

She started clattering pans. "You said you had a good shot at parole."

"I was bullshitting. They were never gonna let me out."

Georgia opened the oven to a faceful of heat. She ducked her head, slid in the biscuits, banged the door shut. Did Brother expect she'd be happy to see him? Did he think he could walk out of prison and come home and everything would be fine?

"Your timing is lousy," she said. "As usual."

"Sorry, Sis. When opportunity knocks... If you'd seen the

way that car got demolished, you would never ride in a little car again. You got a cigarette by any chance?"

Georgia kept a pack of Marlboros in the seven-drawer high-boy, but she was not about to tell him. "You can't stay here, you know that. What about Mama and me? You want to get us arrested?"

"Yeah right," he said. "'Cause I stopped by for a cup of coffee?"

"Well they could," Georgia said. "We'd be accessories, or whatever. Aiding and abetting."

They bickered awhile, their preferred method of communication since childhood. Brother said he planned to stay only a day or two, grab a shower, sleep, get some grub. Then hit the road for some quiet place he could wait out the heat. Georgia asked where that might be. He wasn't sure. He hadn't expected to escape, so he was taking it one day at a time. Probably somewhere out West.

The hall door swung open. Georgia was surprised to see Nathan not only awake and dressed, but all dressed up: white dress shirt, striped tie neatly knotted, navy slacks, shiny go-to-church shoes. All from one backpack? Georgia had assumed he'd brought only basketball clothes.

She had underrated Eugenia Jordan. Any young man who dresses for church without being asked has been very well raised.

Nathan and Brother eyed each other like members of different species. Brother said, "Who the hell are you?"

"That's Nathan." Georgia got bacon from the fridge. "Nathan, say hello to my brother the escaped convict."

Brother put out his hand. Nathan shook, formally.

"Who the hell is he?" said Brother.

Georgia said, "He's my son." There. Now she had said it twice. It was a little easier the second time.

Brother laughed. "No shit? You got a son—and he's black? That's not just funny, that's high-*larious*. What did Mama have to say?"

"I don't think it's really sunk in on her yet."

"When the hell did you have a kid?"

"The summer after graduation." Georgia draped the bacon in the skillet. "Remember I went to stay with that cousin in North Carolina?"

"No," Brother said.

She shook her head. "You were always so oblivious."

Brother turned and stuck out his hand, with a wall-to-wall grin. "Let me shake your hand again, Nathan. Welcome to the family. God help you."

Right away Nathan liked Brother, Georgia could tell. Another good reason not to leave the boy home while she went to church. Brother had never been a positive influence on anybody.

While they ate breakfast, Georgia went to stand in front of her closet. She was trying to work up her nerve to wear the red summer dress from the big Belk's in Mobile, with the scoop neck and sexy low back. It was a little red dress, bright red, far too revealing for church, which is why she wanted to wear it. She was thinking of the scene near the end when Rhett tells Scarlett that all her friends know she's been shamelessly throwing herself at Ashley's head. He forces her to wear the shocking red dress to Melly's party, so everyone will see her for the whore she is.

And wear it she does. Defiantly, beautifully. In the end Scarlett gets the better of Rhett because she looks so damn great in that dress.

Georgia wanted Brent Colgate to see her. To see that she was not afraid of him. See his threats and call him, raise him … She should wear the red dress to show him he could never own her completely.

But standing at the closet, it occurred to her: What if he's never seen *Gone with the Wind*? Seems impossible but you never know. If he hasn't seen it, the red dress would be lost on him.

She twirled this way and that in the mirror.

It was the perfect shade of red with her coloration. Made her hair even blonder. It was not a dress for church but it made Georgia look fantastic.

She pulled off the red dress, and tried on the simple navy-striped twill dress from Belk's.

She checked the mirror. Very attractive. She draped a string of pearls around her neck.

The red dress carried a message Brent might misunderstand. The navy stripe carried no message.

Perhaps it was better not to push her luck. Anyway, she looked damn good in the navy twill.

She went downstairs. "Okay, Brother, you can stay here while I go to church, but do not show your face outside this house, hear? Don't call Sims Bailey, don't call anybody. Just look after Mama till I get back. Promise me."

He promised. She knew exactly how much his promise was worth. But hey, it was his hide on the line. If he got rearrested, so what? Georgia had other concerns. She would say she didn't know he'd come home. They couldn't charge her with being an accessory if she didn't know he was there.

Nathan folded his napkin and stood. Georgia was touched that he woke up assuming she'd be going to church, and he'd be going with her. Walking to the car she said, "Nathan, it's sweet of you to offer, but you don't have to go to church with me. There's a video arcade downtown. You want to hang out there and I'll come pick you up when it's over?"

He shook his head. "It's ah-ight. I go with Mamaw every Sunday."

She slid into the driver's seat. "I don't know if you're going to be comfortable. You'd be the only black person in this church."

He thought about it. "You don't want me to go?"

"That's not what I said," she said—trapped! "You're welcome to go. I just thought it might be more entertaining for you to play video games."

Nathan fastened his seat belt. "I ain't never play them things."

"I've got plenty of quarters, if you want to try," Georgia said hopefully.

"Nah, I'll go to church with you." What he said was "choich." And though Georgia winced inside, she thought, yes, you may go to choich with me, Nathan. And if anyone asks about you—well, I'll think of something.

"I knew what I was getting into," Nathan said. "Mamaw say you the kind that never misses a Sunday."

"Well isn't that nice!" Georgia said. "I'm glad she thinks of me that way."

Six Points people are nosy but maybe their Southern manners would kick in, maybe they would be too startled by the sight of a black boy at the First Baptist to ask any questions. That gave Georgia something to pray for, anyway.

She drove the long way around to keep from passing Krystal's house. She couldn't bear to see that For Sale sign again.

The First Baptist parking lot overflowed. Apparently every sinner in town had decided this was the day to renew his fellowship with the Lord. Or maybe it was the growing star power of Brent Colgate, Studly Pastor, that was filling the parking lot, packing the pews. Georgia drove to the far end of the lot thinking surely there would be one open space, but at last she gave up and went to park along Sycamore Street.

When Nathan got a look at all the white people flocking toward the church, he said, "Is it gonna embarrass you, if I go in there with you?"

There it was, the $64,000 question.

Georgia lied in her most cheerful voice. "Not at all. Thank you for asking, though. Let's go in."

For the first thirty years of her life Georgia always walked up these steps in the company of Little Mama. (Daddy, the unbeliever, slept in.) When Little Mama quit coming, Georgia came by herself. It felt distinctly strange to walk up the steps with this lanky black boy at her side.

She said hello to Steve and Mary Lou Osman. "Hey Georgia, oh my gosh what a pretty outfit!" said Mary Lou. "Love the pearls. And who have we here?"

Count on Mary Lou to just blurt out the question. She always said exactly what was on her mind.

"I'm Nathan." He put out his hand. He shook Mary Lou's hand, then Steve's. They smiled at his formality.

Mary Lou said, "What a nice polite young man."

"He's my son," Georgia said.

Mary Lou blinked. "Why, he looks just like you!"

Nathan burst out laughing, a little too loudly. Georgia said, "Thank you!" and kept moving. She was grateful to Mary Lou for setting a positive tone, now just get in the church with a minimum of fuss. She felt lots of eyes on her, mostly male—but weren't there always eyes on her? She was attractive and took care with her appearance. Why wouldn't they look? Especially since she'd brought an African American for show-and-tell!

She waved howdy to Jimmy Lee Newton, Sandie Winkler, George Thomas, Emma Day Pettigrew and her husband, Floyd—she couldn't decide who among them did the biggest double take.

Veering in at a forty-five-degree angle was Myna Louise Myrick, who had left that unpleasant quilt message on Georgia's answering machine. Georgia maneuvered Nathan to the left of the steps, deftly putting the crowd between Myna Louise and herself.

They stepped out of the bright hot dazzle of a south Alabama morning into the cave of the vestibule. It took a few blinks to see anything.

What Georgia saw was people sitting in her pew.

She counted pews to be sure she wasn't imagining it. Fourth pew on the left. They must be strangers. Everyone in this church knew that had been Georgia's spot her whole life.

From the back she didn't recognize them—then she caught sight of the woman's plump neck. She would have known those pink folds of skin anywhere: Brenda Hendrix.

And beside her—yes indeed, the man himself! Eugene!

He was thinner now, and pale. He had lost the front half of his hair.

And look! The four lovely daughters! Not so lovely anymore. The older two were getting fat, their hereditary tendency to piggishness overwhelming their former adorability. The younger two were still cute but headed for the same fate: you could see it in the snugness of their pinafores. This gave Georgia a kind of pleasure she knew was not right.

The Hendrixes were taking up all of Georgia's pew except for a small space at the end. She was not about to sit with them.

Eugene and Brenda hadn't shown their faces in this town in four years, and just by coincidence they showed up today, to plop down in Georgia's spot?

Impossible. This did not happen by accident.

Georgia noticed that the pew behind them was open.

She put Nathan on the inside and took the aisle seat, just behind Brenda, Eugene, and the daughters. As she settled into her seat, the biggest daughter leaned over to her mother. "Can we go outside now? You said."

Brenda Hendrix said, "Okay but just you and Kaitlyn." The two fat ones got up and squeezed past their mother's knees, into the aisle. The younger girls began whining, and kept it up until their mother gave in and let them go too.

Turning to follow their departure, Brenda came face-to-face with Georgia.

Brenda looked startled. Then she smiled, a satisfied little smile, and nudged her husband. Eugene turned.

When he saw Georgia, his face registered no expression— perhaps because his wife was watching him, ready to pounce.

Eugene stared at Georgia with nothing at all in his eyes. Then he tilted his head and whispered something to Brenda.

This was a setup. The Hendrixes had come to town today to sit in Georgia's pew and show her who won. They were part of the lesson Brent Colgate had come to teach her.

Georgia's heart sank. That hateful smile of victory on Brenda's face told her everything. It didn't matter whether Georgia followed the instructions in Brent's letter or not. He wanted to humiliate her anyway.

Brent and Brenda. Cute names for brother and sister. Georgia didn't remember Eugene mentioning a brother-in-law who was also a preacher, though she had known vaguely that Brenda came from a family of ministers. To look at Brent and Brenda, you would never guess they were related—the piggy pink woman and the handsome blond man—and here came Reverend Wonderful now, in a fancy new robe, trimmed with white racing stripes.

Brent embraced his way from the back of the sanctuary, handing out hugs to the adoring fans clustered along the center aisle. "Good morning!" he exclaimed. "Hello, Betty! Oh hey there, Cathy, how you, praise the Lord!"

A few rows away, he caught sight of Georgia. He smiled and gave a friendly eye squint, not quite a wink.

So handsome. Looking at him, it was hard to remember how evil he was.

Georgia turned to find Nathan already slumped in the pew, chin nearly resting on his chest. His eyes were open but he looked asleep. She nudged him.

"What," he groaned.

"You awake?"

"Is it always this hot in here?"

Georgia liked him more every minute. "Yes. Can you believe it? Once they had a motion to get A/C but they *voted it down!* Have you ever heard anything so stupid?"

She made sure to be talking to him when the Reverend Colgate drew abreast of their row. She did not give him the satisfaction of turning her head. She could feel his eyes on her back.

"Hello Sister," he boomed, reaching over with both hands to shake Brenda's hand. "Hello Brother," clapping Eugene on the shoulder. "So happy y'all could join us."

He turned to Georgia. "Why Miss Georgia!" he exclaimed, as if he'd just noticed her. "Don't you look lovely today."

Brenda sniggered out loud.

Georgia returned his gaze without blinking. She didn't speak. She didn't smile.

Brent broke the stare first. He turned his back, and headed to the pulpit. Georgia had no doubt he had heard her silence.

She was thinking, *I don't know if I can do this.* Not today's ordeal—she could grit her teeth and get through it, church only lasted an hour—but the idea of week after month after year, sitting here in this pew enduring whatever silent torture Brent chose to hand out.

"Hello friends and good morning," he said in that thrilling rumble, "is it not a wonderful morning to be alive on God's earth? Let us raise up our voices in praise!" He motioned to Ava Jean McCall at the organ. "Everyone open your hymnals to page one ninety-seven, 'Though Your Sins Be as Scarlet.'"

Georgia gave thanks she hadn't worn the red dress.

Ava Jean played a brief introduction. A thin wavery howl arose from the congregation.

> *Though your sins be as scarlet,*
> *They shall be as white as snow*

Georgia mouthed the words. Brenda turned her head to cast a little smirk at her.

He'll forgive your transgressions,
And remember them no more

"Hear the word of the Lord, Jeremiah 13:27," the reverend intoned. " 'I have seen your adulteries, and your lustful neighings... the lewdness of your harlotry, your abominations on the hills and in the fields. Woe to you, O Jerusalem! Will you still not be made clean?' "

Georgia saw people shifting in their pews. The First Baptist congregation was not used to that much naughty talk on Sunday morning. Nothing in Brent's previous sermons had prepared them for this ringing assault on fornication, employing all the bad words in the Bible.

"Jeremiah is angry," Brent said. "Angry at the people of Jerusalem. He excoriates them for the degeneracy of their lifestyle choices. Imagine if he came back to earth today! If he landed in Las Vegas and saw that the biggest shrines in America are monuments to gambling, sinning, greed, sexual excess. Imagine if Jeremiah came to earth in San Francisco, and saw the man holding hands with the man—*unashamed!*—in the public square. Or if Jeremiah came *here,* my friends—imagine he came to Six Points today, expecting to find good Christian people of Alabama, and finding instead a town riddled with harlots, and wastrels, adulterers, pretenders who live among us in complete hypocrisy—coming to church week after week posing as pillars of the community..."

Georgia remembered Eugene wincing at his wife for saying "pillow" instead of "pillar"...

"...all while committing the most grievous, the most cunning forms of sin and debauchery seen on earth since the Caesars of Rome."

The last time a sermon went this far off the tracks, Georgia fainted to put an end to it. She didn't think that would work this time.

"... as if they are the very salt of the earth, instead of devils in a lovely disguise. As the Lord tells us in Deuteronomy, 'Thou shalt not bring the hire of a whore, or the price of a dog, into the house of the Lord thy God for any vow: for even both these are abomination unto the Lord thy God.'"

Georgia realized what she had to do.

At first she didn't think she could do it. It seemed like an over-reaction. Wouldn't it be easier to sit here and pretend the sermon was not about her? That Brent Colgate had not just called her a whore, and a dog?

He could do this from now on, every Sunday, without end. As long as he was in this pulpit.

Brenda Hendrix beamed up at him with a beatific expression, as if he were preaching about kittens.

The sound of his voice faded to a droning rumble. Georgia gazed at the stained-glass medallion above the altar, glowing luxuriant deep shades of blue, ruby, and gold. Whenever it got too hot in here, Georgia liked to focus on the deep blue panes, imagine a swimming pool that color, and picture herself diving in.

Now, though, she was unable to summon any scene that peaceful. Her life had been turned upside down by one man. He had her under his thumb. He could play with her anytime he liked. And there was nothing Georgia could do about it.

Or so he believed.

There was one way.

It was scary as hell.

It was like burning down a house to get rid of the termites:

267

you wouldn't have a house anymore, but you would know for certain the termites were exterminated.

You had to really believe you had nothing to lose. Georgia was surprised to find she was already there.

She touched Nathan's knee. "Go out to the car and wait for me," she said. "Please don't ask—just do it right now."

It took Nathan only a moment to see she was serious. He frowned, a question in his eyes.

She nodded. "I'll be right out, I promise."

Every eye from the fifth row back watched the black boy stand up and edge out of the row, to the vestibule.

Reverend Colgate held up his arms. He had the wingspan of a buzzard. He asked everyone to turn to the hymn on page fifty-nine. " 'If We Confess Our Sins,' " he announced.

Georgia looked to make sure Nathan was gone. She stood up in her pew. "I want to confess," she announced, in a voice no one could fail to hear.

A gasp all around. A squeak of benches as certain men shifted their weight. The ardent admirers of Brent Colgate looked confused.

Brent waved his hand for Ava Jean to play. She ignored him, transfixed by the sight of Georgia coming up the aisle toward the pulpit.

A hush fell over the room.

"Miss Georgia," Brent said with a desperate smile. "Are you all right?"

"I want to confess everything," she said. "Didn't you just say confession is good for the soul?"

"Yes, but—why don't we—" He waved vaguely toward the back of the church.

"Oh no, you're not going to shut me up." From her purse Georgia brought forth a cylinder of bills. She snapped off the rubber band and peeled off a hundred, a twenty, three fives. She counted them out on the open pages of Brent Colgate's Bible.

"There's your money back, Brent," she said. "Y'all, I slept with this man, and he tried to pay me for it. Apparently he didn't realize it was on the house. That's me he was preaching about in his sermon."

At least she had wiped that dopey smile off his face. He'd assumed Georgia had everything to lose, when in fact she was fully prepared to throw it all away.

His bemusement faded into transparent rage. He only stayed lost for words for a moment. The wheels behind his eyes began spinning, calculating a counterattack.

"Though your sins be as scarlet," he said, "they shall be as white as snow. The devil is working his will through you, Georgia. He's working inside you right now."

"Everybody here knows me," said Georgia. "They've known me all my life. They know I'm not a bad person."

She turned to the congregation.

A few people smiled, embarrassed, and looked down. No one said a word.

That's what a lifetime of faithful attendance gets you, she thought.

The smartest man in the room appeared to be Jimmy Lee Newton, who got up and rushed out the door, on the right side at the rear. The other men were hemmed in toward the front. There was Ted Horn, his face dangerously crimson. Judge Jackson Barnett and Sheriff Bill, trying to blend in with the wood grain of the pews. Lonnie Chapman chewing on his lip.

With fear in their eyes, they all begged her to keep their secret. Not one of them rose to defend her. Was that any surprise? Not at all. That was always the unspoken arrangement—if anything went wrong, it was always going to be Georgia taking the fall.

"Repent of your sins," Brent was saying, "and ye shall enter the kingdom of heaven."

"My sins?" Georgia's voice rang. "*My* sins? Listen, buster, I have a pretty active love life, compared to some people. But I haven't been doing it by myself."

A buzz rose in the crowd.

"See, there's Ted Horn right there, hey Ted," she said, "and my good friend Jackson Barnett...Y'all saw Jimmy Lee Newton run out of here a minute ago. Over there's Lonnie Chapman trying to be invisible, hey Lon. And our wonderful sheriff, Mr. Bill Allred. If you're wondering why they all look so guilty, it's because they are. Just as guilty as I am."

All those marriages Georgia had been keeping together—all crashed onto the rocks at once. Mrs. Jackson Barnett smacked her husband's face. Mrs. Bill Allred cried, "You hush those lies, Georgia Bottoms!" but the sheriff whispered something and she got real quiet. Poor Ted Horn, never meant to do any harm... but when Brent said the devil was working inside Georgia, Ted had been as happy as everyone else to sit mute.

As long as their secrets were safe, it was fine with them. No matter what happened to Georgia.

She had spent her whole life growing this garden of secrets, guarding them, tending them like dark flowers that only bloom at night. How powerful she felt yanking them up by the roots!

"For every one I named, there are two men in this room who asked me for a date and I turned 'em down," Georgia went on.

"And in case you were wondering, that boy I brought to church today is my son. His name's Nathan. He's twenty years old. Yes, he's black. Just like his daddy."

"Y'all know it all now. Everything about me," she said. "That's all I've got. But you might be interested to know I haven't been the only woman having a good time in Six Points. Brent? You might want to talk to your wife. What you think, Daphne, do you want to tell him, or should I?"

The elegant Mrs. Colgate tilted her slanty hairdo. "Make her stop, Brent! The woman is completely mad."

"Not completely," said Georgia. "At least I'm not dumb enough to leave my car parked in front of the No-Tell Motel next to Jimmy Hodges's red pickup all afternoon, and expect the whole town not to know about it."

That stirred a hum of agreement, as if everyone had already heard about it.

"That's ridiculous!" Daphne cried. "I never did that, I don't even know how to...drive." As she said this last word, Daphne swung around to face her husband.

Brent looked away. Georgia followed his eyes—he couldn't help a guilty glance at Jimmy Hodges, halfway back on the left. Jimmy's face was as red as his truck.

In that instant Georgia knew she had it all wrong. It wasn't Daphne at the No-Tell with Jimmy Hodges.

"Sorry, Brent," she said. "That I really didn't know."

Brenda lunged up from her seat, roaring, "You shut up!"

Eugene caught her, dragged her back down. "That's enough, Georgia," he said in a bitter voice.

"Oh. Eugene. Now you've had enough? Here he is, folks—the fellow who started it all. Understand, Brent and Brenda are here

271

to pay me back for having an affair with Eugene, when he was the preacher here." She scanned the congregation. They couldn't have looked any more shocked than they were already. Georgia wound up gazing straight into Brent Colgate's beautiful eyes. "Now. What else do you want to know? Any more sins you want me to confess? 'Cause I told you, I am a sinner. Damn right. And I will be, to my dying day. Let me tell you one thing I'm not. I'm not a hypocrite."

She turned on her heel and walked out.

22

Driving southwest from Six Points they passed through a region of tall pines and broad, grassy meadows, like horse country without horses. Here and there were some cows, a barn. Underpopulated west Alabama gave way to eastern Mississippi, which was emptier still. Georgia had plotted a circuitous route avoiding all big towns and any road wider than a two-lane. She did not want to meet any law enforcement officials who might be interested in the escaped convict poking her in the back with his knee.

All day they'd been tooling down country roads, stopping at broken-down stores for a Coke and some peanuts, a bathroom break for Mama, Fritos and cigarettes for Brother, a fresh-air stop for Nathan when Brother's smoking made him queasy.

They crossed a sandy shallow river called the Chickasawhay— Brother made fun of all Indian names—and drove into a little town. "Okay we are now in Leakesville," Brother announced, "which means we all gotta take a leak. Anybody? Leakesville?"

Little Mama said, "I wish somebody would tell me where you're taking me."

"We've only told you a hundred times," Georgia said. "It's no use, you'll only forget."

Nathan had more patience with her. "We're going to Na'walyins, Ol' Mama," he said.

"I ain't yo' Mama," said Little Mama. "You black as the ace of spades."

Brother cracked up when she said that stuff, and soon he had Nathan laughing along, the two of them ganging up to make fun of her statements. Georgia felt a little protective—yes, Little Mama was a racist, couldn't remember anything for longer than ten seconds, asked the same question twenty times, and kept re-noticing Nathan as if he had magically appeared for the first time. To Georgia that meant she was a sad case, deserving sympathy. Not a joke for rude boys to laugh about.

Georgia avoided driving on interstates even when she didn't have an escapee in the car. The traffic went too fast, and you never got a sense of having been anywhere except behind the wheel. Once they got out of Six Points, there was no reason to be in a hurry. All day they meandered through Whatley and Grove Hill and Jackson and Chatham, over into Mississippi, to Beulah, where they ate burgers at an old-fashioned Dairy Queen.

Georgia folded the map to a new section. "I think if we follow 57 over here to McLain, then down here it hooks up with 26, we can veer over by Wiggins and on down to Kiln. That'll put us on Highway 90 down around Bay St. Louis. From there it's a straight shot into New Orleans."

She got a little thrill every time she said the words. She could not believe she was finally going. All these years of wanting to go, visiting the place in the pages of magazines... Tonight she would be walking the actual streets.

She could treat them all to dinner at Antoine's, she thought. Or Commander's Palace. Galatoire's. She had read about the menus in these fabled places. There was no end to the fancy preparations, butter and spices and wine. White tablecloths. Elegant waiters, third generation New Orleanians.

In a Civic with her mother, her brother, and her son was not the way she had envisioned herself arriving in New Orleans the first time. She always imagined walking down Royal Street on the arm of Lon Chapman, or some handsome guy. But that had never happened.

She thought of everything she had left behind in Six Points. That great big old pile of a house. So much stuff. She'd spent the last hours walking through, placing yellow sticky notes on things that would come on the truck. The rest of it was headed up to Charlie Ross in Montgomery, for their semiannual estate sale.

Georgia asked Shelley the real estate lady to wait until after they left, so Mama wouldn't see the For Sale sign.

It's amazing how fast you can undo your life, if you have the proper motivation.

Krystal called from Atlanta. She'd always wanted to see New Orleans, she said. She was looking forward to her first visit.

Georgia had to wait until Monday for the First National Bank to open. She told the girl she wanted to draw out every penny. Of course they didn't have that much cash without opening the vault, which they couldn't do because Lonnie Chapman had called in sick—surprise!

The only one who could authorize the transaction was Carole Miller, vice president. She came drifting in just after ten. It was ten thirty by the time Georgia got the money counted and stuffed into that fat zippered pouch.

After that the trip went smoothly, except for all the whining about the radio in the Honda, which had stopped working a couple weeks ago. You'd think it was cruel and inhuman punishment for Brother and Nathan to have to listen to silence or each other.

"I ain't buleeh dat," Nathan said.

"What did you say?"

"I ain't buleeh you ain' gonno music innis car," he said. "Whuh kinda crazyass woman ain' gonno music inna car?"

"The closer we get to New Orleans the less able you are to speak English? I thought we had worked that out."

Nathan grinned. "If you had a radio you wouldn't have to hear me talk."

"You'd just fight with Brother over the station," she said. "Anyway, this is Mississippi. I don't think they allow radio stations over here."

"Now Georgie," said Brother, "remember the eleventh commandment."

"Yeah, what the heck was that, anyway?" Georgia said.

" 'Be sweet,' " Brother said.

"Ah, that's right," Georgia said.

"That's a good one," said Little Mama. "That's what I used to tell y'all."

Georgia settled back in a pleasant daze, the miles rolling under her wheels. This part of Mississippi was a straight road lined with pines and more pines. Georgia imagined the desert was something like this, so blank it made the miles fly by.

Little Mama said, "I wish to God you would tell me where you think you are taking me."

"Mama," said Georgia. "We're going to New Orleans, like you did with Daddy on your honeymoon. We're taking Nathan back to his grandma, then we'll turn around and go home." Nice thing about somebody who can't remember: you can try out different versions of the truth, to see which one works best.

Georgia didn't tell Little Mama about the sticky notes on the furniture. Most of the stuff legally belonged to Mama, but Georgia had power of attorney and that's all you need.

Nathan tapped Georgia's shoulder. "What you mean go home? I thought you was gonna stay down here."

"Oh no, we have to take Mama straight home," Georgia said, finding his eyes in the mirror to give him a wink.

He nodded, relaxed in his seat.

It was late August, hot as hell in Mississippi. The A/C in the Civic was doing its best with four people crammed in there plus Whizzy snoring at Brother's feet.

Georgia flipped on her blinker approaching the I-10 bridge. From the map, she had learned there was no way to enter New Orleans without driving over that long, long bridge crossing Lake Pontchartrain.

Georgia took a deep breath. She could do it. Look at all she'd done that she never thought she could do!

At the on-ramp, an arrow pointed the way to NEW ORLEANS. She gripped the wheel and pressed the accelerator.

In a moment they were up on the highway, flying at seventy miles an hour. Georgia wondered what on earth she had been afraid of. After a day of twisty two-lanes, interstate driving felt like flying down a smooth black runway.

Both lanes on the other side were filled with cars headed out of New Orleans. Could this be rush hour already, three o'clock in the afternoon? Unbelievable. What a city!

There were hardly any cars on Georgia's side of the highway.

What a stroke of luck, a wide-open road to welcome her home. Everything was going better than she could have hoped, considering how dark things had looked only yesterday.

If she followed her heart, Georgia knew she would come out ahead. Look where she was now! Free! Rolling down the road toward a brand-new life. A city emptying out just to make room for her.

Georgia smiled. Her new life was calling. She couldn't wait to get started.

About the Author

MARK CHILDRESS was born in Monroeville, Alabama. He is the author of six previous novels and three books for children. He lives in Key West, Florida.